PUNCH WITH CARE

D0111616

Phoebe Atwood Taylor

PUNCH
WITH CARE

AN ASEY MAYO MYSTERY

The Countryman Press
Woodstock, Vermont

Cover illustration and design by Honi Werner

This edition published in 2005 by
The Countryman Press
P.O. Box 748, Woodstock, Vermont 05091

Distributed by W. W. Norton & Company, Inc.
500 Fifth Avenue, New York, New York 10110

Printed in the United States of America

10 9 8 7 6 5 4 3 2 1

For

Geraldine Gordon of Hathaway House

PUNCH WITH CARE

1

Asey Mayo dropped his empty wooden-slatted clam drainer down on the flagstones of the little terrace by his back door, set his clam hoe and rubber boots beside it, and informed his housekeeper cousin Jennie Mayo that her luncheon menu was changed.

"Your clam chowder's out," he continued as he took the wicker chair next her. "Those fellows at the boat yard," he raised his voice to compete with the music coming from the midget radio on her lap, "they hadn't even bothered to take my new engine out of the crate. They're on strike—for Pete's sakes!"

He suddenly realized that Jennie was sound asleep.

And had been, he decided, since he'd left her some two and a half hours ago, around ten o'clock. The waffle iron she'd intended to mend was lying on the wicker table before her, along with a clutter of wires, nuts, bolts, fuses—and, of course, the ice pick without which she never attempted any mechanical repairs.

The radio's dreamy organ music abruptly gave way to the mournfully dulcet tones of Jennie's favorite announcer.

"*Will* Mother Gaston's adopted daughter go to jail—by mistake? *Should* old Doctor Muldoon tell her that Jimmy has cancer? *Can* Sonia, in her evil zest for brutal revenge, actually plant the stolen bearer bonds on little Beth?"

The studio organ became a violent, roaring tornado.

Three shots rang out, a siren wailed, and a woman screamed in anguish.

Jennie never stirred a hair.

"Listen tomorrow at this time! Find out by what clever device wise old Mother Gaston saves this tensely dramatic situation! And always remember that rigidly controlled scientific tests prove in *nine*—not one, but *nine!*—ways that—"

Asey snapped the radio off, and Jennie at once waked up and glared at him.

"All right!" she said irritably. "All right! I *know* I promised you waffles for lunch if you'd get clams for a chowder. But I never had one single solitary spare moment since you left. Not one!" She glanced down at the empty clam drainer. "Hm. Where are the clams?"

"Wa-el," Asey drawled, "there's a particularly good ball game up-Cape this afternoon, so the boat-yard boys decided to strike again—at least, that's my diagnosis of today's work stoppage. So my new engine's still in its crate, so I got no motor boat, so I didn't get to the south shore. In short, your clam project got washed up. Did the nice May sunshine wash up your waffle iron repair project? Or—"

"If you say that word again," Jennie interrupted, "I'll scream!"

Asey looked at her curiously. "What word?"

"Project!" Jennie said explosively. "*Project!* Don't talk to me about projects! I'm sick and tired of projects—*that*'s why I fell asleep just now. It wasn't the sun. It was that darn project. It just plumb wore me *out!*"

"*What* project?" Asey inquired.

"Of all the silly fool words people've thought up in the last ten years, that's the silly foolest!" Jennie banged her fist on the arm of her chair. "Project! Why, it's got so folks can't hardly go to the post office for one little penny postcard without calling it a Mail Project or a Stamp Project, or some such! Project! How could I *begin* to mend a waffle iron with that fool project crawling all over the place? Jumping on the new grass seed, bouncing up and down in the perennial border, nosey-parkering all over the house—up in the attic, down in the cellar, banging the ice box door, breaking off clusters of the best white lilacs! I never saw people *swarm* the way that project did. Just a bunch of human *ants!*"

"Look, is this somethin' you dreamed about while you were asleep?" Asey asked gently.

"I hadn't been asleep two seconds before you came back," Jennie told him tartly, "and I can prove it—I can tell you every word of 'Mother Gaston' up to the theme music! I just caved in when that project finally left— why, think of that redheaded Air Corps colonel, sneaking a swig of my blackberry cordial!"

"Oho!" Asey said. "So this was some army project that stopped by?"

"Army nothing! It was a bunch from Larrabee College," Jennie said. "Down from Boston to do a project on Town Government." She sniffed. "This was Section B., the towns under nine hundred population division."

"But what in thunder were they doin' *here?*"

"Like every other fool project in the world," Jennie said impatiently, "they'd got sidetracked—only been in town since eight-thirty this morning, but they're already sidetracked forever, if you ask me! Except maybe that thin ex-Wave with the glasses. She kept tryin' to pull'em all together and get 'em going to the Town Hall, but she was just a little squeak in the wilderness. That ex-Wac with the snapping black eyes—*she* was a one, that ex-Wac!"

"I don't think," Asey said pensively, "that I ever felt

3

much more confused. Now just exactly what hap—"

"*You're* confused?" Jennie interrupted. "What d'you think *I* was, being pounced on by a swarm of twenty-odd projecters? Honestly, Asey, I sometimes think that life was a *lot* simpler during the war, when you were away!"

"I promise you I'll be goin' soon again," Asey assured her drily. "Just as soon as they settle the Porter Motors strikes."

"What I mean isn't about *you*," Jennie returned. "I mean about *peace*. Whenever I thought about peace, during the war, I forgot all the things that went along with it. You know, like tourists, and strikes, and sky-high prices, and the roads so packed you hardly dare drive on 'em, and crazy outlanders speeding around curves, and throwing beer bottles and paper plates all over. And silly nonsense like this project!"

"I still don't understand why a college project on Town Government should turn up *here!*" Asey persisted.

"Seems," Jennie said, "they decided that before they set to work projectin', they'd just take a look around the town. There was some word they kept usin'. Or—ori—something or other."

"Orientation, maybe?" Asey suggested.

"That's it! They were orientin' themselves. Somebody —and I bet it was that ex-Wac—remembered that this town was the home of Cape Cod's famous old detective." She glanced at him sideways and continued in tones approximating those of Mother Gaston's announcer. "Tall, lean, salty Asey Mayo, the Codfish Sherlock, the Hayseed Sleuth, the wonderful genius that figured out Porter's miracle tank, the Mark XX. So with a whoop and a holler, they rushed here to see *you*. And drove me crazy asking questions and taking pictures and nosing around— and don't sit there smiling so smug-like, kidding yourself you've ducked 'em, either! You haven't!"

4

"Now see here, Jennie, you didn't promise I'd *do* anything about 'em, did you?"

She smiled. "Thought I could get a rise out of you! No, I never got you into anything, but there's a pile of autograph books inside waitin' for your famous signature—" She broke off as a car rattled up the oystershell driveway and stopped with a great squealing of brakes. "Why *doesn't* Doc Cummings use his new car instead of that battered old wreck?"

"It *is* his new car," Asey said. "He can make any vehicle look like that inside of six months. Hi, doc. Aren't you through work early today?"

"Hi, Asey, hello, Jennie. I'm not through." The doctor eased his short, stocky figure into a steamer chair, and sighed. "I've been too busy with the toys of peace even to get started on my regular rounds. Asey, was peace always like this?"

"You mean sittin' out under a bright sun, watchin' marshmallow cream clouds in a bright blue sky?" Asey said quizzically. "With the bay sparklin', an' lilacs an' apple blossoms—"

"That's not peace you're describing," Cummings interrupted. "That's a butcher's Christmas calendar. Now during the war years, I had a distinct mental picture of peace. All my young colleagues had come home and taken over my practice. I was lovable ol' Doc Cummings, who retired so gracefully. I played golf all day and bridge all night, and lived like a king—my, how lax I am in my terminology! I lived like a labor union head, say, or a commissar, on the royalties of my best-selling memoirs—haven't either of you the common decency to ask me the title of 'em?"

Asey chuckled. "I thought you'd settled on 'Night and Day,' " he said. "Or 'From Mustard Plaster to Penicillin.' Made up another new name?"

"It's a dilly!" Cummings said happily. "Listen! 'Cummings and Goings, the Record of a General Practitioner.' Oh, well, I thought it was funny! But then, I've been up struggling with the toys of peace since five this morning, and that probably makes a difference."

"Whose baby came?" Jennie asked interestedly.

"Oh, nothing's been as normal and sensible as a baby! At five, I was at the newly reopened Sandbar Inn, where the newly arrived chef hadn't bothered to use newly opened lobsters in his Lobster Surprise. Nine fat ladies and six fat men will never be quite so surprised again—and I hope they've learned that proximity to the Cape Cod coast is no guarantee of the age of Newfoundland lobsters. At seven, I coped with a kid whose inland mother let him paddle in the nice back shore undertow before breakfast."

"Collarbone?" Asey asked.

"Uh-huh, and four ribs. That mother'll treat oceans with more respect from now on. Let's see. Then there was that sedan whose driver ignored the big Tonset reverse curve. She's going to see quaint Cape Cod the hard way, from a hospital window. Then two poison ivies who were hunting for wild strawberries, and a really nasty sunburn who wanted to show her office she'd been on vacation—I give you my word, Asey, none of those idiot tourists had any part in my golden haze of peace! And just as I finished extricating a cod hook from the calf of a leg, I was waylaid by a group of college kids—"

"That project!" Jennie said. "Twenty of 'em, weren't there, mostly wearing pieces of service uniforms? From Larrabee College?"

"Well, they mentioned Larrabee, and—yes, now that you speak of it, I suppose some of those seersucker dresses probably were old uniforms. But there weren't twenty. Just four girls."

6

"That ex-Wave with the glasses, I bet," Jennie said, "and those quiet other ones. The rest are probably orientin' themselves at the Country Club! Why, that bunch swooped in here to see the great Codfish Sherlock, and honest to goodness, the way they swarmed around! Let me *tell* you—"

Cummings laughed when she concluded her lengthy description of the project's visit.

"You make 'em sound like a cloud of seven-year locusts," he remarked. "But my four girls were very circumspect, and deadly serious. Came to call on me in my capacity as Chairman of the Board of Health. Wanted vital statistics on Public Health and Welfare. I wasn't exactly in the mood for that sort of thing, after my morning with the tourist trade, so I gave 'em a copy of the Annual Town Report, and excused myself. Very urgent case." He paused and cleared his throat. "Matter of fact, Asey, I *do* have rather an urgent little project—"

"There, Asey!" Jennie broke in. "There, see? All he really means is that he's got some small errand, or chore. But when he calls it a *project*, see, it seems like something big and important!"

"It *is* important!" Cummings retorted. "Furthermore, Asey's going to help me with it. He's got to. It's something I always—well, that is—I mean—"

Asey glanced at him sharply as the rest of the doctor's sentence floundered off into space. For Cummings to run out of words was roughly the equivalent of the Atlantic running out of water. Jennie noticed it too, and stared at him as she got up from her chair.

"If I didn't know you as well as I do," she observed thoughtfully, "I'd say you were setting out to call on your first girl, and wanted Asey to come along with you for moral support. Hm. Got on your best suit, haven't you? And a brand new white shirt. *And* the hand-made

7

silk tie your wife bought in New York and never could get you to put on!"

To Asey's amazement, the doctor neither had any swift, bantering rejoinder on the tip of his tongue, nor did he make the slightest effort to contradict Jennie's comments. He just sat there, silent and red-faced.

"*And* your shoes polished like a looking glass! Hm!" Jennie said. "Hm! Well, before Asey sets out projectin' with you, he's got to have some lunch. You look as if a cup of soup would do *you* good, too! I'll bring it out here."

Cummings gazed after her ample figure as she bustled up the walk and into the kitchen, and shook his head.

"Sometimes," he said, "I'm dazed to a point of speechlessness by the things women seem to know instinctively! How do they *do* it?"

"Meanin'," Asey said with a grin, "that you *are* callin' on a girl? *Is* that your urgent project? Tut, tut, doc! What'll your wife say?"

"I didn't—look, Asey, I don't know how to say this, but look—well, didn't *you* ever read about anyone in the newspapers, or see 'em in pictures, or in newsreels, and think to yourself that you'd like to *meet* 'em?"

"Wa-el," Asey drawled, "when I was a kid, I used to save cigarette box pictures of Maggie Cline, but I can't remember as I ever aimed to meet the lady."

"All right, insinuate that I'm acting like a ten-year-old if you want to! After all, you're in the newsreels and the rotogravures so often yourself, you probably look on other people in 'em as just ordinary run of the mill. Anyway, there's a woman in town I want to meet, and you're going to help me! And that," Cummings wound up with finality, "is the situation in a nutshell!"

"But, doc—"

"No buts, no buts!" Cummings said. "If you don't get out of those fishing clothes, and dress yourself up in your city best, and take your new Porter roadster, and help me meet her, I shall consider it an unfriendly and hostile act. I only want to *meet* her," he hurriedly added. "Just *meet* her, that is, and shake hands, and say how-do-you-do or something—oh, stop chuckling!"

"Who is she, doc?"

"Carolyn Barton Boone," Cummings said almost with reverence. "Carolyn Barton Boone."

"Boone," Asey said. "Boone—oh, sure. Blonde an' beautiful, an' married to a governor, isn't she?"

"She's the wife of Senator Willard P. Boone, and she's the president of Larrabee College, and—"

"Oho!" Asey interrupted. "Now things begin to shape up! So she came to town with this Larrabee project, huh?"

"I don't know. I never thought about that connection," Cummings said. "I was just told that she's staying over with the Douglasses—really, Asey, I've always been a little fascinated with Carolyn Barton Boone. She sounds like quite a person. She's a writer, and she was a judge, and she had a front seat on all the atom bomb stuff, and she visited the Maginot Line, and flew to all the war fronts for the Red Cross, and wrote a book about London in the blitz—and so forth and so on. Now, *you* know the Douglasses, don't you?"

Asey shook his head.

"You *don't?*" Cummings sounded bewildered. "Why, damn it, you must! They've been patients of mine for the last five years! Sure you know'em! You must! You've got to—because *you're* going to take me there to meet Carolyn Barton Boone!"

"If they're patients of yours, an' if you've known 'em

for the last five years," Asey said gently, "what possible difference does it make whether I know'em or not? *You* do!"

"That's not the point!" Cummings retorted. "I know 'em professionally, that's all! *I* can't just barge in on 'em and say I want to meet their house guest, please!"

"Why not, if you want to? You're better known the length and breadth of the Cape than this Boone woman is," Asey said. "Probably the Douglass family'll be only too glad an' happy to have their house guest meet *you!* You see, doc, your perspective's all wrong. You want to consider how many people are goin' to enjoy bein' able to say they knew you even *before* 'Cummings and Goings' was a best-seller. You—"

He broke off as the town's fire-house siren, affectionately known as the Bull Moose, gave its preliminary warming-up yelp for its daily pièce de résistance, the ear-shattering one o'clock blast.

Instantly, Jennie came flying out of the house and snapped on the midget radio, which she'd left lying on the flagstones.

"Golly!" Cummings said. "Time for the Quick Quiz Question! You got paper to take it down on? I've got my pencil ready! I—"

"Ssh, listen!" Jennie said breathlessly. "Listen, now!"

She and the doctor stared at each other in blank bewilderment as a blare of hot jazz issued from the little set.

"For goodness sakes! What's wrong?" Jennie picked up the radio and peered at the dial.

"Wrong station, maybe?" Cummings suggested.

"No! It's smack *on* WBBB! Why, isn't that funny! And the Bull Moose hadn't stopped when I snapped it on! It hadn't hardly *started* to be one o'clock! Asey, what's the time by your watch?"

"Approximately one-four."

"Four minutes *past?* Tch, tch, tch!" Jennie clucked her tongue. "That means the Bull Moose was *late!* Hm! Sylvester'll hear about this! Why, he must've been a good three and a half *minutes* late with that ole siren just now!"

"Sylvester," Cummings said cheerfully, "might as well write his will and pick out his tombstone design. He'll be torn apart by sunset."

"Sylvester?" Asey said. "Hey, what *is* all this, any-way? Who's Sylvester? What were you two expectin' to hear?"

"For a man that's supposed to be so darn great and so darn bright and so darn wonderful," Jennie retorted irritably, "you do seem to miss more that's goin' on around you! I s'pose it's on account of your being away so much! Well, you see, we didn't have any time siren during the war because we saved the siren for an air raid signal—"

"I know all that!" Asey said.

"And when we returned to what we laughingly refer to as a peace-time basis," Cummings said, "it was unani-mously voted to sound the Bull Moose at one instead of the traditional twelve o'clock noon."

"Uh-huh, I'd noticed that," Asey said. "After all, you can't *not* notice the Bull Moose! But I never understood why the time was changed."

"Because of the Quick Quiz Question, of course!" Jennie said. "This way, nobody could *miss* it! When you hear the Bull Moose, you turn on your radio for the Question—oh, you *must*'ve noticed how I always rush to the radio just at one o'clock!"

"You rush to it so many times durin' the day," Asey said, "I hardly pay much attention to any specific hour. Why's this Question thing so important to everyone?"

"Why, you take down this Quick Quiz Question they

ask at one," Jennie explained in the same tones she might have used in speaking to a very young and very stupid child, "and then you run find the answer if you don't know it—and you usually don't—and then when they call you on the phone and ask you the answer in person, you tell 'em—and you *get* things! Free! Only yesterday, a girl in Taunton got an electric fan, and a wrist watch, and a waffle iron—goodness knows *we* could use a new one! And cartons of cigarettes, and theater tickets, and a hundred dollars cash, and a pair of nylons, and five pounds of *butter!* All *free,* and all just for knowing what a Turdus Migratorius was!"

"There, *see?*" Cummings said with irony. "A munificent horn of plenty disgorging rare and precious items on your very doorstep—provided you've equipped yourself with such little smatterings of incidental information as the Latin name for a robin! I personally never miss it—poor, poor Sylvester!"

"Who's Sylvester, an' where does he come in on this Question project—ooop, sorry, Jennie, that word just slipped out! Who's Sylvester?"

"In a sense," Cummings said, "he's the power behind the throne. Owing to some small part or other being currently unavailable—I don't know whether something's struck and not producing it, or whether it's price ceiling trouble, or just a plain shortage—anyway, the automatic mechanism of the Bull Moose is out of order. During the crisis, Sylvester Nickerson sounds the Bull Moose with his bare hands. He—"

"Hold it!" Asey said. "I remember—he's the one they used to call Silly Nick, isn't he? Tall, gangly fellow, always chewin' tobacco, who used to sit on the movie house steps at four in the afternoon so's to be on time for the first show at seven?"

Cummings nodded. "Sylvester owes his fame to always having been at least two hours ahead of time. He made a fortune during the war—standing in butter and meat lines for people. Many's the time I've seen him camped in front of the A & P at three in the morning! Well, while Silly Nick is no mental colossus, he's on time. Never knew him to miss before—by the way, Jennie, did the Taunton woman miss the Doubler? The Doubler," he added parenthetically for Asey's benefit, "occurs when you answer the Question right. It's an unannounced quickie they spring on you, and if you hit it, your loot is doubled. So—"

"Listen! The phone's ringing!" Jennie interrupted excitedly. "What'll I *do?*"

Asey drily suggested that she answer it.

"But s'pose it's Station WBBB calling for the Question answer—and here we don't even know what the Question *is!* Oh, dear, I always *knew* if ever I missed one day, that'd be the day they called—"

Muttering to herself, she rushed indoors only to reappear within a minute, still muttering.

"Getting me worked up like that!" she said disgustedly. "It was only that Mrs. Douglass, Asey. She's lost another house guest. Carolyn Barton Boone, that blonde who's— why goodness me, doctor, whatever are you making such noises for?—in the papers so much. Mrs. Douglass says will you please find her."

"Asey Mayo!" Cummings was spluttering with indignation. "You told me you didn't know the Douglasses!"

"I don't," Asey said. "Except two or three times when I've been home, Mrs. Douglass's called an' said she's lost a guest, an' since I'm a detective, do I mind awfully findin' 'em please. An' then a few minutes later, she calls back an' says they've found the company they mislaid, an' it was awfully nice of me. I never *did* anything about any of her lost guests, I never met her or saw her, an' I don't even know whereabouts they live!"

"Pochet Point." Cummings arose and threw away his cigar stub. "Come on, man, get started!"

"See here, doc!" Asey leaned back in his chair. "In two shakes of a lamb's tail, that flibberty-gibbet'll call back an' say that her company's turned up for lunch. She always does."

"What a wonderful excuse to go there!" Cummings seemed almost to be talking to himself. "Marvelous! If she's really lost, you can find her, and if she isn't, it's a splendid chance just to drop in and meet her casually —come on!" he tugged at Asey's arm. "Get up! And while we're gone, Jennie, call around among your friends and see if you can't manage to locate someone who happened to hear the Question."

"And what about lunch?" Jennie demanded with a touch of asperity. "It's all *ready!*"

"Oh, we'll be back inside of half an hour—come on, Asey, rouse yourself! This way you won't have to dress up, you can be your picturesque self, complete with yachting cap and fishing clothes. Give me thirty minutes out of your life! You'll never miss 'em!"

"Wa-el, all right," Asey said as he got to his feet. "I'll be big. I'll humor you—"

"Not *my* car!" Cummings steered him away from the battered sedan in the driveway. "We're going in your new Porter roadster!"

"Do we *have* to take that confounded Christmas tree, doc? It's so doggone flashy! The old one's so much—"

"The *new* one!" Cummings insisted. "Come along!"

Before the pair reached the garage, the telephone rang once more, and Jennie hurried inside to answer it.

She was at the back door calling Asey at the top of

her lungs as the brand-new Porter roadster glided down the driveway and on to the main road, but neither Asey nor the doctor heard her frantic yells or noticed her wild wavings.

"Oh, dear!"

Jennie shrugged as the chrome-plated car flashed along the shore road, and then she walked slowly back into the kitchen.

"Well," she murmured, "I s'pose there's no sense wasting it!"

Deftly, without any superfluous gestures, she poured soup from a saucepan into a thermos bottle, packeted sandwiches in waxed paper, wrapped up slabs of sugar gingerbread, slid two apple puffs into a covered dish, packed the lot neatly in an oblong basket, and tucked a damask dinner napkin over the top.

She had opened the door of Cummings's sedan and was setting the basket on the floor when the telephone again sent her scurrying back to the kitchen.

"Oh, hello, Emma!" she said. "No, we missed the Question, too. That darn old Sylvester was late with the Bull Moose! Yes, Asey's been back home a day and a half—Porter Motors is striking. You heard rumors on the radio it was bein' settled? Well, Emma, to tell you the truth, I don't think he'll go whipping back to the plant right now, even if a settlement's in the air. Nope, I think he's going to be pretty busy right here in town for a while. I'm just setting out to take him his lunch. Why? Because Mrs. Douglass just called to say that Carolyn Barton Boone—you know, that pretty blonde who's in the papers and newsreels so much—well, she's just been murdered over to Pochet Point."

2

"Mrs. Douglass really isn't a flibberty-gibbet at all," Cummings remarked casually as Asey stopped for the red light at the village four corners. "You've got entirely the wrong impression—you know, I begin to sense what you mean about this car. I keep feeling I should sit up on the boot and bow to the populace and have myriads of rose petals thrown at me."

Asey chuckled.

"It was originally built to the specifications of a Balkan prince," he said. "Didn't I tell you that? We nearly shipped it to him a dozen times durin' the war, but something always cropped up to keep it from startin' to London. Then it turned out he'd strung along with the wrong People's Party, and hadn't enough money left to buy even one of the six horns. So Bill Porter an' I tossed for the thing, an' I lost. I don't think," he added, "that I ever saw a vehicle with more useless gadgets, generally speakin'. That curved hook by your elbow is to hang one of them fancy dress uniform swords on, for example."

"Oh, won't you find *that* handy, now!" Cummings said with irony. "If there's one little accessory you've always needed, it's a resting hook for your jewel-encrusted sword! As I was saying, Asey, Louise Douglass really isn't a flibberty-gibbet. She and Harold Douglass are a pleasant, amusing couple—and believe it or not, their beachwagon's *blank!*"

"How's that again, doc?" Asey inquired.

"The side panels of the front doors of their beachwagon," Cummings explained. "They're blank. You know, no whimsical house-names, like 'Rising Gorge' or 'Wits End', no manufactured family-names, like 'Tom-Mary-Joe', or 'Mywyfanl', or something. No pictures, not even a carefully worked out latitude and longitude. They own the only blank beachwagon on Cape Cod. And that's what *I* call the acid test of restraint!"

"I haven't been over to Pochet Point in years," Asey said thoughtfully, "but the only house I recall there is old Aunt Della Hovey's, with all the fields around it."

"That's it. That's the one. And what's more," Cummings said, "it hasn't been renovated under the guidance of a modernistically minded architect, either. They promised Aunt Della when they bought the place that they'd keep certain things as they were, and they have actually done what they promised—see here, you don't for a moment suppose that Carolyn Barton Boone's *really* lost, do you? There are some pretty treacherous marshes and bogs over this way!"

"If she's followin' the tradition of the Douglass's other guests," Asey said soothingly, "she's just got mislaid, an' they only noticed it because she didn't turn up at lunch time."

As he slowed the car down at a cross roads, Cummings suddenly pointed over toward the edge of a swamp at the right.

"Good Lord, look there! See that thin girl standing by the pines?" he said. "That's one of the Larrabee project group who came to my office. I think she's the ex-Wave Jennie mentioned. Now what on earth is she doing there with a notebook? What *would* that swamp have to do with Public Health and Welfare?"

"Mosquito control's the only explanation I could offer," Asey said. "Huh, I don't see anybody else around! Must be that the projects boiled down to just her, now—which lane here, doc, the left?"

They drove for several minutes along a rut road bordered with post and rail fencing.

"They keep their fences neat an' mended," Asey observed. "Usually the summer folks let 'em go all to rack an' ruin—oh, doc! Look! Look at her!"

He braked the roadster so abruptly that Cummings's head thudded against the windshield.

"Her? Carolyn Barton Boone?" he demanded. "Where? Where is she? Did you catch sight of her?" Rubbing his forehead, he peered anxiously around. "Where? Where is she?"

"Look, doc!" Asey pointed. "Look over there!"

Cummings, staring in the direction indicated by Asey's finger tip, snorted with irritation.

"*I* can't see anything!" he said. "Nothing except the railroad!"

Asey pushed his yachting cap back on his head, then leaned his elbows against the wheel, and stared at the doctor.

"You can't," he said gently, "see anything *but* a railroad? *But* a railroad? Oh, for Pete's sakes, doc! Nothin' but a railroad! Where did it *come* from? An' look—look up back of the house there! An engine—a baby Baldwin! An' a Pullman!"

"Oh, yes, yes, yes, yes!" Cummings said impatiently. "I know, I *know!* That's the Pochet Point and Back Shore Railroad!"

"But whose *is* it? An' what's it *doin'* here? An' how'd it *get* here? An' *when?* I never saw it before! No one ever told me about this! Where'd it come *from?*"

"Oh, for the love of heaven!" Cummings said in exasperation. "I wish you'd stop bouncing up and down with excitement and get along to the house and Carolyn Barton Boone—we came to see her, remember? This old railroad just belonged to Louise Douglass's grandfather, that's all."

"I see," Asey said. "I see! Something the old gentleman used to keep in his hip pocket, I don't doubt, an' one day it just shook out an' landed here? How nice, now! Something to remember grampa by!"

Cummings opened his mouth, closed it again, and then drew a long breath.

"Let's stop being sardonic," he said with icy sweetness, "shall we? Let's just get the hell on our way! Why, man alive, you can see the Pochet Point and Back Shore *any* time! In fact, Harold Douglass won't let you get away from this place without taking at least two round trips— you never went through more childish fiddle-de-dee! First he sells you a ticket in the station. Then—"

"Station? Where's the station?" Asey craned his neck.

"Then," Cummings ignored the interruption, "then he takes off his ticket-seller's green-visored cap and puts on a conductor's cap and coat, and gets on the train, and punches the damn ticket for you—with a lot of dramatic flourishes. Then he takes off the conductor's cap and coat and puts on an engineer's outfit, complete with bandanna, and then he rides you around and around and around—I give you my word, I thought I'd either have to dump the fire or derail the thing to get out of his clutches! Now I promise you faithfully—*after* I've met Carolyn Barton Boone, I'll see to it that you're given the whole silly works!"

"Doc, don't you like railroads?" Asey asked curiously.

"I can take railroads," Cummings returned with dignity, "or I can leave railroads alone, and at this moment, I ask nothing more of life than to leave this one, rapidly! Oh, drive along to the house!"

"A narrow gauge—a two-foot narrow gauge! It

19

must've been an old short line somewhere," Asey said. "Of course, it must've been! Happen to know what line it was in the good old days, doc?"

"It was the Harmony and North Budget," Cummings said. "Or something that sounded like that. Get along!"

"The Harmony and North Blodgett! Why, I knew that line! I used to take it, years ago, to get to old Cap'n Porter's place in Maine!" Asey said. "What a job they must've had to pick this outfit up an' bring it way out here, an' lay track—why, they must have nearly three-quarters of a mile of track!"

He started up the roadster with such suddenness that the doctor bounced back against the leather seat, and then he stopped with such force on the gravel turntable by the Douglass's house that the doctor's forehead again smacked smartly against the windshield.

By the time Cummings had located the push button which opened the car door, Asey was already striding past the house in the direction of the engine and the Pullman, drawn up by the little, box-like station.

"Asey!" Cummings called after him in aggrieved tones. "Asey, come back here! Come—"

After the fourth futile shout, the doctor gave up and hurried after him.

"The old Harmony and North Blodgett! Look at that old Pullman, doc, look at her!" Asey said with admiration. "Isn't she a beauty? They *made* Pullmans back in the days when they made her! That's luxury de luxe! Look at that fine gold leaf stripin', an' the gold filagree work—"

"While I shrink from throwing any monkey wrenches into this nostalgic rhapsody," Cummings said in his most acidulous tones, "may I point out that we came here for a definite purpose? Think back! We came to find Carolyn Barton Boone, so that I might fulfill my desire—"

"To shake hands an' say howdy. I know. But I just got to take a glance—doc, this is the very same Pullman I used to travel on to Blodgett Centre. Look!" he pointed to the ornate gilt lettering running along the side. "The 'Lulu Belle'! Isn't she *something!*"

Cummings stared stonily at the Lulu Belle as Asey raptly walked the fifty-foot length of it.

"Maybe it *is* something wonderful. Maybe *is* an old jim-dandy, a crackerjack peach of a daisy!" he said when Asey finally strolled back to where he was standing. "I've done my level best to look at the thing and see something more than a small green Pullman with a red roof. I'll concede it's shorter, and littler, and narrower than most, and more violently decorated. To coin a phrase, it's quite cunning. But I'm damned if I can see any reason for you to become so nostalgically carried away!"

"That baby Baldwin engine!" Asey said. "I got to take—"

Cummings grabbed his arm and hung on to it.

"You don't need to go inspect that!" he said. "You've already gazed at it hard enough in the last five minutes to have it engraved on your mind forever. Asey, you can play with the nice choo-choo as long as you want to if you'll only just come inside the house first and help me meet Carolyn Barton Boone. Just tear yourself away long enough to walk over the threshold and help get the ice broken, and then Harold Douglass'll probably let you play conductor and engineer and punch tickets with him —oh, my God, no! *Don't!*"

Asey had gripped the filagreed iron grab-rail and swung himself up the single step to the end platform of the Lulu Belle.

With a loud sigh, Cummings followed him.

"Asey—"

"This was the smokin' end, see?" Asey said as he slid

21

open the panelled mahogany door. "Here's where old Cap'n Porter an' his business friends used to sit, in these fancy wicker chairs, an' toss more millions around than you an' I ever dreamed existed. That door—"

"Asey Mayo!"

"That door there's the wash room—all solid mahogany, as I remember. Here's the main part of the car—oh, they must've done a lot of refurbishin' to make it like this, but they refurbished it just the way it used to be, back in the early nineteen-hundreds! Yessir, they even kept the old observation end up yonder, with the red plush settees!"

"Yoohoo!" Cummings, standing behind Asey in the narrow passageway, punched him in the back. "Yoohoo! Asey!"

"Oh, golly, those old chandeliers with the jinglin' glass prisms, an' the old red silk curtains, an' the gold plush swivel chairs, an' the tidies with the red tassels, an' the gilt mirrors, an' the silver-plated spittoons, an' the thick red carpet—the thick red carpet—the—"

Asey stopped.

He couldn't quite bring himself to add that on the thick red carpet lay the body of Carolyn Barton Boone!

3

"NEEDLE STUCK?" Cummings inquired. "Oh, move along, man, get on with your tour of the past! Don't bother considering *my* project! I've altered my objective. My goal now is merely to meet Mrs. Boone before her blonde hair turns to silver and she's taken to a cane!"

Asey swung around suddenly and looked at him.

"What's the matter?" Cummings demanded sharply. "What's wrong?"

"Doc, I never hated to say anything half as much," Asey began unhappily. "I never—"

"What're you blocking the aisle like this for? What've you—get out of the way!"

"But, doc—"

Cummings pushed past him.

His facial expression never changed as he gazed down at the still figure on the thick red carpet.

"Honest, doc, I—"

Asey broke off and watched the doctor's professionally impersonal survey of the situation.

After all, he thought to himself, Cummings knew perfectly well that he was sorry, knew how he was regretting that this projected visit to Mrs. Boone hadn't got under way earlier in the morning. But there wasn't any need for him to run on and on, being sorry, and regretting the whole business. There wasn't anything that could be done now about meeting Carolyn Barton Boone.

As for what had happened to her here in the Lulu Belle, it was all there for Cummings to look at and to put together.

Mrs. Boone, dressed in the perfectly fitting white slacks and white jacket which were almost her trademark in the newsreels, had been murdered. There weren't any two ways about that. By no stretch of the imagination could she have managed to inflict on herself that ugly head wound.

Cummings, kneeling on the carpet, turned and looked up at Asey.

"Actually a rabbit punch, you know," he remarked. "Beautifully placed. Magnificently placed. But not very expert. Right?"

Asey nodded.

"Someone," Cummings continued, "could have achieved

the same result—and a far neater effect!—by using about one-fiftieth as much force and energy. In fact, I'd say that someone hauled off and just blindly smashed away at the back of her head, and landed where they did just by dumb luck! And what a nasty thing to use for a weapon!"

With a brief gesture, he indicated the pointed silver bud vase that was lying in the middle of the aisle a few feet away, apparently where the murderer had casually tossed it.

"They wrenched it out of the ring-holder above Seat One," Asey commented. "See the gap back there? Someone reached out an' grabbed it as they came into the car."

"I will say that your cunning little Pullman is certainly a fertile field for blunt instruments!" Cummings said. "Although I, personally, would never have chosen that bud vase. I'd have taken my chances with one of the silver cuspidors, or one of the little umbrella holders. Or even with one of these mahogany footstools."

"Workin' on the theory that the heavier your blunt instrument is, the lighter the blow you'd have to strike with it?" Asey asked.

"Of course. No need to have been quite so damn brutal with that pointed thing!" For a split second, Cummings's voice betrayed his real feelings. "Well, let's see, now, let's consider!"

He squinted up at the gold plush Pullman seat beside him.

"That's what I thought," Asey said. "She was sittin' there—it's the only chair not lined up facin' into the aisle. She was sittin' there, an' had half-swung it around so as to look out of the window. Then, all of a sudden, she hears a sound behind her. Not enough to make her turn the chair. She just turned her head an' looked, an' then she started to her feet. I'd say she'd almost stood up

24

when she was caught off balance with that blow. That'd explain her pitchin' into the aisle." `

Cummings gave the plush chair an experimental turn.

"It sticks a bit," he said. "That's probably why she just turned her head. Wonder if that particular chair— no," he shoved at the seat ahead of him, "they're all hard to get started. Well, she may have guessed what was coming at her, but she didn't feel it—now, for heaven's sakes, Asey, *don't* say how wonderful it was that she didn't suffer, will you?"

"Why, I never intended to say any such—"

"Because," Cummings went on, "that's an idiot point of view I intend to make quite an issue of in my memoirs. There is no death, however quick or painless, which quite compensates one for the joys of being alive, however dubious they may occasionally appear. What time is it now, one-forty? Well," he got up and dusted the carpet lint from his knees, "if I hadn't gone home and changed into this suit, and then frittered away so much time going over to get you, and listening—or not listening, rather, to the Question—"

"Are you tryin' to say that she hasn't been dead longer'n an hour?" Asey demanded.

"Oh, I'm putting myself way out on the end of a limb, of course. But if I'd arrived here at noon, I think I might have met her." Cummings paused. "Heavily made up, isn't she? Not as young as I'd somehow imagined. There's a phrase I've often heard my wife use about some of the summer people—'well taken care of'. She means —oh, very well-groomed, very carefully dressed, every curl in place. That sort of thing. I never thought before, but she always uses it of women who seem much younger than they really are. I'd have said that she," he nodded toward the aisle, "was about thirty-five or so. She's easily fifty. Maybe more."

"Jennie calls that sort of thing stage-managin'," Asey said. "An' it is, if you stop an' think. With her slim figure, that white suit gives the impression of her bein' youthful, an' that green scarf around her neck is just the right shade to make her hair seem more gold, an' her skin whiter. An' she doesn't wear a lot of sparklin' rings to call your attention to her hands, which might sort of tip you off to her real age—huh! Now I didn't notice that before!"

"What?" Cummings asked curiously as Asey bent down.

"See what she's grippin' in the palm of her hand? I thought it was the edge of a green handkerchief, but it's a ticket!"

"I missed it too," Cummings said. "Hm. It's a punched ticket, furthermore. Looks as though Harold Douglass had started to give her a ride—that's an ugly way for me to put it, I must say! Well, where do we go from here? All hell will break loose on this business, I suppose. And Halbert'll be delirious with pleasure!"

"Albert who?"

"Halbert. The new state cop in charge of this area. Hanson's been transferred to the western part of the state. Halbert's got some splendid new equipment, and I rather suspect," Cummings said, "that he's been praying for something like this to happen so he could use it."

"Experienced man?" Asey inquired.

"Halbert? Experienced? Why, he virtually ran the Counter-intelligence of the United States Army with his own two hands—I assure you," Cummings said with irony, "that no army corporal since Napoleon was ever more essential! I try not to think that his three uncles who actively engage in politics have any possible connection with his present position. In fact, in my official capacity as medical examiner, I try to think of Halbert just as little as possible. But we've got to call him, I suppose—and get my grisly duties properly under way. Think one of us should stay here?" he added, as Asey started to walk to the end platform.

Asey shrugged. "If no one knows she's here except you an' me an' the murderer, I don't think any guard's necessary."

Neither of them spoke until they were crossing the gravel turntable by the house.

"Seems incredible!" Cummings said absently. "I mean that the Douglasses actually don't know about this! But they can't know, or there'd have been some hue and cry, and of course it explains their thinking she was lost, too. I suppose they must be out hunting around the point for her, or they'd have seen us when we drove in—my, my, that couldn't have been more than twenty minutes ago, but it feels like years and years!"

"This is a pleasant place." Asey surveyed with approval the neat white Cape Cod house with its dark green blinds. "Nice lilacs, nice iris, nice lawns."

"Oh, they take good care of everything." After a perfunctory knock, Cummings shoved open the panelled front door. Then, just as perfunctorily, he sang out Douglass's name several times as he stepped across the spattered floor of the wainscoted hall to the telephone. "Notice all their ship pictures, Asey. All of old Aunt Della's family stuff, all the Hovey family ships, and some corking other ones that Louise picked up at auctions—"

He broke off as a tall, dark, powerfully built man in his forties, wearing khaki shorts and a white crew-neck sweater, entered the hall from a door to the right.

"Douglass!" Cummings said in surprise. "We didn't think anyone was home!"

"It's providential, doctor—*was* it you she called? I phoned your house at once, but your wife didn't know where you'd gone. Really, I'm terribly worried about her." He turned to Asey and smiled politely. "Mayo, isn't it? Glad to see you—she's still out, you know, doctor. Out cold!"

Cummings looked from Douglass to Asey, and then back to Douglass again.

"Who," he said crisply, "is out cold?"

"Why, Louise! I heard her making a phone call, and then she called me—but she'd fainted before I got to her. I haven't been able to bring her to. She's in here." He led them into the living room from which he'd just emerged. "I carried her in here—"

The sight of the woman stretched out limply on the chintz-covered couch in front of the long fireplace was awe-inspiring enough, but Asey found that he was almost too impressed with the room itself to notice her much.

He hadn't, he decided, seen so many miscellaneous objects enclosed by four walls since he'd been a small boy living in his sea-going grandfather's house.

And they were exactly the same sort of things.

Like those mercury glass goblets, with ships' names etched on them, that stood on the mantel, and like the vast, gold-tooled family Bible sitting the exact center of the Chippendale table. It was Old Home Week to see again such a collection of sailors' scrimshaw work, and odd chunks of coral, and ivory tusks, and peacock fans.

And shells! Small pink shells from the Indies, and conch shells from India, and one huge African shell large enough to bathe a baby in!

"Golly!" Asey said with a chuckle of pleasure. "Golly!"

He had hardly started to look at the gold-knobbed captains' canes in a Canton stand before he caught sight of a Swiss village under a glass dome, and beyond that, on the wall, a cluster of wax flowers in a wide walnut frame. A set of ivory elephants jumped at him from their teak-wood stands on a whatnot shelf, and an enormous palm fan swept them away in favor of a full-rigged ship in a bottle.

Every inch of the floor was covered with hooked rugs, and every inch of wall space was filled with pictures of ships, with hull models, with framed daguerreotypes and crayon portraits.

"See what you can *do* with her, doctor, even if you haven't got your paraphernalia with you!" Harold Douglass was saying anxiously to Cummings. "*Do* something! Louise never fainted before in her life!"

"She'll be all right!" Cummings said shortly.

"But her color!"

"Her color's all right! Stop worrying!"

"Oh," Douglass said. "It's been changing so—well, I suppose you know!" He turned somewhat hesitantly to Asey. "I notice you've been looking around at the room, Mayo. I do feel I should explain that we promised Aunt Della Hovey when we bought this house that we'd keep certain things just as she'd always kept them. It's rather a clutter, I'm afraid. Of course we're so used to it now, we take it for granted. But it—well, it *is* startling to people seeing it for the first time."

Asey smiled.

"Startlin'?" he said. "This's the first native house taken over by an outlander that I ever felt at home in, if you want to know the truth. Usually, the summer folks paint the walls a sort of sickish pink, or sickish blue, an' the only thing they ever have in the livin' room aside from a few sticks of aluminum furniture is a picture by—what's that fellow's name, doc? Not the sunflower one they all used to have. This other fellow."

"Picasso," Cummings said as he strolled over to the window. "Only lately they've taken to Dali. Guts, and watches."

"Well, anyway, they always call the result a real quaint old Cape Cod room," Asey said, "an' to a real Cape Codder, it sure is just that! But this, Mr. Douglass, is the real McCoy! What's the matter with Mrs. Douglass, doc?"

While he couldn't fathom the expression on Cummings's face, Asey knew that something was wrong. It wasn't the doctor's habit to stand idly by, staring out of a window and drumming his fingers on the sill, when he had a sick patient stretched out before him.

"Well," Cummings said, with his eyes focussed somewhere down the shore, "she's had a severe shock, and she hasn't come to. But she will!"

"I never felt so damn helpless!" Douglass said. "*I* didn't know what to do with her when I found her lying out there in the hall! In a house filled with books, you'd think there'd be something in *one* of 'em about what to do when a person faints, and stays fainted—out cold! But all I could find was an old tome of Aunt Della's that advocated burning duck feathers under the patient's nose —and lacking them, a spoonful of melted ambergris thrust under the tongue! If I'd known where to find either, I'd have tackled 'em willingly—doctor, there must be something constructive that I can do! I can't just stand here doing nothing any longer!"

Cummings swung around from the window.

"Go get a glass of water," he said briskly. "Put two— no, three—put three ice cubes in it, and just a pinch of salt. Three grains."

Asey raised his eyebrows questioningly as Douglass bolted from the room.

Cummings answered with a wink, and then he went

into an elaborate pantomime from which Asey deduced that Mrs. Douglass was not any victim of a prolonged faint, that she never had fainted at all, and that her present condition was just a lot of bluff.

"Huh! Her color's good," Asey said interestedly as he strolled over to the couch and looked down at the motionless figure. Mrs. Douglass, he decided, was a lot younger than her white hair indicated. In her thirties, perhaps. "Color's most normal, wouldn't you say?"

Cummings winked again. "Yes," he said solemnly, "but I don't like her breathing. I'm going to write out a prescription—you can whip up town and get it filled, if you don't mind."

Asey wasn't sure whether the faintest trace of a frown flitted across Mrs. Douglass's face, or whether it was just a passing shadow. But he had no doubts whatsoever about her black, unplucked eyebrows. They had very definitely wiggled.

"Funny about this sort of thing," Cummings said casually as he scratched away on the prescription blank pad which he'd drawn from his coat pocket. "Nine times out of ten, when the patient regains consciousness, you'll find they can't remember a thing. The psychiatrists' explanation is extraordinarily interesting—here, take this and give it to Billy at the drug store."

With some difficulty, Asey managed to decipher the doctor's minute handwriting.

"She's ok," the slip said. "Faking. This is all fishy. You pump D.—I'll pump her. *Both* stalling." "Both" was heavily underlined. "D. took 1st Aid & shd certainly know faints & what to do! I don't get this, don't like it!!!!!"

Asey tucked the prescription blank into his pocket as Douglass came panting back with the glass of water.

"Fine. Thanks." Cummings drank the water, to Doug-

31

lass's obvious surprise. "Now, you go along with Asey and get a prescription filled for Louise."

"But should *I* leave?" Douglass asked uncertainly, clearly not wanting to at all.

Cummings nodded. "Be the best thing in the world," he said with firmness. "You've been under a strain—need a change. She's coming to—needs complete quiet. Worst thing you can have in a situation like this is a lot of people staring you in the face when you recover. She'll want to talk to you and tell you things, and you'll want to ask her questions—can't have that! Bad business! Got to give her a chance to rest. Get long, now. I want that stuff from the drug store!"

Asey herded Douglass toward the door.

"Oh!" he paused on the threshold. "Don't forget about your phone call up the cape, doc, will you?"

"I'll take care of it," Cummings said.

As he got into Asey's roadster, Douglass said diffidently that he didn't feel at all right about leaving Louise like this.

"But I suppose Cummings knows best—what an incredible car! I'm glad to have the chance to meet you, Mayo, after hearing so much about you. Louise and I were thinking of asking you to come to this sort of buffet supper we seem to be throwing tomorrow—we have a house guest, Carolyn Barton Boone. You've probably heard of her?"

"Uh-huh," Asey said.

He didn't have to turn his head sideways to know that he was being stared at sharply. Thanks to the Balkan prince's lavish specifications on side-view mirrors, Douglass's face was entirely visible.

"Louise and I really got thrown, trying to figure out who might want to come," Douglass continued. "After a lot of debate covering five towns, we could only settle on

Cummings and his wife, and you—someone on the party line said you were home. We thought you three might be amused, no matter how you felt about her—of course, asking anyone to meet Boone *is* a tough problem! Fraught with pitfalls, as Louise put it."

"So?" Asey asked. "Why?"

"Well," Douglass shrugged, "you know how it is with that sort of woman. Boone's never been exactly luke-warm in her opinions or her sentiments, or reticent in expressing 'em, either! And then there's always the political angle of Senator Boone in the background. You're not just for Boone, or against her. You're very-very-for, or very-very-against. In fact, *you* stand out as the only person I ever mentioned her to who didn't either spit in my eye at the sound of her name, or else purr like a kitten."

"I'm neutral," Asey said. "Doc, on the other hand, is very-very-for."

"No! Is he? I didn't know! Never happened to discuss her with him," Douglass said. "Anyway, we decided we'd have to sift out the local guests with great care, because God knows if a pro-Boone and a con-Boone took to battling it out in our living room, Aunt Della's early Cape Cod décor would bite the dust! That's not the ideal room for tempers to blow in!"

Asey agreed.

"An' what about you?" he asked in what he hoped was a casual tone. "Are you pro, or con?"

He saw the corners of Douglass's mouth curve upward slightly.

"My role in this, Mayo," he said, "at least, the role I'm working at like a dog, is that of the perfect parent."

"The perfect parent? Er—whose?"

"Layne Douglass, who is twenty-four and an instructor at Larrabee College," Douglass said with a certain amount of resignation in his voice, "might be summed up impartially as pro-Boone."

"Twenty-*four*?" Asey mentally revised his first estimate of the Douglasses respective ages.

"And you do not tell a modern girl of twenty-four what you think of her boss," Douglass said, "or present your somewhat biased personal opinion as a sufficient reason for her taking another similar position somewhere else. Instead, you firmly tell yourself a lot of silly tripe about her being an adult now, and you try to be reasonable, and rational, and fair—mind you," he added, "you don't slop over and pretend you think the whole business is wonderful, either!"

"In short," Asey remarked, "you take it with dignity?"

"With dignity," Douglass said, "with our eyes wide open, and with no illusions. Rather the way that two adults might suffer a dose of castor oil."

Asey chuckled. In spite of Cummings's suspicions about the man, he found that he was beginning to enjoy Harold Douglass.

"To think," the latter continued, "that Layne could have catapulted Carolyn Barton Boone into our house last night—without notice! Without any notice at *all!* *Dar*-lings!" he assumed a very creditable falsetto, "*dar*-lings, we've come to make a check on a *project!*"

"So that's the real cause of the invasion, huh, that project?"

"Yes. Boone suddenly took it into her head to do a little field work and find out just exactly why some of the various projects kept getting gummed up so badly—you know," he said with a reminiscent sigh, "we've seen Layne through a lot—measles, wisdom teeth, that riding master with the moustache, all those pilots suffering from delusions of grandeur, and all those beardless ensigns, and

34

the interne who didn't come up to her chin. But *this!* Bringing Boone here!"

"How long," Asey glanced at him in the side-view mirror, "is she plannin' to stay?"

"Three days!" Douglass shook his head. "Three whole days—of course, as Louise pointed out, if you look back on any three-day period in your life, you find that it passed. There's no reason for me to assume that time might take to standing still now. We've gaily opened our house to the project members, we're throwing this fish fry and buffet supper for them and Boone tomorrow, we've promised everyone a ride on the railroad, and we're doing it all with a fixed smile. If only our faces don't break! Well, to answer your question of way back there by the swamp, Mayo, no. No, I am not a pro-Boone man!"

"Difference in political concepts," Asey suggested as he stopped for the four corners light, "or social concepts, or don't you approve of her college, or her educational notions, or what? I'm sort of curious, because Doc Cummings is so very pro!"

"Purely personal reasons," Douglass said. "One of those emotional reactions that should have faded with the years, but hasn't. When Boone stuck her beautifully coiffed blonde head into our living room last night, I felt that same old urge to rise up—right in the middle of Aunt Della's décor—and murder her in cold blood."

"Oh?" Asey said aloud, and mentally ordered himself to keep his eye on the ball and stop being distracted by details like Aunt Della, and Layne Douglass's beaux!

After all, Cummings had warned that the Douglasses were stalling—and Cummings knew them, and Cummings wasn't easily carried away by unfounded suspicions. While all this light, airy conversation about Mrs. Boone was disarming enough, and informative enough—wasn't it maybe just a little too disarming, when you thought it over, and a little too pointedly informative?

"You see, we knew Boone on her way up in the world," Douglass said, "and that's so often a disillusioning time to know the great!"

"What was Mrs. Boone doin' then?" Asey asked.

Douglass laughed shortly. "What she's done all her life. What she's doing now. Smashing down everything that stands between her and her goal of the minute. Specifically, it was back in the old days of radio. We were all writing for it—Louise still does, you know. In fact, we both do." He was silent for a moment, and then he smiled. "Of course, you would take a professional interest in motivation, wouldn't you? But don't worry, Mayo. It was a long time ago that Louise and I got in Boone's way! I assure you we won't provide you with any new business now—good God!"

"What's the matter?"

"I just thought! *I* shouldn't be going to the village with you!"

"Why not?" Asey said as he swung the roadster to the curb. "Besides, you're already here."

"In all the excitement of Louise fainting, I forgot! We've lost Boone—oh, not really *lost!* She's just wandered off somewhere. And my aunt, Mrs. Framingham, is out hunting for her—I ought to be home straightening things out! My God, to think that could have slipped my mind! But I just forgot everything else when I found Louise lying there in the hall!"

"D'you often lose your guests?" Asey inquired as he got out of the car. "Mrs. Douglass's phoned me a couple of times in great anguish about your—er—displaced persons problems."

"Has she? She never told me that! But Louise does get panicky when people are mislaid. We've had a few grim experiences with guests who foolishly set off in small boats and had to be rescued by the coast guard. We padlock the oars and the boathouse, now, and hide the keys," Douglass said, "and we've put signs on all the marshes, warning people off. It's tricky territory over there at the point. I don't think Boone has met with any dire accident, but I feel I should hurry back—will Cummings's medicine take very long, d'you think?"

Asey looked across the street at the drug store, and decided that there were still enough questions he wanted to ask Douglass to warrant his maintaining the fable of Cummings's prescription.

"I don't think so," he said, "an' anyway, isn't the medicine for your wife probably more important than locatin' Mrs. Boone?"

"Of course!" Douglass said contritely. "You're absolutely right. I didn't mean to rush you—and actually, I don't care if Boone is up to her neck in the bog of the east marsh! My real concern is Louise—she'd go berserk if any little thing went wrong with Boone while she's staying with us. Even a good horse-fly bite would upset her!"

"Haven't you *any* idea where Mrs. Boone went to?" Asey asked casually. "Golly, how could you lose track of her?"

"How? You might as well try to keep tabs on a flea!" Douglass said. "She started off to meet the Larrabee project when it came this morning, but then she had to come back to the house—phone calls were pouring in from all over. She finally decided they were too distracting, and had them all relayed back to her college office. Then as I had her all set for a ride on the railroad, she disappeared—for a phone call, I thought. But when I went indoors, Louise said she wasn't there—oh, you can't keep track of anyone like her!"

"But didn't any of your servants see her?"

"Servants? Are you kidding?" Douglass said. "We haven't been able to get any for years, except for a cleaning woman on Fridays! Layne and some of the project crowd had gone over to the shore earlier, so my aunt set out in our beachwagon to see if Boone might've followed them. I was just starting to take a look around the marshes when I found Louise there on the hall floor—Mayo, I still can't figure out what happened to her! She must have felt ill, and called Cummings—that was how you two happened to turn up, wasn't it?"

Asey evaded the question.

"Cummings'll turn me over his knee if I don't get his prescription filled," he said. "I'll be as quick as I can."

Inside the drug store, he made his way out to the small back room that served as a pharmacy, and asked cheerfully for a four-ounce bottle of tap water.

"Just color it pink, an' label it 'Cummings-Special', Billy," he added. "The doc's humorin' a patient who fainted."

The druggist grinned.

"Last week he wanted dark green—said it was to comfort some woman in Wellfleet who was getting her fourth divorce. Doc sure is busy, isn't he? I just saw his car rattle by here for about the twentieth time today."

"His car?" Asey said. "Rattlin' by here? But his car's over at my place!"

"He parked right around by the post office, Asey—why, I couldn't miss that car!"

While the druggist typed out the label, Asey strolled to the front part of the store and looked out the side window.

There was no sign of Cummings's sedan by the post office.

Neither, he discovered with a start of surprise as he turned his head, was there any sign of his own roadster, out front!

While Billy, brandishing the bottle of tinted water, called out after him, Asey rushed out into the street.

His chrome-plated car was nowhere to be seen.

"Huh!" Asey shoved his yachting cap on the back of his head. "Now what in time would he do *that* for?"

Probably half the shoppers on main street had seen the man go, but there was no sense steaming into the A and P, or the post office, or the fruit store, and asking a lot of silly questions.

The point was that Douglass and the car were gone!

Turning on his heel, Asey strode off to the four corners and hitched a ride on an oil truck that deposited him at the foot of his own oystershell driveway.

True enough, Cummings's sedan wasn't parked up by the house, but Asey dismissed that fact as unimportant after discovering that Jennie wasn't at home, either. Without question, she had taken the car.

"But why the doc's?" he murmured to himself as he walked on to the garage. "Whyn't she take her own coupe, or my old roadster?"

He was still asking himself questions as he took out the latter, and started to drive it back to the Douglass's house.

Who *had* Mrs. Douglass telephoned—providing that she actually had telephoned anyone? And why had she thereupon fainted—or pretended to faint? And why hadn't Douglass guessed that her long drawn out period of unconsciousness was all a fake?

"An' why'd he swipe my car an' beat it? What about that feller, anyway?"

If Douglass had been improvising, Asey conceded that

the man had done a good job. Without in the least seeming to set up a lot of facts, he had in effect done just exactly that. He'd pointed out that Mrs. Boone was, after all, a highly publicized figure, and that many people disliked her intensely. Just the mere mentioning of her phone calls brought out the picture of an active, busy woman whose life was under constant outside pressure.

"Outside pressure," Asey said to himself. "He kept pushin' her away from Pochet Point out into the world, didn't he? Away from himself an' his wife. *They* didn't know she was comin'! That was just the daughter's doin'. Just college business. Nothin' to do with *them!* They don't like Boone for two cents, but they're as nice as Mrs. Post could wish, all for their daughter's sake. Just selfless, that's what!"

And through no one's fault, Boone was lost. Lost, that was all.

"Like a doggone collar button!" Asey muttered.

Yes, he had to hand it to Douglass. His story was good.

"An' if he's asked for more details, like about startin' to give her a ride in Lulu Belle, an' about her disappearin'," Asey added, "why gee whiz, in his excitement at findin' Louise all fainted on the hall floor, why gee whiz, everything's slipped his mind!"

And as the doctor had already sardonically insinuated, Louise probably wouldn't remember much after her prolonged faint, either.

In short, he decided, the Douglass family would remember just what it wished to remember, and not a whit more.

"An' they'll be simply charmin' about it, too! Disarmin' as all get out!"

The gravel spun under his wheels as he braked to a stop in the Douglass's driveway.

There was no sign of Cummings's sedan—that meant

that Jennie, too lazy to walk to the garage, had taken it to go shopping in.

There was no sign of his new roadster—and what that meant, Asey didn't know.

"Where in time did he *go* to in it?" he said aloud as he strode into the house. "Hey, doc—"

He stopped on the threshold of the empty living room. Then he went to the center hall.

"Doc! Mrs. Douglass! Cummings!" He drew a long breath and bellowed out his best quarter-deck roar. "Cum-mings! Cum-mings!"

Nobody answered.

The house was empty. Asey went through it twice, room by room.

As he came down the back stairs to the kitchen, he helped himself to some sandwiches from a plate on the kitchen table, and then went out on the back step and sat there, munching thoughtfully.

He had topped off his impromptu lunch with fruit and some cookies when he noticed the little green slip of paper blowing along the driveway, an inch or two at a time.

A little green slip?

Asey jumped up and grabbed it as it bobbled along past him.

It *was* a ticket. A green ticket.

A punched green ticket!

Asey started off toward the Pullman on a dead run.

Like the Douglass's house, he found that the Lulu Belle was empty, too.

4

"Now you see it," Asey muttered, "now you don't! Rub your eyes, Mayo! Look again!"

But it was no mirage.

The Lulu Belle really was empty, and Carolyn Barton Boone's body was no longer there.

The pointed silver bud vase was back in its holder above Seat One. The gold plush swivel chair beside which Cummings had knelt was now back in line with all the fifteen other gold plush swivel chairs. A Boston newspaper—that morning's paper—which had apparently been casually dropped on the thick red carpet, actually covered the dampish spot where someone had been busy eradicating blood stains.

In another half hour, when the carpet was thoroughly dried out, the presence of blood stains would never be suspected by anyone who wasn't hunting for them. The only extraneous object in the car would be an old discarded morning newspaper, which certainly wouldn't move anyone unduly!

Asey pushed one of the plush chairs around toward him, and sat down.

This situation, he decided, required a brief review!

He and Cummings had left the Lulu Belle at roughly quarter to two. They had spent perhaps a quarter of an hour in Aunt Della's sitting room before he'd driven Douglass to the village. Say twelve minutes for that trip. He hadn't hurried.

He had been in the drug store not more than five or six minutes, Asey decided. Twenty more had taken him from the oil truck at the four corners back to the Douglass's again, via his own house. The oil truck had been

slow, but he hadn't dallied any after taking his old roadster.

And he'd spent perhaps fifteen minutes here at the
Douglass's in stark, lonely solitude.

It all boiled down to the fact that an hour and eight
minutes ago, Mrs. Boone's body had been lying on the
floor of the Pullman.

He felt gratified, on looking at his watch, to find that
his estimate wasn't too far off. It was now five minutes to
three.

Seventy minutes exactly.

And that was just about sixty-five minutes more than
anyone really needed!

For someone who had previously armed himself with
a newspaper and a damp wash cloth, slightly less than five
minutes would have sufficed for the task of replacing that
vase, scrubbing the red carpet, dropping the newspaper,
and making off with the body.

Harold Douglass would have had plenty of time to do
it, after rushing back from the village in the new roadster!

"Without even breathin' hard at the end! Yessir, Mayo,
you went an' gave somebody enough time to make away
with her about fourteen times. Puttin' it the other way,
I s'pose fourteen separate people each had the opportunity—"

Asey shook his head as he stared out of the car window.

Putting it that way wasn't as silly as it sounded. After
all, there were more than fourteen people who could
have been milling around!

There was the project bunch, for example. Twenty of
them. Douglass said they'd been offered the run of the
place. He'd even mentioned that some of them were over
at the beach.

Then there were the Douglasses themselves. And their
daughter.

"An' that aunt Mrs. Somebody-or-other that was out huntin' Mrs. Boone in a beachwagon!"

And Dr. Cummings—where in thunderation was Cummings?

Where were the lot of them? Where'd they gone to? What had become of them?

Twenty-six people, more or less. Call it twenty-six.

Why, twenty-six people—and a corpse!—couldn't just vanish off the face of Pochet Point!

Asey got up suddenly from the plush chair and walked through the car to the end platform.

There was the Douglass house, neat and white, and quiet as a tomb. There were the rolling marshes, bare and empty, looking even a little forlorn with the tide out. The snatch of outside beach that was visible showed no signs of being inhabited. The pine woods were still.

Except for an occasional ripple of wind that moved the marsh grass, the whole place was as lifeless as a tourist post card. Even the sea gulls, huddled on the far side of the point, were quiet as they waited for the tide to change.

Twenty-six people.

And a corpse!

What had become of 'em?

And where were the police? At least by now they should have sent someone here in response to Cummings's telephone call!

Of course, he thought with a grin, explaining the current situation to them was going to be just a little awkward!

"Dear Mr. Halbert, whose uncles are so good in politics," he murmured, "we used to have a body here that would have put you on the front page of every newspaper in the whole country. But it seems like all we got left now is a green ticket with a diamond-shaped punch in it! Huh!"

He swung down from the platform and marched off back to the house.

On this new tour of inspection, he looked under beds, examined closets and cupboards, crawled up into a stifling attic, poked around eaves closets, and subjected the cellar to what amounted to a cross-examination.

Then he tackled the barn, whose sprawling first floor was a combination garage, workshop, tool house and general catch-all.

The more compact second floor was an elaborate guest apartment, obviously where Mrs. Boone had stayed. Her rawhide suitcase was perched on a luggage rack, but she hadn't bothered to unpack more than a pair of green silk pyjamas, a dressing gown that matched, and a few toilet articles. A green pocketbook that looked like a large envelope lay open on the maple bureau, and Asey raised his eyebrows as he glanced at its impersonal contents. A folding check book, a sheaf of Travelers' Checks, a leather change purse, a gold pencil, and a lipstick. Clearly, Mrs. Boone wasn't a woman who believed in clutter!

Asey's footsteps seemed to him to echo hollowly as he descended the stairs to the lower floor, and he began to feel oppressed by the stillness of the place.

As he paused for a moment at the entrance to the workshop, he found himself remembering the stories he'd been told as a boy, of crewless ships that sailed along all by themselves—whole ships, unhurt and uninjured in any way, but just strangely and mysteriously abandoned.

This place was like that, he thought. He couldn't find any signs of trouble, or struggle, or violence, or of anyone's having left with great haste, or under duress.

45

And heaven knew if anything had happened to Cummings, he'd have left some clue behind, even if it had necessitated his amputating one of his own fingers!

The notion that he might have overlooked something bothered him sufficiently to send him searching the house and the barn all over again.

And again he wound up without any scrap of tangible evidence to prove that anything at all untoward might have taken place during his absence.

To all intents and purposes, there never had been any murder at Pochet Point!

"But doggone, there was one! An' I still feel uncomfortable! Something's awful wrong here somewhere—I just keep missin' what it is!"

The only thing left which had escaped his minute attention was the water tower, the relic of an old windmill water-pumping system that plainly hadn't been used in many years.

Asey strode over to it.

A really ingenious person, he thought as he mounted the weatherbeaten side-ladder, would have hoisted Mrs. Boone's body up here. There were blocks and tackles back in the barn workshop, and plenty of good stout rope. And considering that the tendency of the world was to hunt looking down, and not looking up, you couldn't pick a better place!

The idea pleased him so much that he felt genuinely disappointed when he found nothing there—not even a bird's nest. The wooden platform planks were rotten, the seams of the tank had split, and the whole structure seemed to sway with his weight.

"Sensible birds!" he observed. "Know enough to keep away!"

Just as he gingerly started the downward climb, feeling

that at any moment everything might collapse beneath him, he caught sight of something flashing in the meadows beyond the pine grove to his right.

A mirror?

The ladder rung on which his left foot rested actually disintegrated while Asey waited for the sun to come out from behind a bulbous white cloud.

Yes, something *was* shining there through the trees!

Not a mirror, though. That was the chrome-plate of the prince's roadster!

The old water tower was not only trembling like a leaf but groaning as well when he reached ground two seconds later.

But he hesitated for a moment over on the gravel turntable by the house.

While it certainly would be quicker to cut through the woods on foot, he would feel pretty silly if he got there and then had to stand by flat-footed, like a bump on a log, while someone—probably someone named Harold Douglass—went flashing past him in the new roadster!

He slid in behind the wheel of his old car and started down the driveway even before he had the door fully closed.

Five minutes later, he turned off a rut road, parked in a clump of bayberry bushes, made a few brief calculations, and started off on foot in the direction of the place where he had seen the chromium gleaming.

He came on it almost sooner than he expected, standing on another rut lane that ran between the edge of the pine grove and the rim of the meadow.

Asey stopped short.

Then he drew a long breath and surveyed the scene before him.

Just beyond the car's rear fender stood a white sign,

almost standard billboard size, whose primary decoration was a gigantic, leering black skull that surmounted particularly gruesome crossbones.

"MUD MEADOW", the lettering below said. "KEEP AWAY. IT TOOK FOUR MINUTES FOR A COW TO DISAPPEAR ENTIRELY IN THIS HOLE IN 1943. YOU'LL GO QUICKER! YOU WEIGH LESS! KEEP AWAY!!!" It was signed with Douglass's name.

And just beyond the car's front fender, with her back to him, was a brown-haired girl who seemed at first glance to be wearing a brief white woolly jacket, and absolutely nothing else.

But Asey was less moved by her apparent state of near-nudity than by the fact that she was interestedly staring down into the muddy stretch of bog directly in front of her, rather as if she had been watching something disappear from sight.

Asey's eyes narrowed.

Was she the Douglass's daughter? From where he stood, she certainly didn't look much like an instructor in a college, he thought. She looked more like a refugee from the first row of a musical comedy chorus!

He'd soon find out who she was, and what she was doing here, and how she had managed to come into possession of his roadster!

But even as he took a step forward, he stopped again.

The girl had reached over into the car and pulled out a khaki-colored army blanket. Now she was folding it with such meticulousness that she seemed almost to be parodying the gestures of someone folding up a blanket.

In spite of himself, Asey chuckled.

Then, suddenly, as if she were tossing a basketball, she pitched the folded blanket into the mud hole.

Apparently she now knew exactly what results to expect, because she didn't bother to lean over and watch it disappear.

Instead she swung around and took off the short white coat, revealing the sort of bathing suit outfit which Jennie was accustomed to refer to, with a good deal of tongue-clucking, as "those disgraceful baby clothes." In Jennie's opinion, not one woman in a million could get away with the things. This girl, Asey decided, was the one who could.

After stretching herself luxuriously, she got into the roadster, sat back, and lighted a cigarette.

That was not the nervous gesture of someone who had just re-disposed of a body, Asey thought. Nor was there, in her action of folding and of tossing away the blanket, any trace of frenzy, or of hurriedly ridding herself of incriminating evidence.

On the other hand, you couldn't brush away the truth. A blanket was a cover, and whoever had removed Mrs. Boone's body from the Lulu Belle probably had taken the elementary precaution of covering it up with something!

With her cigarette tilted in one corner of her mouth, the girl fumbled with both hands in the pockets of the white coat. Then she got out of the car and started hunting around in the bushes.

Finally, behind the car, somewhere near the foot of Douglass's skull and crossbones sign, she found what she'd been searching for.

Asey felt shivers run up and down his spine as he watched her tie around her head the green scarf that Mrs. Boone had been wearing.

5

IT WAS A GREEN just different enough from most other greens, Asey thought, so that you couldn't miss identifying it. He remembered commenting on the shade to Cummings back in the Lulu Belle when he first saw Carolyn Barton Boone. And again in the guest apartment over the garage, he'd noticed that her silk pyjamas and dressing gown were the same color. Without thinking much about it, he'd made a mental note that it was probably her favorite green as well as a part of her trademark, like the white suit.

This, he decided, was the place for him to come in. Leaving the shadow of the pines, he strolled over toward the girl.

At the sound of his footsteps, she turned her head quickly and smiled, and then her face fell. Asey wasn't sure whether she actually had been expecting someone or not, but he experienced a vague feeling of being a disappointment to her.

"Good afternoon," he said pleasantly, and tried to recall who had recently made some comment about snapping black eyes. Cummings, maybe? Douglass?

"Hello." She wasn't nervous or jumpy, but she was clearly on guard.

"Nice car you got there," Asey remarked.

In her throaty voice, the girl agreed that it sure was.

"Yours?"

She hesitated for the fraction of a second before answering him. "Nope," she said, "I'm just minding it for a friend of mine. He's over in the woods there."

Perhaps she was more nervous than she appeared, Asey

thought, if she felt it necessary to invent a nearby friend who could so conveniently be used as an excuse for the car. He couldn't quite bring himself to believe that she might be improvising in the interests of her own personal safety!

"I see." He saw also that she *had* been dumping something into the mud hole. There were marks in the ruts where some heavy object had been dragged from the roadster. "I'm Asey Mayo," he went on. "I wonder if you've seen Mrs. Boone around anywhere. I'm huntin' her."

The girl suddenly turned as white as her bathing suit.

"What's the matter with her?" Her voice sounded harsh. "Is anything wrong?"

"I'm just huntin' for her," Asey said with perfect truth. "The Douglasses can't find her."

"Gee!" She leaned back against the seat, and her color began to return to normal. "Gee, you certainly scared the beje—you certainly had me scared! I know who you are, of course—gee, I thought for a minute she might have been hurt, or something like that. Say, I met your Cousin Jennie this morning. We was all of us to—I mean, all of the project went over to your house. I always seen—I've seen," she corrected herself again, "you in the newsreels and all, and I always wanted to meet you in the flesh. Your cousin's quick with the tongue, isn't she?"

"It was Jennie who mentioned the eyes—sure, I remember now! I bet you're the ex-Wac!"

She extended her hand. "Roger!" she said. "I'm Gerty Rand. I used to be a sergeant."

"An' now you're a member," Asey said quizzically, "of the Larrabee College Town Government Project, Section B, or Small Towns Division?"

"Beats hell what the GI-bill did, doesn't it?" She grinned from ear to ear. "Every now and then I pinch myself—when I don't giggle too hard! Say, what makes with General Boone? What's happened to her? She missed the beam somewhere?"

Asey nodded. "That looks like one of her scarves you're wearin' around your head," he remarked. "That's her color green."

"It's one of hers. She gave it to me," the girl said simply.

"Oh? I thought a scarf that particular green was sort of her special trademark, like," Asey said.

"Yeah, it is, but she gives 'em away. You know, it's like a Good Conduct Badge at Larrabee," Gerty explained. "She strews 'em around to key personnel when she's in a good mood. I had a general was like that. The day his wife divorced him, he give the whole outfit Bronze Stars—oh, there I go! He *gave* Bronze Stars! Say, do you have trouble with your grammar?"

"Wa-el," Asey said with a chuckle, "bein' a native Cape Codder, I can slip up as much as I like, an' folks just set it down to the quaint an' picturesque speech of the section. Away from the Cape, I try to put on as many 'g's' as I can without gettin' too twisted up. But I don't know as I let grammar haunt me much."

"But boy, oh boy, can't it!" Gerty shook her head. "You start in trying to *do* something about it, and honest to God, you don't have another peaceful moment, never —I mean, ever! This college outfit—say," she broke off suddenly, "say, listen, I got a problem, Mr. Mayo!"

Asey restrained his impulse to remark that she probably had more than she ever dreamed of, and said instead that he had a problem, himself.

"I keep lookin' at those marks in the ruts—see 'em there, an' there? An' I keep askin' myself *what* in the world you could have been shovin' into Douglass's mud hole here!"

"Oh, *that!*" Gerty said. "That's a *part* of the problem —gee, I don't know where to begin! You see, Boone— no. No, I guess I hadn't ought to start off with her, but I don't know where else—"

"What's Mrs. Boone like, anyway?" Asey asked quickly, as she hesitated. "I heard an awful lot of different opinions about her."

"Well," Gerty said, "well, on public relations, she's tops. The girl's solid there. Give her a bunch of reporters and ask her—oh, anything. Ask her like what she thinks about Russia, see? She's right back at you—history of Russia in one little sentence, social and economic problems in another, peace of the world demands such-and-such, and while we may feel thus-and-so, why whoop-de-dee for the global good, and that's *just* the sort of intelligent international citizenship, gentlemen, that Larrabee's trying to instill into its undergraduates—what're you laughing at?"

"You," Asey said. "Mostly that little gesture with your hand. I've seen Mrs. Boone use it in newsreels. Go on."

"Of course," Gerty said, "she always lands up straddling the middle of the fence, but it sounds swell, and you can make a wonderful headline out of it, and everybody loves her to death."

The trouble with this girl, Asey thought, was that after she got you laughing, she froze the smile on your face with something unexpected, like throwing that blanket away a while back, or using a phrase like "loving her to death."

"An' how about you?" he inquired. "What're your feelin's about her?"

Gerty ignored his questions. "Yes, sir, on PR, Boone is there! A swell front-woman. Between you and me, though, Shearing's the one that runs the college and keeps the joint buzzin'."

"Who's he?'"

"She. She's just Miss Shearing," Gerty said. "She don't seem to have any rank, but just you get something good and fouled up, and everybody says to go see Shearing. Not Boone. It's always Shearing gets things back under control. Her father started Larrabee, and she was the head till somebody left the place a lot of dough, see, and the new board of directors stuck Boone in as president. Shearing came down here with us on the project," she added, "but I think Boone sent her right back—for a pencil, or a piece of Kleenex, or something. Boone works the tar out of her. She's really sort of a Chief of Staff. Does all the dirty work but never gets any credit."

Asey mentally put Miss Shearing on his list for future reference.

"An' what," he asked again, "are your own feelin's about Mrs. Boone?"

"Look," Gerty said severely, "I don't stick my neck out on my C.O.!"

"Wa-el, what does the rest of the project think of her, then?" Asey persisted.

"That's another part of this problem I got—I mean, I *have*. Listen, Mr. Mayo, this crowd at Larrabee—well, they're okay. They're right. Only a lot of 'em aren't shook down yet, see? Like Stinky."

"Stinky who?"

"Gee, I forget you don't know!" Gerty said. "The way we been talking, it seems like I known you a long time—oh, God, that's *all* wrong! Honest, what'm I going to *do?*" she asked unhappily. "If I got to stop and try to make it proper grammar all the time, then I get all dried up, and what comes out isn't what I *want* to say!"

She looked at him ruefully.

"If it simmers down to a choice of grammar or of bein' thwarted," Asey said, "I think I'd be inclined to advise your forgettin' the grammar. An' I point out to you that *I* haven't any blue pencil in my hand!"

"Well, listen, see, it's like this—say, whyn't you come in and take a load off your feet?" She moved over obligingly and made room for him on the roadster's seat. "Now, here's the picture, see. Stinky—that's Bill Cotton —he was a fly-boy. Chicken colonel. Big shot. Then, bingo—he's back in school, see, a senior again. Okay! Then there's Jack Briggs. Lousy eyes, see? Glasses. Limited service. P.F.C. Briggs, the desk-drawer commando. So *he's* back being a senior, too. So what's *he* going to do? *He's* going to show Stinky who's the brains-colonel, see? That's what! He's going to be the big shot in school—and the hell with all of Stinky's fruit salad—" she paused.

"Ribbons," Asey said. "I know."

"Get the set-up?" she asked eagerly. "Stinky's such a damn fool—of course, *all* men are, but—oh, excuse me, Mr. Mayo. I forgot."

"Oh, don't mind me!" Asey said. "When Jennie lets her hair down in one of her off moods, she usually claims that all men are fools, an' I'm the *biggest* fool she ever met—look, could you just maybe clarify this situation of Stinky an' his friend Jack Briggs?"

The way this saga of hers was shaping up, he thought to himself, it was going to take considerable clarifying and sifting before she worked her way back to the problem of what had been dumped into the mud hole.

"Friend? *Friend?* That's just exactly *it!* He *is*n't! Jack *is*n't his friend—but Stinky's such a sap, he still thinks so! That's more of this problem, see? Every time we go on one of these—these—" Gerty seemed to be searching for a suitable word, "these *damn* projects, Stinky lands up in a cooler somewhere, see, usually D and D—"

55

"Uh-huh, city girl," Asey said gently, "I know what a drunk an' disorderly charge is."

"Well, so Stinky's in the cooler, and Jack's the bright boy with his work all done. Every time there's an exam, Stinky's in trouble the night before—see? *Jack's* the bright boy again. And Stinky, the big sap, doesn't have sense enough to open his eyes and see what's rolling over him! Just a steam roller, that's all, pushed by his old pal Jack! Now do you get it?"

Asey said that he understood up to a certain point.

"But what's it all got to do with your shovin' things into the mud hole? An' with Mrs. Boone, as you suggested when you first started out?"

Gerty looked at him for several moments, and then she sighed.

"Look, Mr. Mayo. You see this car?"

"Uh-huh."

"Look at it." She waved her hand toward the Balkan prince's fanciful gadgets. "Look. Ten grand!"

Asey, in a position to know, nearly corrected her and said twelve.

"Well," Gerty went on, "Stinky stole it."

"*Stinky?* He stole it?"

"That's right! You heard. It's not his, and I'm not minding it for him. He swiped it. It's hot. Now, what would *you* do about that, to begin with?"

"Wa-el, I been wonderin'," Asey said, "for some time. You see, it's mine."

Gerty looked as though he had thrown the roadster at her.

"Wow!" she said softly. "Wow!"

"Exactly," Asey said. "Just so! You better talk quick, sarge, an' you better get *all* the problems into the record. Begin with Boone, an' work Stinky an' Jack in where they belong, an' this car, an' whatever you stuffed into the mud hole besides the blanket. Put it all together in the form of a nice, concrete, truthful report, please!"

Gerty smoked half of a cigarette before she answered, and then she sat up straight, and reported.

"After leaving your house in the town at approximately twelve noon, Layne Douglass and I proceeded in her car to her house at Pochet Point, where we secured rations— I mean, lunch—which we took to the outside beach. We swam, ate lunch, and she made sketches. Slightly over an hour ago—my watch is being repaired in Boston—I started back to the Douglass's house, leaving Layne still working on her sketches. Owing to lack of knowledge of the terrain, I took the wrong path, found myself on this road here, and the first thing I saw when I came around the curve there was this car, and Stinky in it."

"Wow!" Asey said. "Nothin' wrong with your grammar when you report!"

"But it takes so much time to think first! And so," Gerty dropped her crisp manner, "I said to him, 'Look, Stinky, where'd you steal that from?' And he said what made me think he stole it, and I said, 'So your rich grandfather died an hour ago and left it to you, and get the hell out of that car!'—You see what happened, don't you, Mr. Mayo?"

Asey allowed that he didn't, quite.

"Why, Jack suggested a party, like he always does— on projects, or before exams. So he and Stinky go to the town liquor store, and get a case of beer, and some gin. Then Jack wonders what's the best way to get it to the Inn where we're staying, and says they really need a car. Then he looks out the window and sees this roadster, and dares Stinky to take it. And Stinky does! *That*'s what happened!"

"I thought," Asey observed, "that you were at the beach with Layne Douglass."

57

"I was—but I know what happened! I know what *would* have happened later, too, more or less. It happens in different ways, but the results are always the same. Jack—he always rooms with Stinky—he says he's got an errand to do, and he'll fix Stinky a drink before he runs out. And that's all, chum! However Jack manages, it's as easy as that!"

"An' what was Stinky doin' over *here?*" Asey inquired. "Samplin'? Or just en route somewheres?"

"He was lost. First he took the wrong turn at the traffic light. Then he tried to get to the Douglass's to find the right way back, and he got here instead. So," Gerty said, "I told him to go get Layne, and she'd show us the way back. And the minute he got out of sight, I dumped all the liquor into the mud hole. I know how much dough this crowd has—and I know Jack can't borrow enough to replace what I dumped, no matter how he scrapes around. So," she concluded grimly, "that cracks his little plan for lousing Stinky up on *this* project, anyway!"

"Just how were you plannin' to fix up the car problem?" Asey asked.

"I was going to make Stinky march it back to the owner and apologize like crazy. He *will*, too."

Asey looked at her thoughtfully. Something in her voice made him suspect that Stinky would probably arrive on his knees, dressed in sackcloth and possibly smeared with ashes.

He asked about the blanket.

"Oh, that? That belonged to Jack. Had his name on it. You know, it's been cold on a lot of these projects we been on," she explained. "We learned to go prepared, like with blankets, and red flannels and all. I don't know why the blanket was in the car—maybe the boys took it to carry their bottles back to the Inn in. I was just so damn sore, I threw it in the muck, too."

"Wa-el," Asey said, "that accounts for the roadster, the mud hole department, an' Stinky an' Jack. Now— about Mrs. Boone. You started off with her, an' never got to her. Just where does she enter into this problem of yours?"

"The Sucker Club," Gerty said promptly. "Boone's the founder, organizer, and head girl—oh, there isn't any such thing really, of course! That's just what Layne Douglass and I call it. You see, Mr. Mayo, Boone's the real trouble with Jack, and Stinky too. They're both right guys. It's just that Boone's made suckers out of both of 'em, only they don't know it! You ask Layne— she'll tell you that's the truth. We been talking about it on the beach just now."

"Made suckers out of 'em in what way?" Asey asked curiously. "What d'you mean?"

"Gee, if you was—I mean, *were*—only another girl!" Gerty sounded wistful. "Your Cousin Jennie'd see the picture before I got the words out of my mouth. Well, it's like this, see. Boone'll go to Jack and say she's making a little speech, or writing a little article, and she'd like his point of view—now just what would a former enlisted man think of this?"

Again she made that little gesture with her hand that was so like what Asey remembered of Mrs. Boone in her newsreel appearances, and yet so much a parody of it.

"Then," Gerty continued, "she goes to Stinky and asks him the hero's point of view on the same thing. Now what would a fighting officer with twenty-one decorations feel about so-and-so? Oh, Mr. Mayo, don't you see what she *does* to 'em? Don't you *see?*"

"I think I do," Asey said slowly. "You mean they never

get the chance to stop rememberin' what they was an' what they did in the war, because she keeps bringin' it up."

"That's it! Stinky's flattered that a big shot like her should ask him, and he shoots his mouth off," Gerty said. "And Jack, he's flattered too that she asks him, but he's a little sore because of her still thinking of him as a private, see? Then he goes and cooks up something else that gets Stinky into a mess, to prove that Stinky's really the low boy in civilian life, see, and *he*'s the bright boy. It's a circle that just keeps going round and round. And the suckers—oh, those two big suckers, how they go and fall for it!"

"An' for her, too?"

Gerty sighed as she leaned back against the roadster's seat.

"Uh-huh. Her too," she said.

"No need askin'," Asey remarked, "which one you're feelin' all that anguish for!"

A little smile flitted across Gerty's face. "Layne Douglass would kill me if she thought I said it, but it ain't—ooop! *isn't*—half the anguish she's feeling about Jack and the way he's acting, let me tell you!"

"Oh?"

"They were both in college together, you know, before he went into the army. If she wasn't the refined type, she'd black both his eyes so quick! Honest, people can act *so* crazy, can't they? Jack calls her 'Doctor' Douglass, like she was a professor about a hundred years old, and she calls him 'Briggs', like he was a kid freshman of sixteen, just out of high school! And yet, if you watch, you can see how her eyes follow him when she thinks he isn't looking, and when he thinks she isn't looking, he looks at her—gee! And if you said a word to either of 'em about it, they'd kick your teeth out."

She paused and gazed dreamily at the sand dunes beyond the meadow.

"Either—they," she murmured. "That's wrong, isn't it? Well, if you said a word to either, he—or she, as the case might be—would slap you down. I got to look up that either-they business again, I guess."

With difficulty, Asey suppressed a smile. "How does Layne feel about Mrs. Boone, in view of her makin' a sucker out of Jack?"

"Oh," Gerty said wearily, "she thinks Mrs. Boone is Mrs. God! Sure, she kids about the Sucker Club, but she doesn't hold anything against *Boone*—no, sir! She's just livid with Jack because he don't catch on. Thinks it's *his* fault. Now me, I'm sore enough with Stinky, God knows, but I don't kid myself, see, about whose fault it all is. *I*'m not a one to underestimate the power of a woman—not a woman like Boone, anyway! *I* don't think she doesn't know her own strength—I know very damn well she knows it, and uses it, and but good!"

"On Jack, for example?" Asey steered her back to the angle which interested him most. "I gather he's fallen for her even though he really still loves Layne."

"Oh, Jack and Stinky both!" Gerty said. "They eat Boone up, both of 'em! They're goggle-eyed with her. Punch drunk. And I tell myself," she added with a touch of bitterness, "it can't be only just on account of her lovely correct grammar!"

Asey threw back his head and laughed until he choked.

"Have you bothered," he said when he got his breath, "to tell yourself that she's married?"

"Look, I seen that old, bald, weedy windbag!" Gerty retorted. "Married to Senator Willard P. Boone, a girl might as well be single!"

"Now give the old fellow credit," Asey said with a chuckle. "The papers always call him spry, an' talk about what wonderful golf he plays, an' I'm sure I seen pictures of him tossin' out the first baseball, too."

"Oh, he's *agile!*" Gerty said crisply. "He's quick on the old pins! Every blonde in school gets set to sprint when Old Horse-face comes to the campus! But I don't count the senator. What *I* count is secretaries!"

Asey raised his eyebrows.

"*Men* secretaries, I mean," Gerty said hurriedly. "Boone always has men because she claims girls got too jealous of her. Eric—that's the one she's got now—he's in Washington this week, but Eric's going into the diplomatic service, and so she's hunting around for a successor. It's a sort of a springboard job, being her secretary is. And," she grinned, "and *all* of 'em bounce off into the *nicest* things!"

"So?"

"And *I* think—now look, Mr. Mayo, I'm just guessing at this!—*I* think that Jack Briggs wants to go into politics."

"And he certainly couldn't ask for a nicer place to bounce into 'em from," Asey said, "than bein' her secretary. That what you mean?"

"Yeah. Like Eric said to me last week, you meet such *in*teresting people, working for her! And Stinky, he has some idea he'd either like to teach, or run a school," Gerty went on. "He'd contact some pretty interesting people, too. Now I don't think either of the boys would break down and *say* they covet Eric's job, see? And I'm damn sure neither of 'em knows what they'd be getting themselves in for if they landed it. Our Mrs. Boone," she added succinctly, "doesn't do things for free! Only in their misty-eyed state, Jack and Stinky don't notice that! But there's the nice job, and there's the two of 'em getting through school next month, see?"

"An' if one of 'em should get it—?" Asey left the sentence unfinished.

Gerty winced. "Then either Layne Douglass is going to do some pillow-biting, or I—well, I don't think that mummy'll stick around Larrabee's College to watch, if Stinky wins."

She was looking out over the meadow to the dunes again, but this time Asey knew that she wasn't brooding about her grammar.

"What did you do," he asked curiously, "before you went into the army?"

"Show business," Gerty said. "I was twenty then, and I'd been in show business for five years. I didn't know one part of speech from another, and I didn't starve, and I won't starve again for not knowing all the rules about infinitives—what are you asking all this for?" She turned and shot the question at him suddenly.

"All what for?" Asey returned. "About you? I didn't mean to pry, but I was curious. I don't run into ex-Wac sergeants every day in the we—"

"Don't stall, chum! You didn't care a hoot about your car's being swiped! It's *Boone* you wanted to know all about—it's *her* you been so interested in!"

Asey observed that to his way of thinking, Carolyn Barton Boone was a very interesting person.

"When you first came, you didn't look to see if your car was okay—you didn't even take one little gander at the fenders!" Gerty said. "Instead, you looked for tracks of something that might've been shoved into the mud hole. You must've been watching me some time to know that I threw that blanket away—I'm just beginning to catch on! So Boone's lost? *Lost?* Okay, chum, let's have it! What's happened to Boone?"

Asey shrugged and said truthfully that he didn't know.

"She *was* at the Douglass's," he continued, as Gerty made a derisive sound of disbelief, "an' then—well, they sort of lost track of her."

"Sure! Of course!" The irony in Gerty's voice would have done credit, Asey thought, to Dr. Cummings. "And the minute she slipped out of sight behind that purple lilac, they called in Asey Mayo right away—just to help find her! Yeah, sure! But I got to admit that Little Lame-brain here took a long, long while to get hep—me, *I* was mostly worried about Stinky, and parking in a hot car! And how you eased all that dope out of me!" She paused and looked at him with something akin to admiration. "I just made you a present of the whole damn setup, didn't I? The works, from Shearing to Stinky!"

"I wish you wouldn't be so suspicious-like," Asey said, and meant it. "I told you the truth. I am huntin' Mrs. Boone because—she's lost!"

"To the person sending in the best answer, in fifty words or less, to our question, '*Why* is Asey Mayo hunting Mrs. Boone?', we will give, absolutely free and without charge, a two hundred and forty-eight piece set of genuine, bone-type china, with *real* simulated-gold trim," Gerty said. "Including *two* pickle dishes. And just a tip, folks. The answer is *not*, and I quote, 'Because she's lost!' Unquote. No, chum, I don't think they rushed you into the cast for a bit-part. Something seems to keep telling me that you landed the lead."

Asey sighed.

"I can see," he said, "where you an' my Cousin Jennie have a lot of things in common. She refers to that trait as her perspicacity, an' Cummings calls it her intuition, an' I sometimes feel, myself, that it's something she does with mirrors."

"So I'm right?"

"I'm torn," Asey said. "If I say no, you'll go whisper

things to the project, an' I don't think I want that. If I say yes, you're right, you'll go whisper things to the project, an' I don't think I want that, either. I wonder if you could—wa-el, I don't like to ask you to promise anything. But could you maybe dead-pan till I find out how things shape up? I know she's dead, an' I know she was murdered. I saw her. But I don't know where she is now. I'm huntin'."

Gerty pitched her cigarette stub into the mud hole and watched it disappear.

"I told you a while back," she said, "that I didn't stick my neck out on my C.O. Well, an ex-C.O. is something else. You know what? I've run into a lot of nasties, but she took every prize. And," she added quietly, "I hated her. I hated her guts!"

She turned and looked at him expectantly.

"Oh, I guessed that," Asey returned. "Under the circumstances, I think you've really been very fair to her, too. You gave credit where it was due. After all, she hasn't treated your friend Stinky very nice. She—"

Gerty bit, just as he hoped she would.

"Not because of him! What I think about Boone is strictly personal—it's *me*, it's nothing to do with Stinky! I thought it about her before I knew he existed!" She had never, Asey thought, sounded so deeply in earnest. "I got to Larrabee, see, and I'm minding my own business and going my own way. Then, somehow, Boone sees my records and finds out that I—oh, well, what does it matter *now*, for God's sakes! Let's just skip it!"

While Gerty was smiling, her eyes were suspiciously bright, and Asey decided that he would skip it. Whatever Mrs. Boone had done to the girl, the hurt had been deep enough to sting even now. To bring tears welling to Gerty's eyes, it must have been a sledge hammer blow, and he could always find out about sledge hammer items.

65

It was the other sort of thing, the strange, complex little relationships between Jack and Stinky, and Layne Douglass, and Miss Shearing, and all the rest of the project, that would have taken him so much time to delve into without Gerty's unwitting aid.

Or had it been so unwitting, he asked himself suddenly. If the girl could turn herself into Mrs. Boone with just a simple twist of her wrist and a flick of her finger, or if she could snap out a report like a company commander after a few seconds' thought, then just how far could you trust her? Where did her play-acting begin, and where did it end? And why had he been so dim-witted as to expect that she'd always ring bells to announce to her audience what act was currently on?

Aloud, he asked her where she thought Stinky and Layne might be.

Gerty shrugged. "I never expected he'd be this long getting back!" she said. "After all, I sent him packing off hell-bent in the wrong direction!"

"Whatever for?"

"Your Cousin Jennie," Gerty said with a demure smile, "would catch that one! You'd be surprised, Mr. Mayo, how hard it is to see anyone for five minutes anywhere on a project like this, without about four hundred million other people there too!"

"Wait for him, then," Asey said as he got out of the roadster, "an' bring him an' the car back to the Douglass's —see here," he took a stick and scratched a few lines in the dirt, "here's the way the lanes go. You go here, an' then here—see? An' if he doesn't turn up within a reasonable time, you come along by yourself."

"You mean I should drive this thing? But look," she pointed to the gadgets, "they're all marked funny—what makes with all those 'J's' and 'M's' and 'Z's'? I don't know which is what!"

"It's just Serbo-Croat, or Croato-Slav, or somethin'," Asey said casually, and explained the gadgets to her briefly. "Simple enough, see? After all, you probably drove jeeps, didn't you?"

"Sure, from Casablanca to Berchtesgaden."

"Then I dare say," Asey remarked, "that you'll be able to trundle this job to the Douglass's if Stinky doesn't come soon."

"What about you?" Gerty asked.

Asey pointed to the woods. "Oh, I got another roadster," he said. "I keep a spare."

"Dirty capitalist," she said amiably. "And don't worry, Mr. Mayo. I'll dead-pan. If Sti—I mean, if somebody gets themselves mixed up in a mess like this, you can't *do* anything for them! To tell you the truth, I don't think any of our crowd's got anything to do with it, and I think it may turn out to be the best—"

"Best what?" Asey prompted as she hesitated.

"As my philosophy professor said last week," Gerty returned, "there is a wide abyss between being realistic and being callous—hell, I *can't* say it's the best thing Boone ever did in her life, can I? Well, anyway, I'll dead-pan, Mr. Mayo!"

When he reached the edge of the pine woods, Asey paused and looked back toward the roadster. Gerty had climbed up on the folded boot-top, and was stretched out, peacefully sun-bathing and apparently sound asleep.

"An' I'll bet a nickel," he said to himself with a chuckle, "that she played gin-rummy in fox-holes—an' probably won!"

He had nearly reached the place where he'd left his old roadster when someone called out to him.

"Yoo-hoo! I beg your pardon! Could you—"

Asey swung around.

A tall, thin girl in a striped seersucker dress was hurrying toward him, notebook in hand. He recognized her as the ex-Wave whom Cummings had pointed out earlier, over by the swamp.

"I beg your pardon," she said a little breathlessly as she adjusted her wide blue-rimmed glasses, "but would you possibly know the location of an abandoned mosquito-control project in this area?"

"I'm sorry," Asey said, "but I wouldn't. I haven't been over this way in years until today."

"Oh. Then I don't suppose you'd know anything about where the town's water project was started, either?"

"Out this way? Golly, that was thirty years ago, or more," Asey said, "an' they gave it up within two weeks, as I remember. You're one of the Larrabee College project, aren't you?"

"Yes. I'm investigating Public Health and Welfare." She sounded very nearly as enthusiastic about it, Asey thought, as Gerty had sounded on the topic of Stinky.

"Don't you find it just a mite dull, all by yourself?" he inquired.

"Oh, no! Not at *all!*" she said. "I've managed to see some of the town's points of interest as I've gone along, of course. Where the early settlers made peace with the Indians, for example, and where they planted their first corn, and then the scene of the encounter with a German submarine in the First World War. It's really been *very* interesting! I wonder, though," she added with a puzzled look, "if you could explain one marker I noticed, about an 'Encounter with the British'. Was that during the Revolutionary War?"

"Nope," Asey said. "The British sailed into the Bay Harbor, an' we repelled 'em with our trusty muskets—that was 1812, the war everybody forgets. The one they burned Washington in."

"Washington? But he—"

"Not he," Asey said. "*It.* The city."

She thanked him very seriously, and said it was a very interesting piece of information indeed, but she clearly didn't believe him. She also declined, quite distantly, his casual offer of a lift back to the Douglass's.

"Thank you, but I'm somewhat behind my schedule," she said. "I have five more items to check before I shall feel free to stop. But it was very kind of you to make the suggestion."

Notebook in hand, she marched on through the pine woods.

Asey backed the roadster out of the bayberries.

He felt a sense of relief, on swinging into the Douglass's driveway, to hear the sound of people's voices.

That meant the cops were there, and Cummings. And the Douglass family, and the project. Mrs. Boone's body would have been located. Things were under way!

He found himself blinking as he stopped on the gravel turntable.

His first impression was that he'd never seen so many people outside of the Grand Central Station, or Coney Island on a hot summer's day.

Then facts leapt at him.

Cummings wasn't there. Nor his car.

The cops weren't there. Nor their cars!

He hardly recognized Mrs. Douglass as she wove her way through a quartet playing badminton, and hurried toward him.

In his memory, Mrs. Douglass was a pale, inert figure, lying limply on a couch.

This Mrs. Douglass was gay, animated, and apparently as happy as a lark.

"Where's Cummings?" Asey demanded.

"The doctor? Oh, isn't he with you? Mr. Mayo, I'm sure you'll be happy to know that there was some perfectly frightful mistake! She's all right!"

"Who is?"

"Mrs. Boone! Isn't it wonderful? She's all *right!*"

6

"You mean," Asey sounded as incredulous as he felt, "you know where Mrs. Boone *is?*"

"Well," Mrs. Douglass said, "not exactly *where*, but I know that she's perfectly all right. That—" she broke off to answer the question of a short, chubby boy whose voice still seemed to be in the breaking stage.

As she discussed with him the possible location of some missing croquet mallets, Asey began to realize that the place wasn't anywhere near as crowded as he had first assumed. He couldn't count more than ten members of the project disporting themselves around the lawn. But he suddenly understood with great clarity what Jennie had meant by her repetition of the word "swarm."

"Now, *where* was I?" Mrs. Douglass said a little distractedly, as she turned back to him.

"No," Asey said. "Where's Mrs. *Boone?*"

"Oh, yes! She's with Miss Shearing," Mrs. Douglass said. "I was practically frantic about the situation, and then Miss Shearing phoned and said that Mrs. Boone was with her, and perfectly all right, and for me not to worry. Wasn't it *silly* of me to think she was dead!"

Asey looked at her thoughtfully while the badminton game held a brisk free-for-all almost under the roadster's front wheels.

"Do I sort of gather," he said, "that at one time you *did* think she was dead?"

"Why, of course I did! What on earth d'you suppose I called you here for?" Mrs. Douglass demanded. "I dis-*tinct*ly said she was dead! In fact, *I* thought that she'd been murdered! I *told* you—"

"Hold it just a second, please," Asey said. "I want to go slow an' get it straight. Just exactly when did you phone me?"

"Just after I phoned and said she was *lost!*" Mrs. Douglass returned. "I called you back again, and told your cousin that I'd found Mrs. Boone dead, and I thought she'd been murdered—haven't you talked with Dr. Cummings? Didn't he tell you all about everything?"

Asey ducked back to avoid a shuttlecock sailing into his eye, and then raised his voice over the din to inform her that he hadn't seen Dr. Cummings for more than two hours, and that he'd be obliged if she'd tell him where the doctor was!

"*I* don't know! I thought he must have gone off after you! Mr. Mayo, I simply don't understand this little mix-up about those calls! First I phoned you and said she was lost, and then after I found her—"

"Where?" Asey interrupted.

"On the floor of the Lulu Belle! After I saw her lying there, I rushed in and phoned your house again, and told your cousin—she said you were just leaving and she'd try to catch you! Mr. Mayo, haven't you seen your cousin? Didn't she tell you all about everything?"

"I haven't seen Jennie since—oh, for Pete's sakes!" Asey plucked a shuttlecock out of his lap, and tossed it back at a husky, dark-haired girl with a thick fringe of bangs. "Try an' keep it over that way, will you, sis?"

"She's been here," Mrs. Douglass said.

71

"*Who?*"

"Your cousin! Oh, dear, it's really di*stract*ing here, isn't it?"

"What's that?" Asey almost had to yell to make himself heard.

"I said, your cousin left some things for you!" she yelled back. "A basket—" she lowered her voice during a sudden lull, and then resumed in conversational tones, "and a note. I thought you knew all about them—I thought you'd probably *come* for them! She said the note explained something important, and you must be sure to read every word—she left it indoors, in the house."

Asey got out of the car. "Let's get—I said," he had to bellow again, "let's get it, shall we?"

Aunt Della's cluttered living room was so quiet, after Mrs. Douglass had shut down the windows overlooking the lawn, that the silence was almost as deafening to Asey as the outside noise had been.

"I suppose it's a sign that I'm aging rapidly," she remarked, "but it keeps seeming to me that youth keeps getting noisier and noisier, and somehow knocking over more objects! I told Layne that they simply could *not* step foot in this room, none of them, unless Harold or I was here! Aunt Della would never forgive me if I let that horde mill around among her treasures. Not that they'd ever *mean* to break anything, of course, but I know they would! Just a moment, I'll go get your things."

After she'd left the room, Asey was puzzled to find himself again experiencing that same uncomfortable feeling which had so obsessed him earlier in the afternoon, before he'd climbed the water tower and gone rushing off to the meadow and Gerty.

Something about this place still bothered him!

And certainly, he thought as he strolled over and gazed out at the thickly populated lawn, it couldn't at this point have anything to do with the place appearing so abandoned!

And where in thunder was Cummings? And the cops? *And* Mrs. Boone?

And what *was* this idiotic business of her being "all right"?

He suddenly found himself wanting to jerk open the window and to bellow out at that noisy swarm, to tell them to pipe down, that there'd been a murder!

His hand was on the window catch before he admonished himself not to be a fool. Before he could do any bellowing about murder, he'd have to have slightly more proof than a little green ticket punched with a diamond-shaped hole!

"Here you are!" Mrs. Douglass brought in a basket covered with a white napkin, and held out an envelope to him.

Asey slit it open to find that Jennie had apparently sat herself down and written a short novel on the Douglass's fancy blue house-stationery, which had a sketch of the baby Baldwin and the Lulu Belle running across the top of the page.

"I do hope she explains everything!" Mrs. Douglass said anxiously.

"She should," Asey returned. "It's long enough!"

A smile came to his lips as he read the first sentence to himself.

"Dear Asey, that Mrs. Douglass may be a writer & a wonderful woman & all that but she is certainly a *crazy coot*, that's all I got to say!"

"*Is* it important?" Mrs. Douglass interrupted.

"Not very, so far," Asey answered, "but it's reasonably accurate, I think!"

He continued reading.

"She called our house just as you and the doc were leaving & said Mrs. Boone was murdered! I tried to yell after you & tell you but the wind was the wrong way or something because anyway you didn't hear me. Think of it, think of her getting me all stirred up that way & packing your lunch (there is salt in waxed paper, wrapped up, in corner of basket in case the soup isn't salt enough for you) & thank *Goodness* the only person I told about Mrs. Boone was Emma & how it happened I won't ever know but when I called *her* back just now & said it was all a mistake, why she'd been so busy cooking & particularly popovers she hadn't called anyone else & told them! If it hadn't been popovers & her such a careful fussy cook, I can only say it'd been all over Cape Cod now about Mrs. Boone—you know Emma & how she gabs!"

Mrs. Douglass cleared her throat. "Is she explaining everything?"

"Jennie," Asey said, "isn't leavin' a single stone unturned. Includin' popovers!"

He went on to the next page.

"So just you bless that tea-party she was having! So I took the doc's car figuring you'd want it & he'd want his bag, & your lunch, & on the way I stopped in town to ask about the Question but nobody has heard it & everybody is furious with Sylvester & they say he's run away he's so scared what'll happen to him when folks get their hands on him. Think of it, everybody missing because he was three minutes late with the B. Moose! Someone said someone from Truro said he'd forgotten the Question, which somebody else told him at a gas station, but the answer was *catnip*. I mean the Question was the Latin name for it. So just in case you are anywhere & get called, remember CATNIP!"

Asey sighed, and went on to the last page.

"Does she make everything *clear?*" Mrs. Douglass wanted to know.

"Yes," Asey said. "Just remember catnip."

He entirely missed her nervous, almost frightened glance at him.

"So," the last page said, "I guess I was a little late getting here because I had to stop by the Red Cross on an errand & at the post office—"

"*That*'s how Billy at the drug store saw the doc's car!" Asey said aloud. "Jennie was drivin' it around findin' out about catnip an' such! Well, that's nice to know!"

"I still can't see," the letter went on, "*WHY* I didn't tell everybody about the murder only everybody was so busy fussing at Sylvester & *I* was so busy trying to get hold of the Question, I guess I never got the chance to. The P.O. was empty & at Red Cross only Mrs. Newell & her deaf as a post. Just as well I was late getting here & didn't tell because now Mrs. Douglass says all a mistake & Mrs. B. *not* dead *or* murdered & I *do* think you should speak real firm to her about bothering you this way! You tell her next time she sees a body lying somewhere, why to touch it, & if she ties bells around their necks maybe she won't lose so many guests. In all this mess there must be a cow bell! Jennie."

Asey drew a long breath.

"Well?" Mrs. Douglass said.

75

"There's a P.S.," Asey said wearily. "Jennie always has a P.S."

But it was brief.

> "I got clams & will have chowder tonight—nice ones on the Tonset Rd—& you be home for it. Will take the doc's car back to our house since otherwise he won't know where it is. If Mrs. D should ask you what *I* think, I am mad clear through with all her silly nonsense. J."

"Well," Mrs. Douglass said as he looked up from the letter, "now, if you'll excuse me, I'll leave you—I've got to get hold of Layne and tell her that they simply *must*n't climb up that water tower—it's suicidal! And *look* at that silly little fat boy!"

"Isn't he," Asey craned his neck to look through the window over at the tower, "isn't he a mite younger than the rest of this crew?"

"Oh, yes, he and the girl with the bangs, and a few others," Mrs. Douglass said, "they were just all going to college *any*way. Not ex-G.I.'s, or anything. Just boys and girls—oh, dear, we've yearned for years to find someone who'd take that tower down for us, but I don't want any of them to break their necks doing it! I'm so glad," she was edging politely toward the door, "that your cousin explained everything to you, Mr. Mayo, and you were *so* good to come, and thanks just awfully!"

"I'm afraid," Asey said as he folded Jennie's note and put it in his pocket, "that she explained things of what you'd call a more local nature, like. Mrs. Douglass, let's review this situation, please—they're down off the tower, an' you can relax. First you phoned me an' said Mrs. Boone was lost. Then you found Mrs. Boone in the Pullman, an' rushed in an' telephoned me again, an' said she was murdered. Then, to coin a phrase, as the doc would say, you fainted. What was the reason for that fake faint?"

"Well," her cheeks were very bright, "I—oh, does all this *matter*, Mr. Mayo? Mrs. Boone's all right, and we know she's all right, and the silly thing I did then doesn't make a bit of difference now, does it?"

"Do you, deep down in your heart," Asey said quizzically, "honestly believe this business about her bein' all right?"

"Why, I certainly *do!* Miss Shearing said so!"

And she certainly sounded sincere enough about it, Asey thought.

"Okay," he said. "Then let's work this out on a basis of my just insistin' on knowin' what happened, an' why. Why did you pretend to faint?"

"I was *so* worried about Harold, and what he might do when he learned about Carrie—Mrs. Boone, that is. We knew her long ago, you know," Mrs. Douglass added parenthetically, "when she was just plain Carrie Branch. The only thing I could think of to do that would keep Harold quiet, and with me, and away from the Lulu Belle and her, was to faint!"

Asey raised his eyebrows.

"Oh, I know it seems silly!" Mrs. Douglass said. "But as I told Dr. Cummings, when a woman is in a quandary, she doesn't stop to figure out wonderful modern solutions on a par with the atom bomb! She just damn well pretends to faint, that's all, and solves things just the way her mother would have solved'em!"

"But what did you think Harold might *do?*" Asey persisted.

"As I said to the doctor—I've been through all this with him, you know, once before!—Harold is *ingenious!* He *writes!* He—"

"Harold told me," Asey interrupted, "that *you* wrote!"

77

"Oh, we both do! I do dialogue and script—but don't you see, Harold writes the *plot!*" she said earnestly. "I'm afraid you don't appreciate, Mr. Mayo, what Harold might have thought up to do, if he'd known about Carrie! He never would have let well enough alone, never! It simply isn't his nature! *I* never could have stopped him from moving that body, or—or *some*thing awful! Oh, if only you were a woman, I could make you understand!"

"This is the second time this afternoon somebody's wished I was a girl," Asey said. "I managed to catch on the other time, so maybe I can grasp this. What difference d'you think my bein' a woman would make?"

"You'd listen!" Mrs. Douglass said. "Oh, to the radio, I mean. To *day*-time radio. Like serials. If only you'd followed 'Maida's Lost Love' throughout the years, for example, or 'The Life of Mother Gaston', I'd never have the slightest difficulty in explaining to you why I couldn't trust Harold Douglass *near* that body!"

"*Will* Mother Gaston's adopted daughter go to jail—by mistake?" Asey said. "*Should* old Doctor Muldoon tell her that Jimmy has—was it a broken neck, or cancer? *Can* Sonia, in her zeal for revenge, actually plant the stolen bonds on poor little Beth?"

"My God!" Louise Douglass said. "You've heard some of it! Were you having your hair cut, or at the dentist's?" she added curiously. "Ordinarily men don't hear Mother G. unless they're solidly tied down in a chair! But do you begin to see what I mean about Harold?"

"You win," Asey said, "an' I see. I get your point. Anybody who could think up that stuff *could* think up anything, particularly since he didn't like Mrs. Boone anyway. But why did you keep up the act after the doc an' I got here?"

"I was waiting," Mrs. Douglass said, "for Harold to

get out of the way! After all, when you two entered the room, I couldn't very well look up and smile brightly, and jump to my feet, and say it was all a *hoax!*"

Asey pointed out that Harold had left the room. "Cummings sent him for a glass of water—remember?"

"Oh, but *then*," she said, "by *then* I was feeling too foolish! By then I realized that instead of helping Harold, I'd actually made everything much worse by assuming that he *would* have done something to her—I tell you, I'm just *no* good at plot, I invariably mess it up! And at *that* point, the smartest dialogue in the world wasn't going to help me any! I lay there," she pointed to the chintz-covered couch, "and I wished the floor would open up and take me out of the whole horrid situation! I wished I *had* fainted, and couldn't come to!"

"But Cummings managed to rouse you all right, after Harold an' I left?"

"He pinched me," she said briefly.

"An' after tellin' all this to him," Asey said, "what happened then?"

Because, he thought to himself, what happened then was the crux of the whole matter. Up to the time he and Douglass left for the village, the body should still have been out in the Pullman. Up to then, Cummings was all right and in the picture. Up to that point, the situation was more or less simple.

Some of his impatience crept into his voice as he repeated his question. "An' what happened then, Mrs. Douglass?"

"I cried."

"I don't doubt you probably felt in the mood for cryin', an' gettin' things out of your system!" Asey started pacing back and forth across the floor. "But what *happened?* What did *you* do? What did *Cummings* do?"

"Why, neither of us *did* anything!" she returned. "I

just bawled my head off, and—oh, yes, after a few minutes, the doctor presented me with his handkerchief. Mine was simply soaking."

She had the grace to look a little guilty.

"I see what you mean by plot comin' hard to you." Asey stopped pacing and perched on the arm of the couch. "Let's try straight narration. I told Cummings I'd been faking my faint, and why. I cried. Then what did I do?"

"I went upstairs to wash my face and bathe my eyes and change my clothes and do my hair, of course! And when I came downstairs again, Cummings was gone—I naturally assumed he'd gone out to the Lulu Belle!" Mrs. Douglass said. "I was worried about Layne and how to break things to her—she's very fond of Carrie, you know. And I was worried about Aunt Mary. I *did* feel she should have some warning of what had happened, and not just have this sprung on her—she'd set out in the beachwagon to—"

"To go to the beach to see if Mrs. Boone had followed some of the girls over there. I know!" Asey said. "That's one fact I seem able to get, but I'm tired of it! What did you *do*, Mrs. Douglass? What *happened?*"

She had started out on foot over toward the beach, she told him, and had run into Aunt Mary walking back.

"She'd had a flat," Mrs. Douglass explained. "And Harold had taken out the beachwagon's jack again to use for something else—that man is *always* taking tools from where they belong!—so she couldn't do a thing about changing the tire. She thought that someone going by in a car would have a jack, or that Harold or I would probably come after her ultimately, so she waited around for quite a while before she started home."

"What in time—" Asey broke off his intended question as to why in time a presumably elderly aunt should even have considered changing a flat tire, jack or no jack. "What time was all this?"

"*I* don't know! I can time dialogue, Mr. Mayo," she was beginning, Asey thought, to sound about as impatient as he felt, "but I haven't—and never in my life *have* had—the faintest idea of my own personal time, and when I do things! I couldn't even hazard a guess as to what time it was when I called your house—and what does it all matter now, anyway?"

"Call it my whim." Asey had no intention of going into all that "Mrs.-Boone-was-all-right" business again now. "What did you an' Aunt Mary do after the two of you walked back here? What *hap*—"

"If you ask me what *happened* just once more, in that March-of-Time voice," Mrs. Douglass said ominously, "I will start in pitching Aunt Della's bric-a-brac at you! I'm telling you what happened, just as well as I can, and it's hardly my fault that what happened wasn't more spectacular! But there *weren't* any fires, or floods, or tornadoes, or tidal waves, or strangers with beards—"

"Or mortgages?" Asey interrupted.

"Or *what?*"

"Mortgages comin' due, or sirens like the evil Sonia scurryin' around with them bearer bonds to plant on poor little Poppet," Asey said with a grin. "I know it isn't what you might call very colossal or terrific action, Mrs. Douglass, but I certainly shouldn't keep on ploughin' my way into it if I didn't think that it mattered! So, after you an' Aunt Mary come back—?"

"We went directly out to the Lulu Belle. Aunt Mary is an adamant soul," she said, "and she insisted on going and looking for herself. She absolutely refused to believe that Carrie was dead, and she simply *snorted* with scorn when I mentioned the word murder. She wouldn't believe me."

"So?" Asey said. "Why not?"

"She said it was unquestionably the result of too much soap opera."

"You mean," Asey said with a chuckle, "she thought you were makin' it up?"

"No, I think she thought I was sincere enough," Mrs. Douglass said, "but laboring under a delusion. She said it was unquestionably just a horrid mistake, and that I was unquestionably overwrought with all these project people, and no servants to help me, and that I'd unquestionably jumped to a lot of silly conclusions, and that unquestionably, Carrie had only fainted. She suggested that what I needed was a nice long vacation from Mother Gaston."

"Wa-el," Asey said, "I can see how she maybe might feel that way!"

"She thought, furthermore, that Harold and I should unquestionably have read the riot act to Layne when she came last night, and insisted on her taking Carrie to some hotel—unquestionably the only proper solution! And still furthermore, she never in her fifty-seven years— actually, she's fifty-nine!—saw the equal of this college project for sheer imposition. Does that," she concluded, "give you just a brief hint of Aunt Mary's character?"

"Unquestionably!" Asey said, and decided that maybe the possibility of Aunt Mary's changing a tire wasn't as out of the way as he had at first thought.

"When we looked inside the Lulu Belle and found it empty," Mrs. Douglass went on, "Aunt Mary just purred with satisfaction and said that she had unquestionably been quite right, hadn't she? Absolutely nothing had happened, as anyone not unduly overwrought could unquestionably see at a glance, and for her part, she was starving hungry and wanted a sandwich, and she really didn't think that irregular meal hours were a good thing.

I protested—but she just said why didn't I take a nice nap, and went indoors for her sandwich."

Asey grinned. "Assumin'," he said, "that your sense of plot may occasionally skip a beat, still an' all, what *was* your guess as to what unquestionably had happened? What did you think had become of Mrs. Boone an' Cummings?"

"I assumed that you and the doctor must have taken Carrie away—in books and on the radio, there's *always* an ambulance that comes and conveniently takes bodies away," she added. "That's so you—so the writer, I mean—can get all those grisly things done away from the scene. Spares you no end of technical problems, too. But then, almost at once after I'd gone back into the house, Miss Shearing phoned and said Mrs. Boone was all right, and with her, and not to worry. Of course, Aunt Mary rose to dizzy heights at that point!"

"Unquestionably!" Asey said.

"While she didn't exactly suggest that my brain has been damaged by years of writing Mother Gaston," Mrs. Douglass said with a laugh, "she *did* point out in eight or ten different ways that only in a soap opera world would anyone go rushing off half-cocked, without sensibly checking to see whether or not someone actually was dead."

She looked at Asey as if she rather expected him to concur with Aunt Mary. But instead, he merely asked what she had done after Miss Shearing called.

"I just sat there, dumb with relief," she said. "And then Aunt Mary and I went back to the beachwagon and changed the tire. *I* was perfectly willing to leave it for Harold, but she thought it would be good exercise—and wasn't it! That jack we took kept slipping, and we lost one of those little nut-things, and had to grub around for it—oh, it turned out to be a frightful chore! And when we finally got back, the project was here. And then, you came. There!" She heaved a sigh of relief.

"An' you don't know a *thing* about Cummings?" Asey asked.

"In my work," Mrs. Douglass said, "the detective and the doctor are always in constant communication. Somehow, I assumed you and Cummings would be—after all, he's probably just making a call on a patient! It isn't as if you'd lost him in some vast trackless wilderness, or something!"

Asey strolled over to a window and looked out at the lawn, now just as empty as it had been full a few minutes ago.

Everything, he found as he sorted things out in his mind, was really quite simple—providing you stuck to the simple facts!

He and Douglass had gone to the village. Mrs. Douglass told the doctor her story of the fake faint. She went upstairs, came down, went out, found her aunt, and the two returned to the house to find Cummings gone, and Mrs. Boone's body gone. Then Mrs. Douglass and Aunt Mary departed to change a tire—it must have been during that.interlude, he decided, that he had come back to find everything so completely abandoned in appearance.

"Where's your daughter?" he asked absently.

"Layne's upstairs, changing her clothes. She got back from the beach just before you came."

"An' Mr. Douglass?"

"Oh, Harold came home just before Layne, footsore and weary. He's upstairs, too, taking a shower and changing. He's just a *little* annoyed with you, I'm afraid," she added in a tone which indicated that Harold was good and mad.

"With me? Whatever for?"

"He said he went into the post office for a second, and

while he was in there, you drove away in your roadster. He waited and waited for you to come back, turned down any number of offers of a lift home, and finally had to walk every inch of the way. I didn't tell him *any*thing about Carrie and this silly mix-up—Harold worries so, and there's always his blood pressure to think about."

Asey turned away from the window.

"In your Mother Gaston stories," he said, "you indicate everything with sounds. Clippety-clop, you run upstairs, clippety-clop, you run down, rattle-bang-thud, you change a tire. I have to do it the hard way, an' ask questions. But now I got the background noises settled, let's get to the root of things—just exactly where did Miss Shearing call from, an' what were her exact words?"

"Aunt Mary took the call," Mrs. Douglass said. "And let me assure you," she added, "she's not a person to make mistakes with phone messages! Frankly, if it hadn't been Miss Shearing calling, and Aunt Mary taking the call, I *might* have had some doubts!"

"I think," Asey said, "that I'd like to have a little chat with Aunt Mary—Mrs. Framingham, isn't it? Or is she changin' her clothes, too?"

"I'll see."

Mrs. Douglass ran upstairs to return almost at once with the information that Aunt Mary was taking a tub, and would be down in about fifteen minutes.

"And now, would you excuse me?" she said. "The project is eating at the Inn tonight, thank God, but there are a million things I've got to see to—won't you just sit down and make yourself comfortable?"

Asey started to pace around the living room after she left, but after a moment he picked up Jennie's lunch-basket and went outdoors. The longer he stayed in that house, the less he liked the feel of it, and the basket was a good excuse for his going out to sit in the roadster while he waited for Aunt Mary.

All the little fill-in facts were assembled, and all of Mrs. Douglass's story was simple enough. Just as simple as Harold Douglass's background on Mrs. Boone had been, he thought. And just as disarming.

But he didn't like it, he told himself, as he sat down behind the roadster's wheel and fished out one of Jennie's apple puffs from the basket.

He had eaten up the sugar gingerbread and most of the sandwiches before he noticed the tire in the rear of the beachwagon parked beside him—obviously the Douglass's beachwagon, since it had no name or decoration on the front door.

Asey sat up suddenly and told himself he was a fool.

"Sittin' there right in front of your eyes is the one easy, sure way of findin' out if all this simple disarmin' story is a made-up soap opera, or not!"

He climbed into the beachwagon and examined the tire, and then he hoisted it into his roadster and roared away down the driveway toward the village.

Twenty minutes later, Benny, the garage man, shifted his plug of tobacco from his right cheek to his left, and gave it as his opinion that Asey was right.

"Only thing the matter with this tire is," he said, "somebody just let the air out of it, that's all!"

7

"You sure?" Asey said. "Nothin' wrong with the tube? Or the valve?"

"Like I told you, I know that tire an' I know that tube—both brand-new, an' I sold 'em to Harold Douglass

86

two days ago, an' they're okay! Didn't you just see the tube for yourself when I had it in the tub? Didn't we paw over that tire twice? Didn't I just *show* you how the valve's okay? Nothin' the trouble here but someone let out the air, that's all! An', Asey, I tell you what *I* think—"

Asey waited until Benny's plug of tobacco made its tour back from the left cheek to the right.

"*I* think somebody took—oh, like a ladies' nail file, say, an' stuck it in to hold the valve down—remember them little marks, like, that I showed you? Now maybe not a nail file, but what I'm aimin' at is somebody didn't just use their finger, like a man—say, Asey, what do you look so glum about this for? After all, it ain't *your* tire! What you so bothered about?"

Asey sighed. "It just means a yarn was too simple, that's all! I thought as much, but—"

He broke off as Jennie's coupe bounced into the yard of the garage and up to one of the gas pumps.

"Hello," she said, and leaned her head out of the window. "Your friend Mrs. Douglass lost any more guests lately? Fill it up, Benny, and charge it—I left my purse at home. Asey, for goodness sakes, what *is* the matter with that crazy coot of a woman?"

"That," Asey said as he strolled over and stood by the car door, "is exactly what I'm tryin' to figure out. Maybe you—yessir, I bet you would! Now—move over those bundles, Jennie. I want to get in an' tell you a story, an' you listen careful!"

Pausing only while Jennie bounced the coupe out of the way of another customer, Asey told her what had taken place at Pochet Point that afternoon. His only elimination was any reference to soap operas or to Mother Gaston.

"So there you are," he concluded. "No Mrs. Boone,

no Cummings. There's everybody's stories, an' there's the tire yonder in the garage—Benny swears someone just let the air out. What does it all sound like to you?"

"Well," Jennie said reflectively, "I know how you hate the things, always turning 'em off every chance you get, and leaving the house when I have my favorites on, but that's certainly what it sounds like, Asey! It sounds just like one of my serials. Mostly Mother Gaston."

"That's what I was afraid of," Asey said as he got out of the coupe. "Thanks a lot, Jennie. The Douglasses hate her for somethin' she did to 'em, an' that aunt doesn't sound like a woman who'd stop at much—"

"Wait!" Jennie got out and followed him to his roadster. "Where d'you suppose Mrs. Boone *is?*"

"What's your guess?" Asey returned.

"Not far. Far from the Pullman, I mean. You know perfectly well how hard it is to carry bodies—well, maybe *you* don't, but I'm sure I'll never forget trying to cart people around in Red Cross, back in First Aid!"

"How would you feel about the mud hole, or the swamp?"

Jennie shook her head and made a face. "Too nasty! It's something smarter. Like a secret room—that's what happened in Mother Gaston about a month ago, you know. They found this body in a secret room of an old farmhouse nobody had ever suspected!"

"An' what d'you suppose happened to the doc?" Asey inquired drily. "You think *he's* in a farmhouse nobody suspects, too?"

"I know one sure thing," Jennie said. "He certainly never *walked* far! You know how his wife always claims she has to watch him to see he doesn't take his car from the house across the driveway to his office! And certainly nobody would take him unawares—remember back in the early days of the war, that Women's Volunteer Defense League and Rifle Corps that we had?"

"The Girl Regulars? That's one item in your past that I can't never forget!" Asey said. "Bullets whizzin' past my head, an' you goin' around swingin' people off their feet with a lot of jujitsu, an'—"

"And just you remember," Jennie interrupted, "it was Cummings taught us those holds! He may look short and bulky, and as if he couldn't move quick, but he's scrappy! You go back over there and look around some more for both of 'em, Asey—I'm sure if someone took the doc away by force, he'd have left something somewhere as a clue for you to follow—hurry back there before it gets dark!"

They separated in getting out of the way of a sedan that drew up at one of the gas pumps, and Asey went inside the garage, got the Douglass's tire, and put it back in his roadster.

"I just thought to tell you," Jennie walked over to him as the sedan departed, "Mrs. Douglass and that aunt were just coming back in the beachwagon when I got there with your lunch—"

"Where'd you get *that?*" Asey interrupted, pointing to the green scarf she was holding in her hand. "Where'd that come from?"

"This scarf? I was just going to ask Benny if he wanted it," she said. "The man in that sedan that just left dropped it when he got out to pay for his gas, I think—he must have, it wasn't lying here before he came!"

"Was it someone from the Larrabee project? One of the college bunch?" Asey demanded.

"Oh, no, it was a *man*—I mean, an older man. Dressed in clothes that matched, you know. Dark grey suit with a pin-stripe, and a Homburg, and a plain dark tie. I really," Jennie said casually, "didn't *notice* him particularly—Asey Mayo, what're you doing? Where are you going?"

Her voice rose as he sprinted for the roadster.

"You wait here for me," Asey said, "an' mind you don't go tellin' anyone about Mrs. Boone!"

Jennie clucked her tongue and shook her head as the roadster shot out of the yard and up the highway.

"Tch, tch, tch, if that man doesn't kill himself one of these days!"

"He won't," Benny assured her. "If he'd been goin' to land up in a crash, he'd've piled up years ago. But he most probably'll get himself pinched—why, I bet he's already in Brewster now, at that rate!"

"That's just the trouble, nobody *ever* pinches him!" Jennie said sadly. "He's got his glove compartments full of Honorary Chief of Police badges, and Honorary Constable badges, and Honorary Sheriff badges, and all such, and whenever he gets stuck, he yanks out one of 'em and pins it onto his shirt, and kids his way right out of trouble!"

Asey, speeding along, remembered that the sedan was light grey, almost white, and that it was a sufficiently new model to be sparkling with chrome.

But it wasn't anything that a Porter couldn't overtake!

After ten miles, he began to slow down. He couldn't believe that the grey sedan could have gone any further —it hadn't left the garage at any break-neck pace. The driver, he decided, simply must have turned off the main road.

He wouldn't have bothered to chase after one of the project, he thought as he turned the roadster around and headed back. But one of Mrs. Boone's green scarves in the possession of an older man, someone who didn't belong to the project, was something which had seemed well worth taking a look into.

"Next time," he admonished himself, "keep your eyes open for—ooop!"

He braked the car to a stop, fumbled around in the glove compartment, drew out a badge, pinned it on his shirt, and was standing in the middle of the road with his hand held up when the grey sedan, which he'd spotted at the top of the long hill ahead, arrived on the scene.

The car was still rocking from the force of the driver's quick braking when Asey walked up to it.

"Emergency inspection!" he said briskly, and pointed to his badge.

This was the right man—pin-striped suit, Homburg hat, plain tie.

"Oh? Emergency inspection of what?"

The fellow was thirty-odd, Asey guessed, he was blonde and good-looking, and he was smiling the forced smile of someone in a hurry who has decided to make the best of little, irritating delays.

"Quohaugs," Asey said.

"Er—I beg your pardon? I didn't quite catch that!"

"Quohaugs," Asey drawled the word out. "What you New Yorkers call clams."

"I'm not a New Yorker," the man said seriously, "and I assure you that I haven't any clams—really, I don't even like clams!"

"To tell you the truth," Asey leaned his arm on the car door and peered interestedly into the empty back seat, "I don't much myself, either. But we had what you might call an out-of-town raid on our quohaug beds here today, sort of a high-jackin', as you might say, an' I have to stop all cars an' inspect 'em for quohaugs. You mind very much openin' your rear trunk?"

"If I have to, I suppose that I have to!"

A moment later, Asey helped him slam down and lock the cover of the empty trunk.

"Thanks, mister," he said. "I'll admit you didn't look to me like the quohaug-stealin' kind, but I had to stop you. That's my job."

Taking a pencil and a small notebook from his pocket, he wrote down the car's license plate number on one of the pages, then turned to another page, wrote "Pass", and then hesitated, pencil in air.

"Who'll I say to pass, mister?" he inquired. "What's the name?"

"I don't see why my name—oh, I suppose it's quicker. It's Manderson. Eric Manderson. Anderson, with an 'M'!"

Asey wrote down "Pass Eric Manderson," and tore out the notebook page.

"Now just you show this if you're stopped anywhere in the next two towns—I can't begin to handle everyone here, of course," he felt that he had to proffer some explanation for the cars which had gone merrily past during his examination of the trunk, "but we manage to cover all the outgoin' vehicles, one place or another. Thanks."

"You're welcome, I'm sure." Mr. Manderson summoned up another of his forced smiles, and then drove off in the grey sedan.

Back at Benny's garage, Jennie listened to Asey's brief recital of the quohaug inspection episode, and announced that in her opinion, he'd been a fool.

"You say that Gerty said that Mrs. Boone's secretary was named Eric, and you say this fellow you just stopped was named Eric, and this scarf I found *certainly* came out of his car! Now why," she said disgustedly, "why for goodness sakes didn't you corral the fellow? You didn't pass him—*or* overtake him! That must mean that he drove *off* of the main road after he left here! And for all *you* know, or bothered to find out, he dumped Mrs. Boone's body somewheres before he drove back *on* to the main road again!"

"Uh-huh, I realize that."

"If I must say so, Asey Mayo, you're a fool! Why on earth didn't you grab him?"

"Wa-el," Asey said, "it's just a mite difficult to grab or corral anybody in connection with a murder that to all intents an' purposes hasn't happened."

"But it *has* happened!" Jennie said impatiently. "You know perfectly well it has!"

"Uh-huh, an' I got a lot of proof, haven't I? A green ticket with a diamond-shaped punch." He took it from his pocket and showed it to her. "See?"

"Why, *that's* nothing special!" Jennie looked at it. "*I* got one of those—one day, oh, just after they got that railroad set up, Mr. Douglass asked the Men's Club at the church to all come up and have a ride, and before he got through, he had the Sewing Circle and the Women's Club and the Girl Scouts and the Boy Scouts and the Board of Trade, and I don't know who all else besides. We *all* got tickets like that. Mr. Douglass, he gets a great kick out of that railroad. Puts on a visored cap—"

"An' sells tickets," Asey said. "An' then a conductor's cap, an' conducts, an' so on an' so forth. I know. The doc told me."

"Did you go inside of the station?" Jennie asked. "It's not much bigger than a pint of cider, and it has a little pot-bellied stove in the middle, and benches to sit on, and a lot of old-time excursion posters and timetables hung around the walls. It somehow even *smells* like an old station, if you know what I mean—why *did*n't you?"

"Grab Eric? I thought I'd gone into that up to the

93

hilt!" Asey said. "After all, if Eric Manderson is his real name, an' if he bothered to give it to me, he can't be so very scared of bein' identified. We got his license plate number, an' the cops can always track him—"

"Who's talking about that Eric? I mean, the *station!*" Jennie said. "Why in the world didn't you go inside of it? Why didn't you even *look* inside of it? I must say it's the first place I'd have gone to myself, to hunt for Mrs. Boone's body after it disappeared! It's so *near!*"

"An' it's just the one place," Asey said a little ruefully, "that I somehow missed! Probably because it *was* so near, maybe because the engine hid it an' I didn't think of it—oh, I glanced at the place when I swung up into the engine cab, durin' one of my hunts while I was all alone over there, but I never went in—"

"For goodness sakes, look!" Jennie interrupted, pointing in amazement at the car swinging into the garage yard. "*Look*, will you!"

It was his own new roadster that was pulling up to the gas pump.

"And *him!*" Jennie sniffed at the sight of the driver and only occupant, a dark-haired young man, hatless, and wearing sun glasses. "That *nasty* one! Well, unless you *lent* him the car, just you give him the works. He's the nastiest—"

"Hey, you!" The young man made a peremptory gesture in Asey's direction. "Hey, you—Rube! Service! Get started!"

"Well, for *good*ness sakes—"

Under his breath, Asey told Jennie to hush. Aloud, he said, "What's the matter, bub? You want me?"

If anyone ever deserved the nickname of Stinky, he thought to himself, this fellow was it. From his thick black eyebrows to his belligerent chin, he looked like a Stinky. He was sullen-faced, he was arrogant, he was rude—and that foolish little black moustache didn't add any endearing charm, either.

"Who d'you think I'm calling?" His battle jacket fitted him like a corset, Asey noted, and he wore one of Mrs. Boone's green scarves, tied Ascot-fashion, around his neck. "What the hell's the matter with you hicks? I want some service!"

Benny, standing in the doorway of the garage, caught Asey's warning glance just in time to bite back a comment.

"Okay, bub," Asey said. "Want me to fill her up?"

"What d'you think I stopped at the gas pump for, a small beer? Of course I want you to fill her up!"

Asey walked slowly around the roadster. "Say, just where *is* your gas tank, bub?" he inquired. "Can't seem to see it no place."

"It's—" The young man stopped short. "Don't you hicks know anything about a *good* car?"

"We never seen one like this before," Asey said. "Hey, Benny, he wants me to fill this up, but I wouldn't know where the gas tank was, would you?"

"Nun-no, dunno's I would." Benny entered into the spirit of the thing. "Can't see any tank cap. S'pose it's controlled by one of them dashboard gadgets, maybe?"

Gravely, they played for several minutes with the dashboard gadgets while the young man fumed.

After a particularly vehement outburst, Benny shook his head reprovingly.

"What I think is," he observed, "if you don't know where the gas tank on your own car is, bub, you shouldn't hardly expect us to!"

"What I think is," Asey observed as he idly played with several of the gadgets, "you don't need any gas anyways, bub!"

"Look here, you, the tank said 'Empty'! The—"

"Thought you didn't know where the tank was, bub," Asey interrupted.

"There!" The young man, now a rich dark purple in color, pointed to one of the dashboard indicators. "That one—it said 'E'—it's empty!"

"Look, bub, turn your ignition key," Asey said gently. "Now watch them needles. What you were pointin' at is an oil gauge—can't you tell an oil gauge when you see it? The next dial's the gas, an' if you'll look close, you'll see it's three-quarters full, bub—"

He broke off as the young man impatiently lighted a cigarette—with Cummings's own outsize platinum lighter!

Asey *knew* that lighter. He'd given it to the doctor himself. And Jennie recognized it. He heard her startled exclamation.

"So, you got enough gas," Asey went on. "Enough to last until your friend that owns this car can tell you where the gas tank is located. It *does* belong to some friend, doesn't it, bub?"

"What of it?" The fellow's voice was trembling with anger. "And stop calling me bub!" He jammed his finger on the starter button, and then raced the engine until Asey winced.

"Okay, bub!" he said. "Glad to have been of service. Drop in any time!"

Very slowly, the roadster started away from the gas pump, and turned out on to the highway.

"Funny," Benny remarked, "*I'd* of sworn he meant to slat away from here hell-bent for election, but he's still only creepin' along—did you do somethin' to the car, Asey, when you played with them gadgets?"

"I'm introducin' Sonny Boy to one of the prince's fancier bits of equipment," Asey said with a grin. "A special speed just for parade work. He can't go more'n ten miles an hour in that thing right now—an' I don't think he's enough of a mechanic to find his way back to normal through them gadgets in much of a hurry!"

"What was you intendin' to do to him, exactly?" Benny asked. "Seemed to me you broke off your plans there, didn't you?"

Asey nodded. "I *was* hopin'," he said, "to wangle him out of the car, an' under it. Then—wa-el, he was goin' to be an awful greasy boy if I hadn't spotted Cummings's lighter in his hand!"

"And *what*," Jennie inquired crisply, "do you intend to *do* about it? Wait all night while he gets away with it *and* your best car? That nasty thing, if he hadn't left early when the project was over at our house, I'd have slapped his nasty face! Get after him, Asey—don't you think he'll lead you to Cummings? How would he have that lighter if he hadn't taken it from the doc? Don't you mean to follow him?"

"Uh-huh, but at ten miles an hour, I can afford to let him get a mite of a start. He's only to the traffic lights, see?" he pointed. "An' they just went red on him. Huh, I wonder how Gerty ever fell for *him!* An' why didn't he know that was my car? I wonder—"

"What d'you want me to do?" Jennie asked as he got into his old roadster.

"S'pose you go along home," Asey said, "so I can call you there if I need you. Now I'll see where Sonny Boy's goin', an' what he's up to. An' how he came by that lighter of the doc's—if I have to throttle it out of him!"

"Throttle him anyway," Jennie said. "He needs it— and *do* remember the railroad station!"

Asey swung out on the highway just as the traffic lights changed to green, and the chrome-plated roadster ahead started its slow, tortuous crawl over toward Pochet Point.

It was, he decided, the most leisurely chase in which he had ever participated. Most of the time he found himself stopping entirely in order to keep out of sight of the car ahead.

When they finally arrived at the point, Sonny Boy elected to turn off on a lane leading not to the Douglass's house, but toward the shore.

"The old boat house road, huh?" Asey murmured. "An' a very short lane, as I remember it. I guess I'll just stop right here an' listen to where you go—"

He waited until the sound of the other motor stopped, and then he parked in a clump of bushes at the side of the road, and started off on foot.

His new roadster, he found, had been left directly in front of a boat house—but it wasn't the rickety, tumble-down old building which he remembered from the past. This was a new model, sturdy and well-built, and well-kept in what seemed to be the Douglass tradition.

No windows anywhere, a heavy door—you really couldn't ask for a better place to put someone, Asey thought to himself!

Sonny Boy was staring at the padlock on the door, fingering it uncertainly, as if he weren't sure whether to unlock it or not.

"Oh, make up your mind!" Asey muttered impatiently under his breath. "Make up your mind! Give me something to pin you down on! If only I just had something to hitch up you, an' the doc, an' this place—oh, wouldn't I tie your ears into knots! Wouldn't I wrap your teeth—"

Something dangling from the branch of a pine tree near the boat house door glinted for a moment in a final burst of light from the setting sun.

Asey stared at it in fascination.

The only thing in the world which that dangling object resembled was a stethoscope!

Cummings's stethoscope?

"Who else's, for Pete's sakes!"

Asey smiled, and stepped noiselessly out from the cover of the pines.

Five minutes later, he had finished binding and gagging Sonny Boy, and was unlocking the padlock of the boat house door with the key which he had taken from the fellow's pocket.

"Cummings!" he called out. "Cummings!"

Stepping inside, he peered around the dim interior and bellowed the doctor's name again.

A figure rose from a couch in the far corner.

"Ah!" Cummings said acidly. "Ah, Dr. Livingston, I presume?"

8

"Doc, ARE YOU OKAY?" Asey hurried over to the couch.

"Why, I'm *fine*, my dear Livingston! Fine! Bully!"

While Asey guessed that Cummings's hearty irony had been very well rehearsed, he also conceded that there'd been plenty of spare time for him to rehearse in!

"Probably haven't had such a fine rest in years," Cummings went on. "Little stuffy, of course—someone left a few dead fish in here last fall, and nature took its course with 'em. Little dull. Little dark. No good books to read and no light to read 'em by if I'd had 'em. But I'm simply delighted that there's no chance of your catching cold— you have no idea how I've worried about your catching cold!"

"Okay, doc," Asey said. "I'll bite. Why would you suspect I'd catch cold?"

"Got a match? Give me that flap! D'you realize," he

said bitterly, "that I've been months without a cigar? No, Asey, if you'd rushed and steamed yourself into a lather just coming after old *me*, and then caught cold from the lather, why I'd just *never* have forgiven myself, that's all! I'm *glad* you just took your own time and went at it leisurely and slowly, at your own sweet damn convenience!"

"Now listen, doc!" Asey protested. "You sent me off on a fool errand for fake-faint medicine, an' when I come back, you've disappeared into thin air! How in time could you expect me to know you were *here*? How could I do any rushin' an' steamin' after you when I didn't know where you *were*?"

There was a little silence in the dim interior of the boat house while the doctor puffed at his cigar.

"I'm counting to two hundred by tens," he said at last. "I promised my mother that whenever I felt that tendency coming on me to throw boat houses at people, I'd always pause and count to two hundred—Asey Mayo, I left clues all over the place for you! I littered Pochet Point with clues! Short of erecting large signs with red arrows for you to follow, I'm sure I don't know what *else* I could possibly have done to lead you here!"

"Name three," Asey said. "Name three clues!"

"My lighter, for one," Cummings said promptly. "I left my lighter—the one you gave me—sitting on a freshly cut tree stump, right at the junction of the lanes —on *this* side. There it stood, my little beacon, flashing madly in the sun, easily visible—can *you* think of a brighter way to point out that I went *this* way? *I* thought it was a stroke of sheer genius! You couldn't have missed it, my fine Codfish Sherlock! *No*body in God's green world could possibly have missed that lighter!"

"Nobody did," Asey said gently.

"Then why didn't you march straight here when you

spotted it? Or did you merely decide that I'd gone to the beach for a brisk swim?"

"When I spotted it," Asey said, "it was in the possession of one of the project boys up at Benny's garage—not what you'd call an easy place to pick this lane junction from! I only happened here because I trailed him."

"Well, it *work*ed, didn't it?" Cummings demanded. "And then, before I came inside here, I hung my stethoscope on the branch of a pine—I must say that when I'm following murderers, I use my *wits*!"

"I spotted that stethoscope," Asey said, "because of divine intervention, an' nothin' else. The sun just happened to catch it right—honest, doc, be sensible! How could you expect me to find you from a stethoscope hung up in a tree branch?"

"I suppose," Cummings returned as he got up from the couch, "I *could* have left a paper trail, or dragged an anise bag, or tossed snippets of gingerbread in my wake—well, I'll break down and admit that to a lesser mind than yours, my clues might possibly—just *possibly*, mind!—appear slightly on the obscure side. But you *got* 'em, didn't you? Now, tell me, how are you getting along with Halbert?"

"Er—did you phone him, doc?" Asey inquired.

"The facilities for telephoning anyone from this enchanted grotto," Cummings said, "are somewhat limited—d'you resent my pointing that out?"

"Doc, I—"

"*If* I'd had a phone," Cummings ignored his interruption, "I might conceivably have been tempted to phone a lot of people! *If* I'd had matches, I might even have started a fire to lead people here—now *you*, no doubt, know exactly how to rub two sticks together and achieve a flame. But *I* grew up in the pre-Boy Scout era. Fire is beyond me, and I never learned to wigwag, or bang out the Morse code—how could I have called Halbert?" He paused in the middle of the floor. "Good God, man, haven't *you* called him? You *have*n't?"

"Doc," Asey said, "what became of her?"

"She waited until I walked in here—tiptoed in, rather —and then she slammed the door and locked the padlock. No violence," Cummings said, "on either side. She was quiet and refined, I was quiet and abashed—*I* thought she was already in here, you see! Yes, the whole episode was carried out with the utmost decorum. No loose yelling and howling—*I* know when *I'm* stuck in a boat house, and I accept the fact. As to what became of her, I frankly wouldn't know. She didn't tell me. In fact, she never uttered a word. The quiet type."

"*Who?*"

"Who? I regret that I don't know who. I'd even rather hoped," he added with a touch of wistfulness in his voice, "that *you* might. Oh, it was Louise Douglass, or that aunt, Mrs. Framingham, or Layne, or some other girl, or some other woman. A female. Not a man. When did it get this dark?" He looked out of the boat house door. "Hm! Fresh air! No wonder I keep recommending it so highly to my patients—there *is* something tonic about—"

"Now we've had our fun, doc," Asey said, "what in blazes happened?"

"Fun? *Fun?*" For several minutes, Cummings delivered a caustic monologue on Asey's misconception of the word. "And what's *that?*" he broke off suddenly and pointed to the ground. "What's that lumpish object? *Another* corpse?"

"Just the fellow who had your lighter," Asey explained.

"Where is it? I never missed anything more!"

"Probably in one of his pockets—I didn't wait to find

anything but the padlock key. Doc," Asey followed him down the boat house steps and over to the trussed-up figure, "after I left with Harold Douglass, what happened?"

"You keeping him tied up indefinitely?" Cummings inquired.

"At least till I get this story out of you!" Asey returned. "If I let him distract you, I never will—an' his story can wait!"

"Ah, here it is!" Cummings extracted his lighter from a pocket of the battle jacket. "Well, Louise went upstairs to wash her face—haven't a spot of hot soup on you, I suppose? I keep feeling if I could only get my teeth into some nice nourishing soup, my sense of narration would take a definite spurt for the better. You don't think concisely when hunger gnaws at your vitals. Some nice hot soup—"

"Come along!" Asey took his arm. "There's a thermos full of it in the car."

"Oh." To Asey's pleasure, the doctor for once seemed slightly nonplussed. "Where are you going?"

"The other roadster's up the road a piece."

"Oh!" Cummings made a swift recovery. "How'd you get 'em both here, use your astral body? Really, Sherlock, if a man can drive two cars at once, I *do* feel he might spot a stethoscope on a tree—"

When they reached the roadster, Asey removed the beachwagon's tire from the seat, slung it into the rear baggage compartment, and then presented Cummings with the thermos bottle of soup.

After he had made away with a cupful, Cummings condescended to tell what had occurred.

"Louise went upstairs to wash her face—I never suspected that she was the hysterical type," Cummings said reflectively, "and I know she's going to regret every

103

word she poured out to me. 'Throwing herself on my mercy' is the only descriptive phrase I can think of that's suitable to cover the way she acted after you went."

"Let down her hair, huh?"

"And combed it. I was there in the living room, thinking her over, and starting to go to the hall to phone Halbert, as I recall—actually," Cummings said, "this all seems so ante-bellum! And then I heard a strange noise. I've spent most of the afternoon trying to think how to describe that sound to you, Asey, and I can't. It's like a certain type of pain that patients helplessly sum up as a funny little pain. They aren't able to enlarge on it. It's just a funny little pain. This noise was just a strange noise, that's all!"

"Well, was it loud, or soft, or—" Asey began.

"I've run through every sound word that I know," Cummings interrupted, "and I can't put my finger on it! Did it ring? No. Was it muffled? Sort of. Did it creak? Some. Hiss? No, definitely not sibilant. Rattly? No! Nor twanging or jangling, or clanking, or whirring, or droning. Not resonant. Not strident. Not a sudden or a violent sound. There was simply a noise, and it was strange! I've racked my brains, and I can't do any better, much as I loathe admitting myself at a loss for words! Anyway, I went out to the Lulu Belle, even though the noise didn't seem to come from there—and the damned Pullman was empty! That was—hm. Perhaps twenty minutes after you left."

"Time enough," Asey said, "for Stinky to have whipped back in my car, or for Harold Douglass to have hitched a ride—did you hear a car?"

"I've thought later that I did, but I wouldn't know," Cummings said honestly, "how much of it is wishful thinking. It would all be so much simpler to understand if there *had* been a car! And it could have got to the

Lulu Belle without coming directly up the driveway. There are several back lanes. No, I couldn't be sure on the car issue."

"Did you happen to look inside the little railroad station?" Asey asked.

"That was my first gesture," Cummings told him. "I frankly felt dazed at the turn of events, and I kept assuring myself—I can't think why, now!—that no one could possibly have moved that body *far!* And the station was so near, so handy! But it was empty. Then I thought I saw something—or someone—moving in the woods. And idiotically, as I will now publicly concede, I followed that will-o'-the-wisp—Asey, this place is *very* close to the house! Did you realize that?"

"Oh, I don't think it's *very* close," Asey said. "Near, but not—"

"It's very close! Stop and think of the layout," Cummings said. "I had to before I figured it out. The direct lane to the Douglass's driveway curves around a lot—hairpins back on itself, almost. This lane is straight. But—from the house over here is actually only a very short walk. It surprised me."

"Jennie claimed you wouldn't have walked very far," Asey said with a chuckle.

"I didn't. Well, in a nutshell, the boat house door was open, and I thought the woman had gone inside. So after draping my stethoscope over that branch, I came in. And there, to coin a phrase, I was. Where did you find her, Asey? Where was she?"

Asey gravely quoted his own words back at him.

"I regret that I don't know. I even rather hoped that *you* might!"

"I'm not referring," Cummings said impatiently, "to that unknown female who so deftly incarcerated me! I mean Carolyn Barton Boone!"

105

"So," Asey said, "do I."

"Merciful heavens, man, haven't you found that body yet? What have you been *doing?*"

Asey told him.

Cummings shook his head at the conclusion of the recital.

"It's macabre!" he said. "It's too preposterous! Climbing tottering water towers, chatting with ex-Wacs, pumping Louise—and maintaining the while the silly pretense that everything was just dandy! Putting inner tubes in tubs of water! Playing quohaug inspector—oh, Eric must be a first-class dodo to fall for that one! Tieing up Little Arsenic yonder—man alive, do you realize how bizarre it all is? Do you realize that few sane people would believe you? No wonder you haven't managed to find her body, with all *that* madness going on!"

"Wa-el," Asey said, "I've had some success. At least I located you!"

"Even that's fantastic, when you think it out!" Cummings retorted. "D'you suppose that fellow just saw my lighter, and took it?"

"Uh-huh, I suspect so. I suspect he liberated my car in the same casual way."

"So that's how you happen to have two cars over here! Who *is* he—oh, from the project, you said. I remember. That all the food you've got?" Cummings pawed around in Jennie's basket. "No more sandwiches? Not even a candy bar?"

"I noticed an old stale peppermint thing in the glove compartment yesterday," Asey said, "but I assume no responsibility. It's been there six months."

Cummings fumbled around, found it, and then flashed on his lighter and read the label.

" 'Baby Doll'. Hm. More sustaining than three pieces of raw liver, eight slices of fortified bread, two glasses of milk, or four average servings of spinach. Hm. Ingredients—desiccated cocoanut, corn syrup, soy beans, cotton seed oil, peanut oil, dried skimmed milk powder, dried egg whites, vegetable gums, various imitation flavorings and added vitamins. Sounds simply delicious, doesn't it?" He bit into it cautiously.

"What's it taste like?" Asey inquired interestedly.

"Laundry soap and pink mouthwash," Cummings replied without hesitation. "Asey, Mrs. Boone was alive at twelve o'clock. I pried that out of Louise on the basis of Aunt Della's cuckoo clock. While she has apparently no sense of time whatsoever, she *did* remember Mrs. Boone watching the cuckoos—you know, it's one of those things where all hell breaks loose at noon. And Harold—I *think* Baby Doll is ruining my new bridgework!"

Asey advised him to throw the candy away.

"What I start," Cummings said, "I finish. And Harold had promised to give her a ride on the railroad. That's how she got *into* the Lulu Belle—did he happen to give you any explanation of why they thought she was lost? If he'd got through enough of his railroad routine to have given her a ticket, got her on board, and punched the ticket, he certainly must have known she was *there!*"

"Harold skipped very lightly over that," Asey said. "Something about her leaving for a phone call and not coming back, and his going inside to get her. Why does he hate Mrs. Boone so, d'you know?"

"I pried that out, too—strictly speaking, I sorted rather than pried. Louise has just the slightest tendency to run on—oh, you found that out? Briefly," Cummings said, "Boone pulled a very fast and nasty one on the Douglasses years ago, when they were all young and writing for the radio, and she was Carrie Branch. Seems she not only wangled the job that Harold and Louise should have had, but she told such a pack of lies about 'em that they landed on their ears in the gutter—it was really nasty feline stuff, with claws, and spitting. Of course, it turned out to be a very good thing in the end for the Douglasses, because in their desperation, they invented Mother Gaston. And Mother Gaston is the modern equivalent of a gold mine." He paused. "Er—would you *know* Mother Gaston?"

"By now," Asey said, "I feel like a member of her family. Whyn't you tell me that was what they wrote?"

"Because I didn't know till this afternoon. They never confided it to me. Apparently they keep it very dark," Cummings said. "Very secret. Like a bar sinister. But after Boone got them fired, and before Mother Gaston materialized, they had a period of very grim sledding. Early depression stuff—not enough to eat, and sickness, and Layne just a child. A lot of Harold's bitterness, I gathered, stemmed from things like Layne's having to go to a charity ward in a city hospital when she was sick. That sort of thing. It was the child's deprivations that infuriated him."

"An' yet," Asey remarked, "he seemed to me less mad about what had happened in the past than just mad in the present at her, if you see what I'm drivin' at."

"That's my point," Cummings said. "In her hysterical mood, Louise virtually admitted to me that she thought Harold had killed Boone, and when I commented that the motivation was a little tarnished with time, she said that the past hadn't really goaded Harold quite as much as what Boone was doing to Layne now."

"An' what in time did she mean by that?"

"Well," Cummings said, "Layne is sold on Boone. It's Boone, Boone, Boone, Boone this and Boone that. Louise didn't say so in so many words, but I gathered that the Douglasses themselves play a very small second fiddle to Boone in Layne's mind. Louise accepts it philosophically.

Harold doesn't. He reacts as if she actually were their own daughter, you see."

"As if she *were* their own—*isn't* she their own?" Asey demanded.

"Oh, no, she's adopted. The child of friends of theirs who were killed in an automobile accident. I'm really rather surprised that you didn't catch on to that," Cummings said. "While they never go out of their way to make the distinction, they usually make it casually clear. Layne was seven or eight, I think, when they took her."

He took a big bite of "Baby Doll."

"Douglass didn't—yes, come to think of it," Asey said, "he never actually *did* refer to her as his daughter! He just said he was tryin' to act like the perfect parent. An' he begun with the measles when he told about seein' her through things—an' I remember wonderin' why he slid over the early problems like teeth an' colic. Huh! When I talked with him, Harold pretended nothin' had happened outside of Mrs. Boone's bein' lost. But you say Louise thought *he* killed her. What do you think, doc?"

"What goes for one of 'em," Cummings said, "goes for the other. They both have perfectly good motives—revenge for the past, jealousy over Layne. But I found myself thinking of Mrs. Framingham—Aunt Mary, that is—as I followed that woman over here. Somehow she *sounded* like Aunt Mary. I mean, her footsteps did—oh, if only I'd been a Boy Scout in my youth, Asey!"

"Did you aim to build a fire under her, or just wigwag to her?" Asey inquired.

"I mean, I can't even trail people properly! She was always just enough ahead of me so I couldn't see her, and I didn't dare gain on her too much and let her know I was following—and I was *so* sure she'd lead me to something! I don't know why, but I assumed she'd go straight to that body!"

"Why are you so positive that you followed a woman?" Asey asked.

"Because it wasn't a *man!*" Cummings retorted. "Of course, it's occurred to me that Louise had only to go up the front stairs and come down the back stairs and march out to the Lulu Belle, herself, and—oh, so you've already figured that one out, have you?" he added as Asey made an exclamation of assent. "Maybe it *was*n't Aunt Mary. Maybe it was Louise! But I'm positive I followed a woman. I never stopped to look at the Pullman carpet after I discovered the body was gone, but if you say that the stains had been scrubbed off, that *proves* it was a woman!"

Asey wanted to know why he felt that was any particular proof.

"Oh, women always know exactly how to take out stains!" Cummings returned. "The average man doesn't, or else he doesn't think of 'em, or else he makes a terrible botch of the job if he tries. My wife pointed that out to me once. She said furthermore that men always use hot water, which only sets the stain deeper. And Louise had the time to get out there and scrub, and move the body. I dallied in the living room after she went upstairs—oh, damn it, Asey, what happened? How can we find that body? *Why* was Boone moved? *What* are we going to do about it?"

"*How* would kindly old Doctor Muldoon solve this one for wise old Mother Gaston?" Asey said in sepulchral tones. "Listen in to*mor*row!"

"That Muldoon! *There*'s a man I cordially detest!" Cummings said with feeling. "My wife's always throwing him at me because the kindly old fool's grateful patients are always giving sweet old *Mrs.* Muldoon the prettiest diamonds—and my wife feels the discrepancy keenly. She implies that if *I* were only kindlier, more diamonds might fall *her* way! Hm. I'm sure that she or Jennie would know in a *flash* where that lovable old mush-mouth would go to find that body!"

"I asked Jennie," Asey remarked. "*She* suggested a secret room."

Cummings snorted his scorn at the suggestion.

"Of course, a secret room! Oh, just the thing! Or I suppose we could always send away and *get* another body! Sherlock, who took it? Everyone was wandering around, apparently—and even if they weren't actually wandering around here, they could *get* here—Harold could, for example, as you said. But what would anyone *do* with her body? Why hide it in a secret room or any other place?"

"I been askin' myself what anyone hopes to gain from it," Asey said. "For no matter what anyone *has* done with it, we know that it exists, an' we know where it was!"

"What they hope to gain is obvious enough!" Cummings said. "*Time!* They're stalling us!"

"I wonder, doc. I been thinkin' it over," Asey said slowly. "I wonder if it's turnin' up some other place, as it will sooner or later, doesn't just mean that someone's tryin' to get it away from here—I mean like away from the Douglass's, or any connection with them. All the time Douglass talked to me about Mrs. Boone, I felt he was tryin' awful hard to accent her bein' a public figure, tryin' somehow to shove her away from him, an' Louise, an' here!"

"You've really had what amounts to a life history of Boone, haven't you?" Cummings commented. "From me, as one of her public—although I'll admit that much of my early enthusiasm has now waned—and from the Douglasses, who knew her when, and from Gerty, who gave you the college, or in-time note!"

Asey said that the picture of Mrs. Boone was filling out.

"Now, doc," he continued, "s'pose we knew where the body was. S'pose things had progressed in what you might call a normal fashion. Just what different things would we be doin' *now?* What different things would we *have* done? How different would things be now, d'you think?"

"Why, everything would be completely different!" Cummings said without a moment's hesitation. "There'd be cops all over, getting under foot and driving me bats, and there'd be a million photographers and reporters milling around in your hair, and I suppose old Senator Willard P. Boone would have rushed here with his beard waving in the breeze! All the town would be here, all the surrounding towns would be here, all their cousins, sisters, aunts—the place would be a damned madhouse, man alive, and you know it!"

"Uh-huh. But what about the people? You think they'd have broken any bones fallin' over themselves to give us vital tidbits of information?" Asey asked.

"Oh, they'd be on guard—getting information would be like pulling hens' teeth, of course. We've had enough experience with this sort of thing to be sure that everyone would be just as difficult as possible!" Cummings conceded. "Humpf. I suppose I can't say I wouldn't still have spent the afternoon in the boat house, and I don't know but what you still would have been peering into Aunt Mary's inner tube, or chatting by mud holes with ex-Wacs. Humpf. I see what you're driving at, Asey. Actually, we've been less stalled than distracted."

"That's about what I figured," Asey said. "In fact, when everything proceeds accordin' to Hoyle, a murderer has a certain advantage—he can lots of times tell what you're goin' to do next, an' prepare accordingly.

But if I were the murderer in this particular business, I sort of think I'd be kind of on tenterhooks. I wouldn't be sure how much had been found out, or what was known, or what anyone guessed. I wouldn't know whether or not to start any counter-action, or even what to counter."

"You mean, Pollyanna, that you're glad-glad-*glad* that we have no corpse?" Cummings asked acidly.

"Nope, I'm not that glad. But I think we found out quite a lot," Asey said. "I don't think we're stalled, an' I don't even see that we need to let ourselves get distracted. Let's just s'pose you've called your ambulance an' Halbert's men have taken her away. Let's draw a line across the page an' start from there. Start back at noon—say from twelve to twelve-fifteen, until the time you an' I came, around half past one. Durin' that period, you got the Douglass family at their house—"

"And we've got their motives. Check."

"You got Aunt Mary wanderin' around in a beachwagon, an' you got a fake flat—"

"I can't see any obvious motive for her killing Boone," Cummings said. "Certainly Boone never did *her* out of a job, or forced her to any privation! But there's admittedly something fishy about that flat tire business, and about her insisting to Louise that no murder possibly could have taken place! And remember—the woman I followed *walked* like her!"

"Then," Asey went on, "you got the project all over the lot. Take that ex-Wave. Take that fellow I got tied up back there. Jennie said he left our house early, before the rest of the bunch—I'm goin' to look into him in just a minute. Then you got that Eric Manderson floatin' around in the vicinity. You got this Miss Shearin' phonin' from somewhere an' sayin' everything's okay. You got Gerty an' Layne over on the beach—"

"Layne really would be the perfect one, wouldn't she?" Cummings interrupted thoughtfully. "I mean, the perfect murderer."

"Layne? Why?" Asey asked. "She seems to be the only real genuine pro-Boone person I've run across—outside of you, earlier!"

"I know. But I can't believe she doesn't know that many of her childhood hardships were due to Boone. She certainly knows what Harold and Louise feel about Boone! And yet she seems to worship the woman—it could be one of those reversals, you know!"

"What reversals?"

"Oh, there's a five-dollar word for it," Cummings said. "Boils down to—well, for example, you work your fingers to the bone to prove you're *for* something, when really you hate it to death and want to crunch it under your heel like a spider. Had a case of it in the paper last week. Wife stopped loving her husband, covered up by meeting him at the gate every night when he came home from the office, cooking his favorite dishes—just knocked herself out being the perfect little woman. People were awfully surprised when she killed him with the ice pick, but the psychologists understood it all at once. *That* sort of thing. Reversal."

"Sounds a bit complicated," Asey said. "Seems to me it'd be easier to work out Layne by way of Jack Briggs—she wants him, but Boone has the Indian sign on him. I told you about that. Gerty's contribution."

"But that's so commonplace—love, revenge, all that!" Cummings complained. "My idea is—well, it's different! Asey, know what I thought of all afternoon in that damned boat house?"

"Food, phones, food, a word to describe a strange noise, food, phones, an' how to get a light for your cigar," Asey said promptly.

"Your insinuation that I'm a slave to my stomach is libellous!" Cummings said. "Those were merely intermittent reflections—my *real* preoccupation was with that damned rhyme—d'you remember it?—'*Punch*, conductor, *punch* with *care*—'"

"'*Punch* in the *pre*sence of the *passen*-jaire!'" Asey finished up. "Sure. I remember. I've thought of it every time I've thought of that green ticket with the diamond-shaped punch."

"Well, there's more of it than that," Cummings said. "A blue trip-slip for something, and a something-else-trip-slip for something else—I tell you, it's driven me crazy! I've torn my memory apart!"

"It's a *pink* trip-slip," Asey said. "At least, I think it's pink! And for a—golly, I can't recall it, either! A pink-trip-slip, a—"

"Just you take my advice and put it out of your mind and never let yourself think of it again!" Cummings said. "Once you get started, your thoughts start stuttering—*was* there a passen-jaire, d'you suppose, besides Boone?"

"*I* been thinkin' of the murderer as the passen-jaire all along," Asey said. "Well, let's stroll back an' see this fellow that I got tied up. Maybe by now he'll be a little chastened—"

"And of course you've decided *exactly* how you're going to justify this apparent mayhem on his person?" Cummings demanded. "And I mean justify, as explain without going into detail on the topic of murder?"

Asey chuckled.

"Fumble around in that glove compartment in front of you an' pick me out a badge—"

"Pick a card, just *any* card?" Cummings interrupted.

"There's one in particular that I want—an oval, gold-plated job named 'Special Deputy'. It's really very impressive."

"Don't tell me," Cummings said, "that you have some mad notion of playing quohaug inspector again! You never could get away with that twice!"

"I wager I can," Asey returned. "Remember we're not dealin' with natives, or with summer folks—this project crew is all outlanders. An' I don't know but on the whole we can find out about as much that way—don't snort, doc! People be a lot more likely to discuss odds an' ends with a quohaug inspector who's askin' about quohaugs they haven't swiped than they will with someone who's third degreein' 'em about a murder they maybe committed! Hold it—that's the badge I want! Then after Sonny Boy, I think we'll look into Miss Shearing—she's presumably stayin' at some Inn in town—"

"And presumably," Cummings said with irony, "will be fascinated to the core by a visit from a quohaug inspector? No, Sherlock, you might make it with the kids, but I don't think you can play quohaug with her!"

Asey said that he didn't know who had a better right to consult with her, in her capacity as leader of a project on Town Government, than a Special Deputy.

"I can always give her the keys of the town," he added. "Then after we find out a few items, includin' what she actually said to Aunt Mary over the phone, we'll come back here an' see Aunt Mary—"

"In your capacity as tire inspector, no doubt! You can't get away with it! You—Asey, do you keep seeing lights over that way?" The doctor pointed over toward the lane junction.

"You mean car lights? I've noticed some. Every now an' then you can catch a glimpse of light from the Douglass's, too, when the wind blows the branches just right. This *is* close to the house, doc!"

"I'm not talking about car lights!" Cummings said impatiently. "I mean that—see? There it is again! Watch that way!"

"Looks to me," Asey said, "like one of them little pocket flashlights that's like a fountain pen—"

"Maybe," Cummings began to sound excited, "maybe it's that woman—my jailer—coming back to let me out! Look, the light *is* coming this way—oh, damn, they'll see us!"

"Nobody's goin' to notice this car that wasn't expectin' it to be here," Asey said. "I parked with that in mind—stop bouncin' up an' down, doc! Wait—hey, don't get out! Don't—"

"But we can't *see!* We—"

"Turn around an' kneel on the seat—an' shush! Just wait!"

When the figure finally walked along the lane past the car, Cummings's voice breathed in Asey's ear.

"That's Layne Douglass!"

9

"There, see? I *knew* I was right about her!" Cummings's whisper grew louder as the figure moved out of earshot. "*She*'s the one with the motives! *She* took Boone out of the Lulu Belle, and then she did something that caused that strange noise I heard, and then I fooled her by coming on the scene! She never would have guessed anyone was in the house then—no cars outside—and so she lured me away and over to the boat house, and then after locking me up, she went back and *really* hid the body—"

"Not so loud, doc!" Asey reached down and took his flashlight from its clamp on the steering gear.

"And now that it's dark, she's sneaking over to unlock that padlock! Probably she figures I'm asleep and won't hear her, and if I should, she can rush off into the night—" Cummings got out of the roadster and at once stepped on a twig which snapped and sounded to both of them like the explosion of a blockbuster. "Oh, God, I'm sorry, Asey! No Boy Scout in me at *all!* I'm as contrite as—"

"You better shush—an' watch your step!"

Asey spoke with such firmness that the doctor meekly obeyed, and kept silent as he followed Asey on tiptoe along the lane.

The pair paused on the edge of the clearing by the boat house.

Ahead of them, the beam of Layne's little flashlight was focussed on the trussed-up figure on the ground.

"Jack?" she said uncertainly. "*Jack!*"

Asey suddenly found himself grinning from ear to ear.

"Jack Briggs!" Her voice was suddenly sharp. "What happened to you!"

While Asey gave himself a certain amount of credit for having wondered once or twice about the fellow, he had never felt more pleased to discover that he'd guessed wrong. He should have put more faith in Gerty's judgment, he thought. He should have known at once that this couldn't have been her colonel, even though the nickname had seemed so apt and appropriate.

"I thought you said he was *Stin*—" Cummings began hoarsely.

Asey shushed him.

"Oh!" Layne said irritably. "Oh, damn! Of all times for you—"

Turning suddenly, she climbed into the roadster and swung her light over the dashboard.

"Trying to find headlights!" the irrepressible Cummings announced in a whisper. "Silly, *silly* girl! She

118

couldn't find 'em without a guide book in *that* monstrosity of a car! Couldn't—"

He broke off as Asey stepped forward and snapped on his own light.

"All right!" he said briskly. "Hold it! What's going on here? What's the idea?"

Layne gave a little start, and stared into the darkness for a second before she turned her light back at Asey.

"What *is* going on here?" she retorted evenly and without apparent fear, but Asey noticed that the light wavered in her hand. "What are you doing here? This is private property! Who are you?"

"I'm Asey Mayo. Dr. Cummings," he spoke the doctor's name very distinctly, "who is this girl, d'you know?" In an undertone, he added, "Yes, you do, an' to your great surprise!"

"Why, it's Layne Douglass!" Cummings sounded sincerely bewildered. "I must say this is a surprise, Layne! You are probably the *last* person we ever expected to find—merciful heavens, what's *that?*" A note of real horror crept into the doctor's voice. "Who's that bound up there, by the steps?"

"It's Jack Briggs—and I don't—I can't *imagine*—I don't *know* what's happened, doctor!" Her bewilderment, Asey thought, was not just genuine-sounding, but genuine all the way through. Unlike the doctor, with his fluent improvisation, she was hesitant and stumbling—and she was just a little frightened, too! "Whatever are you doing here?"

"We've had a lot of trouble today with people stealin' whole beds of quohaugs an' clams, Miss Douglass," Asey said smoothly before Cummings had a chance to speak. "An' since I happened to be home, they asked if I'd take a hand helpin' to find the thieves. Doc an' I are special deputies—only they ran out of badges before they got to him! We're keepin' an eye on the shore, because we don't think all the crowd's got out of town yet—incidentally," he added, "one of 'em—or *some*body—pinched my car. That's it you're sittin' in, you know!"

Layne got out quickly, as if the roadster were red-hot, and burning her.

"An' I guess that whoever took it," Asey went on, "must have taken your friend here, too—you know this young man?"

"Of course! He's one of the Larrabee College project! Would you two help me untie him, please? There's been some frightful mistake, really! Jack wouldn't steal quohaugs! He must have run into some of the men you're after, and been overpowered!"

"Poor chap!" Cummings said solicitously, as he walked over and looked down at Briggs. "Hold the lights, Layne —come on, Asey, let's get him free!"

With his gag and bonds removed, Jack sat up, looked into the flashlights, and blinked.

Then he looked up at Asey and blinked even harder.

"This is Dr. Cummings, Jack," Layne said. "And Asey Mayo. You know, the detective—"

"Didn't I," Jack seemed to find difficulty in swallowing, "didn't I—uh—weren't you up town at the garage a while ago?"

"Garage?" Asey said politely. "What garage?"

"Well," Jack hesitated, "well, maybe I'm wrong, but you look a lot like a man at the gas station near the traffic lights!"

"Oh, he means your Cousin Josh, Asey!" Cummings said brightly. "There *is* a certain resemblance—same height, same coloring, same general build! Feel all right, do you, Briggs?" he hurried on. "No ill effects?"

"I'm stiff, and I've got a cramp in my right leg, and—"

"What *happened* to you?" Layne interrupted impatiently.

Jack started to shrug, and then he winced.

"Oh, my *shou*lder! I don't know what happened—someone just jumped me, that's all! I was waiting here for you, Layne, as you said to. And just as I was starting to unlock the padlock with that key you gave me—well, that's all, brother!"

The fellow, Asey thought to himself, was speaking with far more truth and accuracy than he guessed. There, in a nutshell, was everything which he'd hoped to find out: Jack was meeting Layne, according to her instructions, and he was unlocking the padlock with the key which she'd previously given him!

That took care of the whole situation—except Layne's motive for wanting to meet him so surreptitiously. But that, Asey surmised, was probably simple enough. Probably, like Gerty, Layne had felt slightly hemmed in by all the project milling around, and merely had wanted to get Jack to herself.

"But the people who jumped on you, Jack! They must have come in Mr. Mayo's car—didn't you hear them? You must have heard the car!"

In a small voice, Jack told her that *he* had come in Mr. Mayo's car.

"You did? Jack, where did you get it?" She sounded, Asey thought, like a very cross mother scolding a very naughty child.

"Outside on the turntable, up at your house!" he retorted a little defiantly. "I thought it belonged to your family, naturally! I certainly shouldn't have taken it, otherwise!"

"You shouldn't have taken it at *all!*" Layne was obviously furious. "I suppose that Stin—that someone put you up to it! But you should have *known* better, Jack! What an utterly idiotic thing for you to do! How could you have been so *stupid!* How—"

She continued to enlarge on his stupidity to an extent that caused both Cummings and Asey to feel uncomfortable, and that made the latter wonder if his first guess about a romantic rendezvous hadn't better be summed up as an error.

"Er—*fancy* your car being at the Douglass's, Asey!" Cummings said quickly when she finally paused for breath. "I wonder *how* it could have got there—let's see, when did you have it last, anyway?"

"Someone pinched it this afternoon, up on the main street. I'm sorry this happened to you, Briggs," Asey said. "Haven't you any clue at all as to who jumped you? Didn't you hear voices?"

The fellow wasn't deaf, after all! He couldn't have missed hearing them!

"Well, yes," Jack said. "I guess I was knocked out for a few minutes first, but then later I heard the sound of voices inside the boat house. You know. Just the sound. Then after a while, I heard people walk out. I think it was two men."

"What did they sound like?" Cummings asked with deep interest.

"Well—gee—like anyone. Like," Jack hesitated, and then he came out with what Asey had been expecting, "Well, they—as a matter of fact, they sounded rather like you two!"

Cummings leaned back against the roadster and laughed and laughed.

"Ha ha! Must have been quite a crack you took," he said, "to hear voices that sounded like *ours!* Ha ha ha! But that's what Jim Higgins claimed, too, Asey—remember? Said one man talked like a Cape Codder, and one sounded more like a summer person. Well, Briggs, I can only tell you that you're damned lucky to have come out of this so easily! Higgins was really hurt—I had to take a couple of stitches in his scalp!"

Jack was confused, and he looked confused.

"Well, I guess—I guess—" he even sounded more confused than he looked.

Asey restrained a smile. While Briggs wasn't convinced by a long shot, he thought, the fellow still wasn't sure enough to open his mouth and make any accusatory statements.

"Wa-el, doc," he said, "we better get along!"

"Oh, absolutely!" Cummings said. "They'll be waiting for us. Sorry we—er—broke up your tryst, Layne!"

"Oh, that doesn't matter at all!" Layne told him casually, without even noticing Jack's quick look in her direction. "I almost started to phone you myself a while ago, Mr. Mayo. I'd felt terribly worried about Mrs. Boone—Carolyn Barton Boone, you know—who's staying at the house, but Louise finally convinced me that I was just being over-anxious."

"Say, doc," Asey prodded him, "isn't she the one you wanted to meet so badly?"

"She certainly is!" Cummings said. "By George, I don't suppose you could arrange a meeting, could you, Layne?"

"I'd be delighted to!" Layne smiled for the first time since he'd met her, and Asey decided suddenly that she really was an attractive girl. "You'll love her, doctor—she's really a wonderful person! I was worried because she's been away from the house since noon without letting us know where she was going, but Louise said that Elizabeth Shearing—she's overseeing the project—said that she was with her. Some business—Jack Briggs, what *are* you grovelling around on all fours for?"

123

"My glasses—they came off when I was hit. You might break down and help me, too!" Jack said. "You know how much the damn things cost!"

While they all helped him search for the glasses, Cummings unostentatiously retrieved his stethoscope from the pine tree branch, and quietly tucked it into his coat pocket.

"I got 'em! I found 'em—here they are, over by the step!" Jack said. "Turn your light this way a second, will you, Layne? I want to snap off the sunglasses—okay. Thanks," he added as an afterthought.

If those dark lenses hadn't been clipped on over the regular frame, Asey thought to himself, he never would have made that mistake in identity. Gerty had specifically mentioned Briggs's poor eyes.

He prodded the doctor gently and whispered in his ear.

"More Boone!"

"Oh!" Cummings said. "Oh. I hope we can make some arrangements for my meeting Mrs. Boone, Layne!"

"I'm sure that Louise has already phoned Mrs. Cummings about the buffet supper tomorrow," Layne said, "but you'd have a much better chance to talk with her if there weren't so many people around, of course. She always has every single minute planned, but I'll find out if she can't spare you some time—why, this door padlock is unlocked, Jack. The key's in it. I simply assumed that they'd broken in, of course! Did they take the key from you?"

"Yes, I just realized that," Jack said. "They must have swiped it when I was knocked out, just after they jumped me. Then when they left, they took the cigarette lighter—it was a lighter I'd seen on a tree stump, and thought someone had lost, and picked up. Say, Mr. Mayo, that might be a clue! One man seemed to know I had it, and the other man said it was his—and say, I've just remembered another thing! The first man called the other '*Doc*'!"

"Asey, there's no question about it in my mind any longer!" Cummings at once rose to the occasion. "I'm sure these fellows we're after are local people, and they're trying to throw everyone off the track by pretending that they're *us!*"

"Now that could be!" Asey said. "It could *be!*"

"I'm positive of it! You know Higgins said that one man called the other something that sounded like 'Macy' —Macy and Doc! Get it? *Asey* and Doc! By George, that's just what they're doing! Those scoundrels are pretending to be *us!*"

"Huh!" Asey reached out in the darkness and gave the doctor an approving pat on the arm. "I wonder— neither of you happened to see anything unusual goin' on about the shore here this afternoon, did you, Miss Douglass? This bunch must have been around this way if they left cigarette lighters—"

"*Ob*viously a signal of some sort!" Cummings interposed. "*Ob*viously!"

"An' they knew the lay of the land, so to speak," Asey went on, "an' about this boat house here an' all. Huh! Didn't you happen to hear *any*thing they said, Briggs? Like any specific comment?"

"The way that I was gagged with that handkerchief of mine," Jack said, "I couldn't hear too well—but there was something about somebody washing her face, I think—"

"Code!" Cummings said. "Code, without doubt!"

"And—oh, yes. Something about—well," Jack said, "it sounded to *me* like hot soup!"

"*Soup!*" Cummings said. "Soup—that's *dy*namite, isn't it, Asey? Hot soup—humpf! I don't like this business! I don't like it!"

"Neither do I!" Asey said truthfully, and gave the doctor a warning poke. Enough, he thought, was enough! "Are you *sure* nobody saw anything unusual goin' on about the shore here this afternoon, Miss Douglass?"

"I've been thinking about it, but I can't recall seeing anything at all out of the way." Layne said. "Gerty—one of the girls from the project—and I were on the far beach, where we could see everything, and we were there all afternoon, too, from a little after twelve till long after four. We never saw anything the least bit strange. Or any strangers—I'd have noticed, I'm sure, because I was sketching—where were you, Jack?"

"Oh, I was all over," he said. "All over town, I mean. Not around here, or the beach, though. Believe it or not, I did some work. I investigated Public Safety. Fire and Police."

"Oh, *did* you!" Layne didn't sound as if she believed him.

"I did! I talked with the traffic cop and peeked inside the fire station windows!"

Their respective whereabouts that afternoon, Cummings decided, must have been what Asey had been waiting to find out about, for he suddenly announced with briskness that they had to be on their way.

"Which car'll you drive, doc?" he added.

"Neither!"

"Neither?" Layne said curiously. "Have you *another* car here?"

"Asey has his spare," Cummings said. "He's lousy with Porter roadsters, you know. No, Asey, I refuse to drive either of those things! I'm afraid of 'em. That's final!"

"Look, doc, you *got* to!" Asey said. "Only just as far as the Douglass's—I'm sure they won't mind our leavin' one there!"

"I will not drive either a single inch!" Cummings was adamant.

"Let one of us," Layne suggested. "Let me—Jack's in no condition—"

"I'm perfectly all right!" Jack protested.

"But I *want* to—I've always yearned to drive a Porter! After all, it's the least I can do, after causing you this delay, Mr. Mayo!"

"But I wouldn't want to break up your—uh—no, Miss Douglass, don't you bother!" Asey said. "I'll send—"

"Don't be silly! You're not breaking up anything! Jack and I were simply going to talk over a problem that we can discuss any time. I'll drive one of the cars—only," she paused, "this one here seems a little strange!"

"*Strange!*" Cummings said with scorn. "Is that the best adjective you can think of to describe a car that is equipped with a built-in sword-holder? Come along up the road with me, Layne. I'm sure you can manage the old model. Let Asey take this thing himself—oh, better lock that door up, hadn't you?"

After Layne snapped the padlock, she and Cummings walked off up the lane.

As the sound of their footsteps receded, Jack cleared his throat rather noisily.

"Er—Mr. Mayo."

"Uh-huh? Get in." Asey stepped into the roadster.

"I guess I was pretty fresh up there at the gas station."

"Wa-el," Asey restrained his impulse to turn his flashlight on the fellow's face, "you were a bit on the nasty side."

"I recognized you right away," Jack went on, "only I didn't want to—I mean, in front of Layne—that is, *she* thinks I'm stupid enough without my giving her anything more to find fault about—oh, hell, you see what I mean! And I *did*n't know this was your car! I really thought it was the Douglass's! I shouldn't have taken it anyway—oh, the whole damn trouble was, I was *sore!*"

"Oh?" Asey said.

"I was burned *up!* Look, I couldn't say this when Layne was around, because I didn't want her to know where I'd been. But I had a date over on the beach this afternoon—that is, I *thought* I did!" he amended with some bitterness. "And I *did* see something odd over there!"

"So?" Asey withdrew his finger from the starter button and leaned back against the seat. "An' what was that?"

"This man—this fellow that was sneaking around through the pines. From where I was waiting, you see," Jack went on, "I could see Gerty and Layne, and I felt a little worried about them with him prowling around. Only I couldn't *do* anything without giving myself away to Layne, and—well, of course, I could have gone after him easily enough if I'd seen him going after *them!*"

"What time was all this?" Asey asked.

"Well, I was already over there waiting when the girls came, and I stayed there till after they went, and I saw him at least three different times—I couldn't tell you just exactly when. I never bothered looking at my watch to see."

"Huh!" Asey said. "I don't suppose you could describe him?"

"I wasn't near enough to see his face, but he was wearing a darkish suit and a felt hat. He wasn't anyone from the project—none of us dresses like that," Jack said, "and he certainly didn't look like any of the townspeople I've seen around."

"Think that you could sum up his felt hat as a Homburg?" Asey was thinking back to Eric.

"I really couldn't say. Only man I ever knew to wear one of those," Jack said with a laugh, "is Mrs. Boone's secretary, Eric Manderson. But he didn't come down with her. You know," he sounded a little self-conscious, "if I hadn't seen that man, and if I weren't sure that someone was prowling around, I honestly would have thought that you and the doctor were that pair in the boat house! Gee, they certainly sounded like you!"

"That 'Macy' and 'Doc' business isn't good!" Asey returned. "I don't like it—tell me, when did you find that cigarette lighter?"

For just the fraction of a second, Jack hesitated.

"On my way back from the beach. I got mixed up with these lanes—one of 'em looks just like another when you're on foot—and it took me a good hour to get back here. Somehow I landed way down there by where this lane here meets the one that goes to the Douglass's house."

"I see." Asey said. "Well, that's all very interestin'. Between you an' me, of course, there's a lot more *to* this business than just the theft of a few quohaugs!"

"I thought so!" Jack said. "I didn't think that you'd be called into action for just a few stolen clams! I guessed there was more. What's the story?"

"Looting." Asey thought to himself that was one way to describe the removal of a corpse!

"Oh. Just looting." Jack sounded disappointed.

"It's pretty serious lootin'," Asey said honestly. "But we're not talkin' about it now. What happened," he started up the roadster, "to your date? Do I gather you got stood up?"

"Don't tell Layne," Jack said, "but I was supposed to meet Mrs. Boone. Purely on business, of course."

"Oh, sure," Asey said. "Why else would you be meetin' the head of your college?"

"Exactly! Only Layne would—well, you know how girls are! Anyway, when I went back from the beach to the Douglass's, I saw this car of yours, and—oh, I was sore, and I'd been sitting around since before noon, waiting, and griping, and I was hungry, and generally burned up—I just took the car. I only intended to go to the village and get something to eat before I met Layne! Now that I see that dashboard lighted up, I wonder how I ever managed to start it—and say, *what* did I do to make it go so slowly? Or did *you* do something to it at the garage?"

Asey chuckled, and explained to him about the parade speed.

"You mean that it really was originally built for a prince? Wow!" Jack whistled. "I thought when I first saw it on the turntable, gleaming in the sun, that it was the car to end all cars—it just burst on me! It knocked my eyes out! It *sent* me! I couldn't help throwing my weight around when I drove into that gas station! Why, by then I was *feeling* like a damn Balkan prince!"

Asey found himself remembering Gerty's theory of Jack's egging her friend Stinky on to take the car, earlier. But if Jack had never seen it before it burst on him at the Douglass's, then that notion of hers wouldn't work out at all.

Get an explanation of why one took it, he thought wearily as he started off down the lane, and it only led you to wondering why in blazes the other fellow had swiped it!

Over at the Douglass's, Cummings and Layne were waiting on the turntable with the other roadster.

"It's marvelous to drive! It's simply *super*, Mr. Mayo!"

Layne stood for a moment in the full glare of the

headlights, and Asey had his first real chance to take a good look at the girl.

She was tall—taller than Gerty—slim, dark-haired, graceful. She had none of Gerty's bounce, Asey thought, and she certainly wasn't the type anyone would automatically put in the front row of a chorus. But she had charm. And when she smiled and her face lighted up, Asey decided that she could give Gerty a run for her money any day in the week.

"It's simply the *keenest* car—"

"Hey, what's all *that?*" As he got out of the roadster, Asey interrupted her and pointed to the floodlights glowing beyond the house. "What's going on out there? Something wrong with the railroad?"

"Oh, no!" Layne said. "That's for Aunt Della!"

"For who?"

"Aunt Della. *Damn* her!" Layne said vigorously.

"Layne's just explained it to me, Asey," Cummings said. "Seems that Aunt Della Hovey always planted dahlias on this day of May—in the evening if it hadn't rained, and in the afternoon if it had, or was. The Douglasses are carrying on the tradition."

"It's more of that idiocy from the book!" Layne said. "I'm so tired of it and so bored with it. That's the *keenest* car—"

"Er—*what* book?" Asey wanted to know.

"We have this silly book full of Aunt Della items—you see," Layne said, "when Louise and Harold bought this house from her, they faithfully promised her that they'd do all sorts of things—and they actually *do!* For my part, I can't think *why*—can you, doctor?"

"I don't know that I ever bothered to think why," Cummings returned. "It always seemed to me that they just enjoyed doing all those things."

"*I* think it's some sort of compensation—possibly for

their lack of roots," Layne said quite seriously. "*Think* of it! *Think* of our having to live in that sitting room, crammed to the ceiling with Hovey family litter! *Think* of our always having to burn apple wood in the fireplaces because Brother Willie—that was Aunt Della's brother—*always* said that apple wood should be burned in his fireplaces, and *nothing* else! And we have the Bible facing east, because that was how Aunt Della's great-great-grandmother said it *should* be! And *all* those graves in the cemetery!"

"You mean," Asey said, "you even have to tend to them?"

"Tend them, and take flowers on prescribed days—and prescribed flowers, too! Costs a small fortune, because no one ordinarily grows what's prescribed any more—you simply can't imagine how much Harold had to pay for a certain variety of mignonette that Aunt Della insisted on!"

Asey laughed.

"It isn't funny!" Layne said. "We have to have goose at Christmas, though none of us like it very much, and salmon and green peas on the Fourth of July, and baked Indian pudding on someone's birthday—Brother Willie's or Brother Tom's, I forget which. Frankly, hardly a day passes that we're not stewing around doing something for Aunt Della or one of her clan! And tonight is Dahlia Night."

"Who's doin' the plantin'?" Asey asked.

"Harold and Louise and Aunt Mary. Aunt Mary withstood Aunt Della for a long while," Layne said, "but I notice that she's given in lately. It finally wore even her down. She attends to putting the January first headlines of the Boston newspapers into the secret drawer of Cousin Lucy's mahogany desk that Uncle Willie—*never* to be confused with *Brother* Willie!—brought from Jamaica. That headline business was a whim of Young Elisha, a stray cousin who used to live here. And Aunt Mary also—oh, I do wish you all wouldn't roar so. It may sound terribly amusing, but it's simply hideous to live with!"

"Annual headlines in a secret drawer!" Cummings said weakly. "That's one *I* never heard of before! Haven't any secret rooms, have you, that you have to tidy and put clean starched curtains in annually?"

Layne said wearily that seemed to be the only item they'd been spared.

"And please!" she went on, "*please*, doctor, don't ever bring up the topic of secret rooms in *this* household!"

"Why not?" All the laughter had disappeared from Cummings's voice.

"It's a very sore subject," Layne said. "You see, secret rooms are Aunt Mary's hobby."

10

Cummings's foot ground down on Asey's instep, and his fingers pinched Asey's arm.

"Is that so!" he said. "Well, well! I didn't know that, Layne!"

"Oh, yes. Secret rooms have been a lifetime hobby of hers. Practically her only hobby, as a matter of fact. She found one by accident in England, on her honeymoon, and it simply went to her head." Layne stopped and lighted a cigarette. "She's never stopped hunting them since. Why, for years and years, she rushed around here waving a hammer and a chisel, banging and prying!"

"She ever find any trace of one?" Asey inquired casually.

"Of course not—but she nearly ruined the wainscoting in the front hall near the chimney," Layne said, "and Louise and Harold finally had to make her promise to stop being so destructive. But she still goes wandering around with tape measures, hopefully measuring—oh, I forgot! D'you want to ask the family any questions about this afternoon, Mr. Mayo? I'm sure if they'd seen anything strange, they'd have spoken about it—and it's only fair to warn you they'll probably thrust a spade into your hand and set you to work."

"Could I maybe just take a peek at 'em?" Asey asked. "I'd like to see this Annual Dahlia Festival of Aunt Della's in action."

"Come along, then!" Layne said. "But do be quiet—if they catch sight of us trooping around the drive, we'll all be digging for Aunt Della!"

The quartet tiptoed around to the back of the house and silently watched the dahlia planting that was taking place with the aid of two floodlights that had apparently been swung around from the railroad station.

Asey's eyes narrowed as he got his first glimpse of Aunt Mary.

Harold Douglass wasn't a short man, but Aunt Mary gave the impression of towering head and shoulders above him. Actually, Asey realized as the dahlia planters stood up and stretched, she wasn't more than an inch or two taller, but her erect carriage and her broad, powerful shoulders created an illusion of great height.

He grinned suddenly as he recalled his previous surprise on finding out from Louise that an elderly aunt should have contemplated changing the beachwagon's flat tire all by herself!

This particular elderly aunt looked to him entirely capable of changing flat tires by the dozen—and doubtless she could also throw in a complete engine overhaul without batting an eyelid!

Cummings moved close to Asey.

"No impromptu grave-digging there!" he whispered. "Looks like plain, honest planting to me!"

Asey nodded. "Same here."

"Don't you think," Cummings went on, "that you'd better see about Aunt Mary before you go to check up on that Shearing woman? *I* do!"

Asey hesitated, and then shook his head.

"Why not?"

"I want to, doc, but I can't."

Asey turned and walked over to where Layne and Jack were standing, and waited for them to finish their whispered conversation. "Miss Douglass, I can only sum that up as a mighty interestin' sight!"

"But doesn't it appall you?" Layne asked as they all started back toward the turntable. "I mean, to think that people can live that way—and like it? With those silly schedules? Doing this for Brother Willie, and that for Aunt Della, and something else for Cousin Lucy—and *all* people they never even knew?"

Asey chuckled. "You ought to meet my cousin Jennie, Miss Douglass, an' find out why we plant peas when we do, an' just how our annual spring house-cleanin' date got set! Nun-no, this really don't dumbfound me so much. I'm used to roots—come on, doc, we're late! I still wonder," he said as he pocketed the keys of the new roadster, "how this vehicle got here!"

"I'm getting to be *aw*fully afraid it must have been someone from the project who's responsible!" Layne said. "I'll look into that, and see that you're apologized to. Sometimes that crowd lets themselves get carried away. I *do* hope you find those men you're hunting—and I'd really adore to drive either car anywhere for you!"

"Thanks—just let it stay here till I can send someone for it," Asey said as he and the doctor got into the old roadster.

That extra car, which had at first seemed such a nuisance, would provide an excellent excuse for him to return at any time, he thought to himself.

"If you're going to the village, could I hook a ride with you?" Jack asked.

"Why don't you wait," Layne spoke up before Asey could answer, "and settle things? The crowd's gone, and the house is quiet. Wait, and I'll drive you up later. Good-bye, doctor! Good-bye, Mr. Mayo!"

Cummings waited until the old roadster was speeding down the lane to the main road before he pulled out a cigar.

"Slow down enough for me to light this, will you, Asey? I honestly haven't dared to smoke, I've been so afraid I might take this lighter out of my pocket without thinking! Tell me, did we fox that Briggs fellow, or didn't we?"

"I'm not sure, doc."

"Humpf!" Cummings said. "Neither am I! Asey, they were all planting dahlias innocently enough while we watched 'em, but that doesn't mean they *could*n't have buried Boone before we came!"

"Uh-huh."

"And that business of Aunt Mary's hobby being secret rooms—I tell you, I nearly forgot myself and let out with a wild yelp at that one! Secret rooms, *think* of it! Asey, there's no reason why there *could*n't be a secret room in Aunt Della's house!"

"Uh-huh."

"It couldn't be anywhere near the front hall, or around the center chimney, of course," Cummings went on with enthusiasm, "because *I* was right there in the living room and could have seen—Asey, I'll bet the old girl *was* starting to bring the body into the house when I went rushing out, after hearing that noise! Then, because I was in her way, she lured me on down to the boat house—I always *thought* it sounded like her walk! And then, after she'd locked me up out of the way, she went back to the house and hid the body in the secret room—which, of course, *she*'d previously found, but never told the Douglasses *about!* Yes?"

"Uh-huh."

Cummings said acidly that because he'd been playing the part of a quohaug inspector, there was no reason for him to *act* like a damned quohaug himself!

"*Say* something! Don't just sit there, letting me ramble on!"

"I like it, doc. There's nobody else I know," Asey said appreciatively, "that could begin to twist so many stories out of a simple set of facts, like your hearin' a noise, an' followin' someone, an' gettin' locked up! First you worked it out with Layne, then with Louise, an' now—"

"Why didn't you talk to her—I mean, to Aunt Mary?" Cummings interrupted. "Why didn't you tackle her out there among the dahlia bulbs, anyway?"

"Too many people were around, an' too many explanations would've had to be made, doc," Asey said. "I certainly want to talk to her, goodness knows, but I want to know first exactly what this Miss Shearin' actually said over the phone. For all we know, maybe she *did* tell Aunt Mary that Mrs. Boone was all right an' with her! Maybe Boone *is* with her, for that matter! Could be!"

"Yes, I suppose you couldn't very well have said anything without going back to the murder," Cummings said thoughtfully, "and to judge from the general mirth and gaiety of that dahlia planting, the Douglass menage has put murder firmly out of its mind—d'you realize, Asey, that Layne has absolutely *no* inkling of *any*thing? I pumped her just a bit as we drove over—Louise never even told her that you and I had been there! Humpf! D'you think that fool quohaug act was worth all the effort?"

Asey said that he did. "After all, your favorite suspect —as of half an hour ago—got an alibi. Layne's story of bein' on the beach with Gerty checks with Gerty's story of bein' there with Layne!"

"Now why do you call her my favorite suspect?" Cummings demanded indignantly. "Oh, I'll admit that things *did* look somewhat suspicious for Layne a while back, but I never seriously considered *her* a suspect! She's a nice girl. Little high-handed, maybe, and a little too opinionated—but that's just being young. Got a nice smile, hasn't she? And after all, she and that ex-Wac were together—it'll be simple enough for you to check up on 'em before noon! By the way," he added, "how *did* your new car get over there? We improvised so much so quickly, I've actually lost all track of the truth!"

"I left it with Gerty, over by the mud hole," Asey said. "She planned to bring Stinky back in it. I assume they came, and then went off in someone else's car—one of the project's, I suppose. Only Layne didn't see 'em."

"Know what *I* think?" Cummings remarked.

"Think you got that secret room located?" Asey said with a laugh.

"Oh, that!" Cummings spoke as though the secret room angle were something that had been brought up several centuries before. "I think that Briggs is a nasty character, Asey! I mean, when you come right down to it, Aunt Mary Framingham is a nice person. Little high-handed, perhaps, and a little too opinionated—"

"But she's got a nice smile?" Asey interrupted drily.

"You know what I'm driving at! You can build up any amount of circumstantial evidence about her, but she's a decent person! But this Briggs fellow, though—now I don't *like* him!"

"I didn't at first," Asey said, "but I'm not sure it isn't just his face. When you don't see his face, you don't mind him—oh, I forgot to tell you about how he spent the afternoon, an' about the stranger he seen prowlin' around the shore. Seems—"

Cummings snorted at the conclusion of Asey's recital.

"That's absolutely nothing but quick thinking on his part, Asey! He heard Layne say that she and Gerty had been on the beach, and because she'd planted them there, why *he* planted *himself* as being near, and watching—you know damn well there's no earthly way to back-check a yarn like that! Humpf! So Boone stood him up!"

"I can understand why," Asey commented.

"That's not the point!" Cummings said. "Point is, the fellow's trying to accent the assumption that she's *alive*, in his estimation—don't you get it? He's smart! It was smart of him to throw in Eric in such an indistinct fashion, too! And *much* smarter to insinuate Eric than to invent a common or garden stranger with a beard! Brought him in very disarmingly, I must say!"

"Lookin' idly over this whole bunch," Asey said, "I don't think I ever seen a more completely disarmin' crew! They're all so doggone innocent about the things they did, they can't even tell you the time of day they did 'em! Seems to me I've asked a thousand people what time something happened, an' they just all shrug careless-like, an' say, 'Oh, from maybe perhaps about a quarter-to-this to aroundabouts-half-past-something-else—more or less!' Nobody's got the time of anything down pat. No, sir, no definite, split-second nonsense with *this* crowd! Fifteen minutes one way or another, or even an hour—"

The roadster came almost to a complete stop.

"What's wrong?" Cummings asked. "Why are you slowing down?"

Asey didn't answer for a moment.

"Just an idle passin' thought that struck me," he said as the roadster picked up speed again. "Nothin' important. But I agree with you about Jack Briggs, doc—we'll look into him some more later. Jennie said he left our house earlier than the rest of the project, so he's got quite a lot of time there that could stand explainin'."

"By George—I didn't tell you! *I* discovered what Layne wanted to talk over with him!"

"So? An' how'd you go about findin' that out?"

"Easy enough," Cummings told him. "I just asked her. Seems he's been offered a job he's not very keen about, but Layne think's it's a wonderful opportunity and he ought to grab it. I asked her about Boone, too, but she just said Carolyn was with Miss Shearing. No use talking, apparently Louise and Aunt Mary just made up their minds that Boone is fine, *and* with Miss Shearing, and not only is that their story to which they've adhered, but they've even sold it to Layne and Douglass!"

"Funny Layne wouldn't have checked up more," Asey said, "if she was so anxious about Boone that she nearly called me!"

"She told me she *simply yearne*d to call Carolyn, but Carolyn was furious if her schedule was disturbed, and that obviously she'd been swamped with some unforeseen college work—wonder what Briggs's job could be?"

"Wa-el, Gerty told me—" For the doctor's benefit,

Asey recalled her contribution about Mrs. Boone's opening for a new secretary to replace Eric, and her suggestion
that either Jack Briggs or Stinky might be a candidate
for the job.

"*Motive!*" Cummings said at once. "Motive for Eric,
I mean. Kicked upstairs, and doesn't want to go—oh,
stop chuckling, will you?"

"I can't help it, doc!" Asey said. "You've hopped
from the Douglasses, one by one, to Aunt Mary, an' from
her to Briggs, an' now to Eric! I wish you'd pick out
one an' stick to him! Or her!"

"*I* wish," Cummings retorted, "that you'd just break
down to the extent of picking *one!* Oh, there's another
thing. Layne made that date with Briggs this morning
when the project arrived, and gave him the padlock key
then. Humpf! That must mean there's a duplicate key
that was used by whoever unlocked the boat house so
that they could shut me up in it later—" he stopped
abruptly.

"What's the matter?"

"Why, damn it, they *couldn't* have known they were
going to shut me up, *could* they, *if* I surprised them when
they were removing the body, so—oh, stop laughing!
Stop it, you old hyena! I give up! I've shot my bolts!
From now on," Cummings said acidly, "*you* may have
complete charge of the Brilliant Solutions and Deductions
Department! What particular hostelry is this project
crowd staying at," he added as they approached the
traffic lights at the four corners, "d'you know?"

"Nope, but I'm sure we can guess easy enough by
the noise an' the swarm of—golly, I *never* made these
confounded lights in my life!" he jammed on the brakes.

"Hoo-hoo! Asey! Hoo-hoo!"

Jennie came running up to the roadster from the side
of the road.

"I thought you'd turn up here at the lights *some* time," she said breathlessly, "and I didn't want to go rushing out there to the point asking where you were—hello, doc, so he finally found you, thank goodness! I got your car over there, and your wife says to tell you if you don't come home and take care of your darn ole business, *she*'s going to Reno! I took down a list of calls you got to make that she gave me over the phone—here."

"Ah, yes, business!" Cummings said. "I'd completely forgotten it for the first time in years—what've you got in that basket there, Jennie?"

"Some chowder, and some supper—for Asey!"

"Do I have to play little tunes on your tender heart-strings?" Cummings demanded. "Do I have to tell you how I've been locked up—foodless, waterless, and practically airless—in what amounted to a Black Hole of Calcutta? Do I have to enumerate my grim sufferings to get a wee snack to revive my famished frame and—"

"All he means, Jennie," Asey interrupted, "is that he's had nothin' since lunch but a quart of soup, an' half my lunch, an' a candy bar more sustainin' than fifteen steaks an' twelve bottles of milk!"

"And to gain sufficient strength," Cummings continued, ignoring him, "to take up once again my selfless role of healer?"

"Selfless! At five dollars a visit?" Jennie sniffed. "Hm! Isn't it lucky that by the merest chance I *figured* on something like this happening, and put in enough for two! That's Asey's side, doc, and this's yours, and don't poach—you know you don't like mustard! Asey, I've made an awful mistake! I told you something that's all wrong. It's *not* catnip!"

"How's that again?"

"Catnip," Jennie said, "was *last* week!"

"Catnip was *what* last week?"

"Why, catnip was the answer to a *last* week's Quick Quiz Question! Somebody told me wrong, and I forgot there'd already *been* catnip once. It's coypus."

"What coy puss?" Cummings asked with his mouth full. "Or coy puss *what*?"

"C-o-y-p-u-s! One word. That's the answer to the Question we missed today!"

"If that's the answer, what in the name of God is the Question?" Cummings demanded. "Coypus! I never *heard* of coypus—is it singular or plural?"

"The Question," Jennie said, "is what's *something*—I never was able to find out *what!*—and the answer is, *coypus!* And nobody they called so far has got the answer yet! And listen to me, Asey, who d'you s'pose has been over at our house, pumping me for all she's worth about *you*, and where you *are*, and what you're *doing*, and what you're *up* to?"

"Shearing!" Asey and Cummings said at once, in unison.

"Who?" Jennie said. "Who's *that*?"

"No matter," Asey said. "Tell us who's been visitin' you."

"That ex-Wave. Alicia Grant, her name is."

"You mean the project one?" Asey asked. "Tall, thinnish girl, wearin' glasses with blue frames?"

"Uh-huh, that's just who! Claimed she wanted to interview me in my capacity as head of the Red Cross—seems her job's investigating the town's Public Health and Welfare. That's what she said! *But*," Jennie added with emphasis, "the only thing she talked about was *you!* I don't know as I ever saw anyone more anxious to find out where another person was! And furthermore—" she paused.

"The radio influence, Asey," Cummings said in resigned tones. "That's a mannerism straight out of Mother Gaston. The dramatic hesitation. 'What do you think—space—Mother Gaston? Is it—space—a boy?—two spaces—or a *girl*?' You should hear my wife do it. What do I think we're having for dinner? Pause and count three. Stew!"

"I'm not pausing because I'm trying to be dramatic," Jennie said indignantly. "*I'm* pausing because I'm afraid you'll think it's crazy! But I *did* hear of one person, one *local* person, I mean, who promised to kill Mrs. Boone this morning when he heard she was in town!"

"You mean, 'I hear tell Miz Boone's in taown? Why, land's sakes, I cal'late I got to *kill* her? I—' "

"Stop it, doc! Who, Jennie?"

"Well, I don't know that I think so much of it, myself, except that after all, people *are* sometimes queer about some things, and this person's queer about women—women who *do* things, in public life and all, that is. *He* says the whole trouble with the world today is women fussing around in politics, and sticking their noses into all sorts of things while their homes and children go to rack and ruin, and their husbands get stomach ulcers from not getting proper food—and of course, Asey, he *has* disappeared! Nobody knows where he is!"

"Who?" Asey asked patiently.

"Well," Jennie said, "I almost hate to tell you because I'm so sure you'll laugh—but no one's seen him since the Bull Moose. It's Sylvester!"

11

"AND FURTHERMORE," Jennie raised her voice to make herself heard above the sound of the doctor's roars of laughter, "of all the women in public life that Sylvester hates anyway, he hates Mrs. Boone the most! He talked about her *terribly* today while he was waiting in the sugar line for someone."

"Did he really say anything about killin' her, actually?" Asey asked. "Or did he just say he hated her an' all her kind—an' you just threw in the rest?"

"He told Amy Waters, that was standing in the line behind him, that if *he* ran across that Boone woman in some lonely, secluded place while she was here in town, he could promise her—Amy, that is—that he'd kill Mrs. Boone with his bare hands! He said he thought it would be a mighty fine thing for the world if someone did, and the best contribution he could make for a lasting peace. Not in *just* those words, but pretty near 'em!"

"Oh," Cummings said weakly, "I haven't laughed so hard since I was a boy! Why, if Sylvester had put it all in writing—even if he'd announced that he intended to snatch that silver bud vase from the Lulu Belle and kill her specifically with that!—I think we could still take it for granted that Sylvester is *not* the person we want! Jennie, it's funnier even than coypus!"

"Where'd he go?" Asey asked.

"Oh, now, look, Asey!" Cummings said. "You can't take that nonsense seriously! Sylvester! Silly Nick—oh, it just isn't sensible!"

Asey reminded him of the quohaug inspections, and of Aunt Della's Annual Dahlia Planting over at the Douglass house.

"They're not very sensible, either! An' you summed up the story of my afternoon's actions as bizarre an' fantastic an' preposterous! Why carp, doc, why carp? Where'd Sylvester go, Jennie?"

"That's it! *No*body knows! People were sore when the Bull Moose was late and they missed hearing the Question, and of course right away they tried to find Sylvester to see what the matter was—but he'd just disappeared! And of course everyone claimed he must have run away because he was afraid of what people would *do* to him!" Jennie said. "See? But then, of course, everybody *got* the Question from someone who'd listened somewhere else, and they're not mad at Sylvester any more—only curious to know *why* he was late! They've even got to thinking it's all sort of funny, now— because of course he *never* was late at anything before, never in all his born days!"

"An' still no sign of Sylvester," Asey said, "in spite of the general change of mood about him?"

Jennie shook her head.

"Everyone's sure it's on account of him being late with the Bull Moose. Nobody ever thought that there might be any other reason—"

"Like his having killed Carolyn Barton Boone, and fled!" Cummings started to shake with laughter again. "Oh, that is *so* idiotic!"

"Sylvester," Jennie said coldly, "is *queer*. You know it, doc! He's queer, and he always *was* queer!"

"While I freely concede," Cummings said as he started on another package of sandwiches, "that Sylvester is a 'character', as the saying goes, and while I admit that in this town he's labelled 'queer', may I also point out that in some larger or urban center, he and his little eccentricities wouldn't even cause a ripple? Why in Hollywood, for example, he'd pass for quite normal!"

"I don't know about Hollywood," Jennie said with a sniff, "but I know I was at a town meeting here once when he got mad about having the new flag pole put across from the Town Hall instead of by the square, and he nearly *killed* Uncle 'Bijah Knowles! They had to *pry* Sylvester off him! I've seen him lose his temper, and I

146

know what happens when he does—Asey, what're you wearing that fool 'Special Deputy' badge for? I just this minute caught sight of it when you turned and the street light struck it—Asey, have you been speeding again and wangling your way out of it?"

"He's only been inspecting quohaugs," Cummings said.

"Humpf! Whyn't you go inspect Sylvester's quohaugs, and see what you can dig up? Sylvester's got a dozen beds, and I'm sure he'd love to meet a quohaug inspector at his age!"

"Ever watch gulls, doc?" Asey asked suddenly.

"Watch gulls? I can't say I've made the process my life work, but I've noticed one or two. Why, Sherlock?"

"Ever notice a bunch of 'em swoopin' around and around in circles after a fish, an' then all of a sudden one fellow comes up from a mile away—an' bang!—*he's* got the fish?"

"If you mean to insinuate that Sylvester is a remote gull, I must say that's an entirely *new* angle on his character! *Swoop?*" Cummings said derisively. "Man alive, Sylvester never moved any faster than a slow crawl—and let me assure you he moves a whole lot quicker than he thinks! Where's my list of calls, Jennie? I must get on with my morning chores—oh, my God, why have you let me sit here and stuff myself like a pig?" he added as he read the list by the flickering light of his cigarette lighter. "I ought to have been at the Harrimans' hours ago!"

"Was it *me*," Jennie returned with asperity, "that brought up the Black Hole of Calcutt—"

"Jennie, you're a wonderful woman, a fine cook, it was a dandy meal, and thank you! Good bye, Inspector Mayo —I shall think of you trying to dig your way out of quohaug beds without my invaluable aid!"

"Keep your stethoscope handy!" Asey said. "Never can tell when you might want to drape it over some handy tree branch for me to rescue you by an'—"

But Cummings's old sedan was already rattling off down the highway.

"Never even asked me if he could drop me off anywhere!" Jennie commented as she took the seat that the doctor had vacated. "He—why, he *is* a big pig! He's eaten all your sandwiches, mustard and all!"

"That's fair enough," Asey said. "I took all his chowder —where are you bound?"

"Oh, I thought if I got through with getting his car to him in time, I might go to the Ladies' Aid meeting —unless," she said hopefully, "you got something you'd like me to do for you. Asey, you don't seem to feel that this business of Sylvester is as crazy as the doc did."

"I might have," Asey told her, "if I hadn't already thought back to somethin'—Jennie, I tell you what. While I go see this Miss Shearing that I been tryin' to get to since the lord knows when, you drop by the Ladies' Aid, will you, an' see if you can't find out any tidings about Sylvester an' what's become of him? An' one more thing—who's the oldest person that might be there tonight?"

"Well, let's see," Jennie considered. "It's a nice night, not too cold—if her son's home, I don't know but what he might bring old Mrs. Phinney. She's ninety-eight and a half—is that old enough? Mrs. Collins is ninety-nine next month, but she don't go out much."

"Ninety-eight an' a half ought to do," Asey said gravely. "Providin' her memory's okay."

"Okay? Why, when they revised the church history this winter," Jennie said, "Mrs. Phinney sat down and ran back ninety years without stopping to *think!* She's a wonder—and not just on *church* history, either. I don't think Emma'll ever forgive her for what she brought up about Emma's grandmother's marriage to Emma's grandfather! Of course, she's a bit deaf in one ear!"

"Wa-el," Asey said, "s'pose you plant yourself down next to her good ear, an' pump her about Aunt Della Hovey's house. Say you heard tell there was a secret room in it, an' was there really, an' so on."

"So I was right!" Jennie said delightedly. "So *that's* where Mrs. Boone's body is! I knew it! I *told* you so! *Just* like Mother Gaston!"

Asey advised her not to get carried away.

"I don't know that there's any secret room, or that the body's in it if there is one. I just decided," he said, "to stop workin' on the sane, sensible angles, an' to try a few Mother Gastony approaches instead. So—you find out about secret rooms, an' about Silly Nick, an' I'll stop by for you in a little while. If anything happens I shouldn't get there before it's time for you to leave, you hitch a ride home, an' I'll get back there eventually."

"To my way of thinking," Jennie remarked, "the silliest thing in all this business is that you got *this* far, and with absolutely *nothing* to work on! I must say I don't understan—"

She broke off as a sedan that had been going through the green traffic lights suddenly stopped, and backed up to the roadster.

The woman driver, whom Asey recognized as the druggist's wife, leaned her head out the window and called to him.

"Asey! Billy said for me to take this and give it to Jennie at the Ladies' Aid, so she could take it home to you—but you might as well take it now. I think it's some medicine you rushed away and forgot this afternoon."

"Medicine?" Jennie asked curiously. "Asey, *what*

149

medicine? When did *you* get any medicine, for goodness sakes! Billy's made some mistake!"

"Nope, it's my faintin' medicine," Asey informed her with a laugh. "An' I *did* forget it!"

Getting out of the roadster, he walked over to the sedan and took the neatly wrapped bottle that Mrs. Gill was holding out.

"Thanks a lot," he said. "Tell Billy it slipped my mind."

"Billy said that he called after you, and he tried a couple of times to yell at you as you drove by—he said he didn't know that this was so *very* important to you, but you asked for it and probably wanted it. It's lucky I saw you—isn't Jennie going to the meeting?"

"Maybe you'd give her a lift," Asey said. "It'd be a great help to me, because I got some errands to do—would you? Thanks. Hop in with Mrs. Gill, Jennie. I'll pick you up later."

Left to himself, Asey pawed around optimistically in the supper basket, ate the single molasses cookie which Cummings had somehow overlooked, and then started off toward the main street of the town.

His idea of picking the inn where the project was staying by their noise was not, he discovered, going to work out. Both the larger inns and the neighboring guest houses were all peaceful and quiet, and entirely devoid of any youthful swarm.

He drew up at the nearest, an old-fashioned, rambling, yellow-frame structure with a cupola, to ask for some information.

The roadster had hardly come to a stop before a tall, lanky, boyish-looking fellow with curly red hair jumped briskly from a rocking chair on the porch, and fairly leapt to the side of the car.

"Sir!"

Asey surveyed his white flannels and blue, brass-buttoned coat, and at once diagnosed him as an assistant manager eager to provide service.

"Is the Larrabee College project stayin' around here anywheres, do you know?" he asked.

"Here, sir. Mr. Mayo, I'm Bill Cotton."

"Oh?"

"Stinky, sir," he explained as he saw that the name didn't register. "I think Gerty mentioned me."

Asey looked at him thoughtfully for several moments.

"So *you* are—for Pete's sakes, *why* Stinky? Why not just plain *Red?*"

"Little problem in elementary chemistry, sir, that's followed me since I was a kid in grammar school," he said with a laugh. "For a long while they called me 'Eggy'. But never Red. I never liked Red. Sir, I'm sorry about taking your car—that fancy job. I thought it was Manderson's. Eric Manderson's. Mrs. Boone's secretary's, that is. Case of mistaken identity."

"How's that again?" Asey inquired.

"Eric Manderson. Mrs. Boone's secretary. I thought it was *his* car."

"That's what I thought it sounded like. Er—how come?"

"Well, sir, I saw Eric going into the telephone office in the village—"

"When?"

"Oh, I don't know exactly when—" Stinky paused. "Did you say something, sir?"

"I said that was a fool question," Asey told him, "an' I certainly ought to know better than to ask it, by now! Go on."

"I'd guess it was somewhere between one and one-thirty," Stinky was obviously trying to cudgel his memory. "Anyway, I called to him—I didn't know he was

151

coming down here, and I was surprised to see him. We talked a few minutes, and he said he had a batch of calls to make, and I said swell, and could I take his car to transport a case of beer that Jack Briggs and I were promoting. And then—"

"You rehearsed this very much?" Asey asked him casually.

"Oh, yes, sir! Gerty made me. She said I was to deal it out quick," Stinky said. "No hesitations. And then Eric said he'd prefer not to lend it to me because this was his brand-new car, but *brand*-new! So I said wasn't he being just a little damn snooty about his new buggy, and kidded around—you can't help kidding Eric, Mr. Mayo," he added earnestly. "That guy just stands up and begs for it. And he swallows it—whole!"

Judging from his own experience of the quohaug inspection and the 'Pass', Asey felt that was an accurate summary of Eric.

"I said," Stinky continued, "I didn't think I'd ruin his car, just taking a case of beer over to the Inn, and all right, if he didn't want to be helpful and cooperative, why the hell with it, he didn't have to be—I didn't really give a hoot, you understand, sir. I was only just needling the guy! And Eric put on a long face, and laid his hand on my shoulder in a fatherly kind of fashion—that's a habit he's got that burns me up!—and said I just didn't understand, that was all!"

"Understand *what?*" Asey asked.

"Understand what a wonderful new car his new car was. He said actually, I probably couldn't handle anything so new, or even start it, for that matter. And while he always tried very very hard to be cooperative with the undergraduates, he didn't feel—oh, stuff, stuff, stuff, and so on and so on, far into the night!"

"In a nutshell," Asey remarked, "he wouldn't let you

have his wonderful, brand-new car, an' so you took mine?"

"In a nutshell, yes, sir—only I want you to get more of the picture first, see?" Stinky said seriously. "Here's this stuffed shirt patting me paternally on the shoulder—why, he's a year younger than I am, the big fat-head—and yapping about his wonderful, wonderful car, and how it isn't that he hasn't got the true Larrabee spirit of friendly cooperation, it's just the principle of the thing, and how hurt and upset I'd be if I hurt and upset his car! And—well, sir, I'd started it all just kidding, but then I got plenty sore, and I decided I was damned if I wouldn't take his car. See?"

"Uh-huh," Asey said, and thought how Gerty's influence crept out in little spots, like that explanatory "see?". "I think I begin to get the picture."

"Well, sir, I got the beer, and then I saw that car of yours—mind you, I hadn't seen Eric's. He didn't ever point the gorgeous creature out to me. But your road-ster was so exactly what his sounded like when he'd told me about it—well, I took it! It was wonderful, and brand-new, and shiny, and complicated—and I said to myself, bingo! Eric's new toy!"

"You didn't feel it was maybe a mite too costly for him?" Asey suggested.

"Oh, no." Stinky shook his head. "Eric's family are lousy with dough. That's how he got that job with Mrs. Boone—they gave the college a nice new wing, and Eric got the nice job! Anyway, it's the sort of car he might've had, and God knows it certainly sounded like the one he'd been describing to me!"

"How in time did you land out on the point in it?"

"I took the wrong turn at the traffic lights, sir, and found myself on the road going out to the Douglass's, and I suddenly took it into my head to show Eric's new car off to Gerty. I thought I might as well get him good and sore while I was at it," Stinky said with a grin. "Then I took another wrong turn and landed on the lane by the mud hole, and met Gerty coming back from the beach, and she gave me hell! Honestly, sir, there's nothing you can dish out that I haven't already had thrown at me!"

"Let's see, now," Asey said. "Gerty told me she'd sent you off to find Layne. Where did you go? What became of you? What happened to you and Gerty later? I'm curious," he added, "because my roadster finally turned up two other places, an' bein' driven by someone else!"

"But we left it at the Douglass's for you, sir!" Stinky said with a touch of anguish in his voice. "Just as you told Gerty! The rest had left, and she and I hitch-hiked back here to town on a truck full of live hens—it isn't smashed up or anything, is it, sir?"

"No, the car's okay. What happened after you went for Layne? I'd sort of like," Asey said, "to figure out this mess!"

"I went off in the direction Gerty said I'd find Layne," Stinky told him, "and almost just around the corner from the mud hole, I spotted Eric—yes, sir, Eric! He was stomping around on another of those lanes, and looking as mad as anyone I ever saw. The guy was livid. I ducked him. I thought, of course, that he'd got hold of another car and come after me, and I didn't feel like being bawled out again quite so soon. Not by him in that mood!"

"So?"

"So I sat down under the pine trees, waiting for him either to find the roadster, or go away," Stinky said. "I thought if he found Gerty, he'd at least prove to her that I'd been telling her the truth when I said that the car belonged to somebody I knew, and I wasn't stealing it! So I sat there and sat there, and Eric disappeared, and nothing happened, and the sun was hot, and I just fell asleep—did you say something, sir?"

"Just cleared my throat. Go on."

After all, Asey thought, he couldn't quite come out and tell the fellow that in all his experience involving corpses, this was the first time that anyone whom he'd been questioning in such detail had nonchalantly brushed off a few vital hours by going to sleep in the sun!

"Gerty finally found me," Stinky went on, "and gave me another tongue-lashing, and told me who the car really belonged to, and we took it back and left it at the Douglass's, on the turntable there. Honestly, sir, I'm sorry about the whole thing! I don't know who could've taken it from there!"

"What d'you think Eric was stomping around the point there for?" Asey asked. "Now that you know it wasn't his car that you made off with, an' that he wasn't huntin' for you?"

"Oh, I suppose he must have been trying to locate Mrs. Boone," Stinky said. "But I never thought of that at the time. I didn't understand till later, from Gerty, that it was yours. I'm very sorry, sir. The whole damn thing sounds so crazy!"

"No crazier than—"

Asey paused and thought better of commenting on Aunt Della's Annual Dahlia Planting Party, and the quohaug inspections, and the pink fainting-medicine.

"Than I'd expected," he continued. "Tell me, what's become of all the project crowd? No one's gone an' chloroformed 'em, I hope?"

"No, sir, they've scattered for the evening," Stinky said. "Some to the movies, some to the juke joint, and some to the library, believe it or not. And very, very quietly, too. You wouldn't guess that we were in town any more."

"My Cousin Jennie," Asey remarked, "makes a sound that's the perfect answer to that. It's sort of half way between 'Phooey!' and 'Yeah?'"

"But I mean it, sir! We've all been chastened. Been beaten over the head by Miss Shearing—see these?" He pointed to his clothes. "Orders! For once on one of these tours, Miss Shearing hasn't been called away, or sent on errands by Mrs. Boone, and did she go to work on us when we came back for dinner! Lined us all up and let us have it—she can make it stick, too! Gerty thinks they were just about to boot us out of this place when Miss S. took over."

Asey chuckled, and gave it as his opinion that maybe the change might on the whole be for the good.

"That's just what Gerty said, in an unexpurgated sort of way. Uh—she's waiting for me at the sandwich joint next to the drug store, and I haven't eaten yet—she was positive that you'd come by here some time, and she planted me in that rocker with orders to wait until you did. Er—will that be all, Mr. Mayo?"

"Run along," Asey said, "an' tell her it was a very complete explanation!"

After Stinky had departed at a fast gallop, Asey got out of the roadster and walked up the wide wooden steps to the inn.

He was thoroughly unprepared, after viewing the same old rows of the same old cane-seated, weather-beaten rockers on the porch, for the renovations which had taken place inside, in the lobby.

The transformation struck him like a slap in the face.

The old rattan furniture and rubber plants and lace curtains had disappeared. In their place were quantities of chromium-framed, imitation leather chairs of a brilliant vermilion color, with little matching tables. The walls were alternate strips of glass brick and mirror, the windows were a sea of Venetian blinds, and the lighting was so indirect as to be almost nonexistent. Pale blue neon signs pointed the way to the Dining Salon, the Cocktail Lounge, and the Grand Ball Room.

Asey's immediate curiosity as to where such innovations as cocktail lounges and grand ball rooms could possibly be located in such modest-sized premises was quenched by a crudely lettered placard under the neon signs. It said simply, "Under Future Construction."

While his footsteps made no sound on the new blue linoleum floor as he crossed over to what another neon sign designated as an 'Office' in the corner, Asey found that he was automatically side-stepping the inserts of vermilion porpoises and assorted small white fish. It was something about their mouths, he decided, that gave the impression that they might jump up and snap at your ankles if they had half a chance.

But with all the alterations, he noted with amusement that the service remained unreconstructed.

There was no one behind the glass brick counter of the office, and no one appeared when he thumped the old-fashioned round bell.

No one even materialized to answer the wall telephone, an obvious relic of the past, when it suddenly began to ring.

After listening to its imperious pealing for five solid minutes, Asey vaulted over the counter, and answered it himself.

"Desk!" he said briskly.

An agitated voice wanted to speak at once with Miss Shearing.

"It's vitally important! This is Mr. Manderson calling from Boston!"

"Oh, yes," Asey said. "Want me to take the message? She isn't available right now."

Mr. Manderson said excitedly that Miss Shearing absolutely *must* have Mrs. Boone call him at once, at college. Absolutely, without fail!

"Okay," Asey said. "I'll tell her."

Replacing the receiver on its hook, he turned around to the register on the counter, and ran his finger down the names of the guests who had arrived that morning.

" 'Elizabeth Shearing. Suite A.' Okay," Asey murmured, "we'll go find it!"

The modernization of the inn, he discovered as he walked through the lobby to the hall, did not extend beyond the ground floor. There were the same old creaking stairs, carpeted by the same old straw matting that was held in place by strips of pock-marked metal. The second floor landing even had a brass spittoon and a few of the refugee rubber plants standing in its corners.

The door to Suite A was wide open, and from where he stood, on the threshold, Asey could see that the bedroom décor, like the office telephone, was not only prewar, but pre-several wars.

The carved headboard of the walnut bed directly in front of him reached to within an inch of the cracked ceiling. And once your eyes became focussed on that ceiling, Asey thought, you were lost. You couldn't possibly tear them away.

First there was the outer molding, a network of leaves and fruits and flowers, and then there was the inner molding, which confined itself merely to flowers. In the middle of that was the electric light fixture, a cluster of six small globular jars. Wires sprouted from five of the jar-tops, and only when you got to them, Asey thought, could you let yourself begin to look down again.

Then, of course, came the fascinating task of trying to figure out just which wires and which extension cords went to which of the five table lights.

By the time Asey finally found himself staring at the faded peonies of the carpet, he felt almost too tired to look up again and attempt any diagnosis of the scenic wall paper. He merely noted that it was mostly a mustard color, and exceedingly busy—nowhere near as busy, however, as the chintz curtains, and the easy chair's slip cover.

He hardly wasted a glance at the huge walnut clothes-press, the marble-topped walnut table, the gilded wicker rocking chairs, or at the numerous steel engravings scattered over the wall.

After all, he had to get to Miss Shearing some time that evening!

He knocked, and then after a moment, he knocked again.

"You'll simply have to wait!" a harassed voice announced from the bathroom. "I don't dare to leave this shower thing—or *are* you the one I asked to fix it, several years ago?"

"No, ma'am," Asey said, "I'm not, but I might be able to help."

"Come in then!"

The bathroom was considerably larger than the bed-room, and at the far end there was an enormous, old-fashioned claw-foot bath tub, with a short flight of steps leading up to it.

Perched on the tub's rim, her hand gripped firmly around a pipe running up to the overhead shower fixture, was Miss Shearing.

Asey at once told himself that she couldn't be Miss Shearing. She wasn't old enough. She didn't look much older than Gerty, or Layne. She was tall, slim, and dark-haired, and she wore a smart yellow tweed suit and harlequin glasses with green rims.

"Miss Shearing?" he said hesitantly.

"Yes. Look, the trouble is, if you let go, it spurts—see where it's spurted there against the wall? And see that frightful lake behind the tub? I've mopped it up with bath towels, but the place was simply afloat when I came in. And you have to hold this pipe—I tried adhesive tape, but it just blows right off!"

Asey surveyed the situation.

"Can you play Dutch boy a minute or two longer," he said, "an' keep your finger in the dyke while I go an' get some tools?"

Five minutes after his return with a wrench from the tool kit of the roadster, he managed to locate the shut-off, and stop the flood.

"Of course," he remarked, "I sort of doubt if you'll have any water in here at all, this way, but it ought to be a lot simpler than sittin' here stemmin' the tide with your bare hands—golly, I missed that wreath of blue flowers runnin' around the inside of the tub! Now isn't that something special!"

"The brown wreath in the wash bowl is much worse. One flower has two petals missing, and you keep hunting for them. I suppose," Miss Shearing said as she looked thoughtfully at her hand, "that I'll probably be able to use this again some time, but it certainly doesn't feel that way now—oh, dear, which one of my little charges is it this time? I just noticed."

"Noticed what?" Asey said.

She pointed to his badge. "That. When I see things that say 'Special Deputy', I have no further illusions. I can no longer let myself believe that you were asked to drop up here by those charming incompetents who run this horrible spot, and render first aid to my pipe. Just who's in trouble now?"

"Look, are you really Miss Shearing? Miss Elizabeth Shearing?" Asey asked.

" 'That Old Hag Shearing',' " she said with a grin, "is very misleading, isn't it? But of course, from the project's point of view, anyone with a few academic degrees is virtually toppling into the grave. Please tell me what they've done now, Mr. Mayo!"

Asey raised his eyebrows. "Oh, you know me?"

"I recognized you when you drove up to the front door a while ago. I was in the lobby—that was just before I came up and found the flood and phoned down for help. Until I noticed your badge, I innocently thought that the Smalleys had called on you to pinch-hit as a plumber—is it Stinky Cotton again?"

"S'pose," Asey said, "that we detour out to them gilt rockers. You know," he added as she preceded him into the other room, "I originally intended to flaunt that badge at you, an' then I thought of playin' messenger boy, an' then you gave me the part of plumber. I could still use any of 'em, but now that I see you, I wonder if it isn't goin' to be easier to tell you the truth."

"I have a nervous feeling," Miss Shearing said, "that this is something more than just Stinky Cotton on the loose! After I whipped them to ribbons an hour ago—oh, listen! Is that water running again?"

Asey went in to see.

"Is it all right?" she asked when he returned a moment later. "Did—oh, what have you got? Where'd you find that?"

"The little silver bud vase," Asey said. "From the Lulu Belle. An' as smart a place to hide it, down among the wet bath towels behind the tub, as I could ever imagine!"

12

ELIZABETH SHEARING looked at him blankly.

"The little silver bud vase from *what?*"

"The Lulu Belle. An' a very bright place to hide it, Miss Shearing!" Asey said. "If I'd had any ideas of huntin' for it, which I hadn't, I don't think I'd have wasted any time gropin' around behind the tub in all that slosh. Not very much time, anyway. Was it my comin' here that scared you?"

She continued to stare at him.

"Must have been," Asey continued. "You saw me, an' you panicked. But you planned it fine, just the same. First you come up here an' gave that pipe a good kick— oh, I should have spotted that one, right off the bat! That pipe never bust by itself! Then you phoned for help, an' sat there holdin' on for dear life. It didn't matter who came first, whether it was me or someone else. The bud vase is all hidden in the wet towels!"

"Just a minute! There was no vase—"

"Happens that I come," Asey went on, "an' you know you're safe. That's one place Mayo won't look. Mayo's been there. He knows you just tossed the towels there in a hurry to mop up the water. No bud vases there! No, sir!"

"Are you," Elizabeth Shearing said, "*mad?*"

"On the contrariwise, I'm delighted," Asey purposely misunderstood her. "This is the first tangible thing I've been able to get my teeth into! As long as you stayed away an' minded your own business, you had me licked. I was stymied. But now that you got panicky an' sneaked that bud vase away—" he paused and smiled. "Wa-el, Miss S., we got something to work on, now!"

"Mr. Mayo," her low voice was controlled and even, "I do not know what it is that the project has done. I do not know what you think *I've* done to aid or abet them! But until you tell me, all this somewhat sinister talk of yours isn't of much avail, is it? Just tell me, please, what the Larrabee group has done!"

"Let's stop playin'," Asey said. "The project crowd hasn't done anything, an' you know it. Where's Mrs. Boone? What did you do with the body?"

Miss Shearing reached out on the marble-topped table, shook a cigarette from an opened package lying there, and lighted it with steady fingers before answering him.

"I'm trying to think," she said, "which one it might be. Such an amazingly horrible way of getting back at me for giving them a scolding they damned well knew they all deserved! The only one with sufficient imagination to think of hiring you would be Gerty—and Gerty wouldn't think this was funny. Neither, Mr. Mayo, do I!"

"Why'd you panic in the first place, I wonder?" Asey seemed almost to be asking himself. "I understand your putting the vase in the towels when you saw me come here—that was smart. The mistake you made was callin' my attention to the pipe again. But why'd you take that bud vase away from the Lulu Belle? Bothered about fingerprints, maybe? I don't understand it!"

"Is the Lulu Belle that juke joint they were going to?" Miss Shearing asked. "Is that where the vase came from?"

"I must've guessed right when I was talkin' to the doc about the problems of counter-action that you'd run into when everything was kept quiet an' under cover," Asey said. "When you don't know what action to counter, you can counter awful wrong—an' didn't you! Didn't—"

"Mr. Mayo, will you stop just long enough to let me ask one question—is this a joke?" she demanded. "Has the project's sense of humor gone completely berserk? Or—have you?"

"If it had been anything else in the world," Asey said, "except that bud vase that was used to kill her—an' goodness knows you wouldn't have bothered to take any of the others!—I might feel inclined to string along a while with this wonderful, well-bred, blank amazement of yours. But under the circumstances—"

"When you came into the lobby downstairs just now, Mr. Mayo," she interrupted, "was there anyone in the so-called office?"

"No," Asey said.

"Did you ring? Did anyone answer?"

"I punched the bell, but nobody came."

"And did anyone ask your business?" Miss Shearing went on. "Did anyone stop your coming up to this floor, up to this room here? If I hadn't been in, was there anything to prevent you from putting a bud vase behind that tub? Or a Maharajah's emerald? Or a small atom bomb? Or anything else you might care to name?"

"No, but—"

"The Smalleys, who run this place," Miss Shearing continued, "are occupied with dirty dishes, with a faulty hot water heater, a broken refrigerator, a stove with a missing part or two, a sick chef, and a few other similar problems. Except when we came this morning, there hasn't been a soul in that office all day!"

"But—"

"But," she wouldn't let him get a word in edgewise, "the situation doesn't seem to be considered at all unusual. In fact, I gathered it was quite the normal state of affairs.

Anyone—and I mean anyone at all—could come and go at will and at random anywhere in this inn! So under the circumstances, Mr. Mayo, let's concede that if you found anything behind that tub, it doesn't necessarily follow that I'm the only person who could have placed it there! I can't prove to you that I didn't, but there certainly does seem to me some basis for reasonable doubt in your mind!"

"But why—" Asey paused. After all, she was as likely a person to plant things on as anyone!

"I thought you'd hesitate," she said. "Now, tell me what's happened, please!"

He noticed, as he told her in a few crisp sentences about finding Mrs. Boone's body over in the Lulu Belle, and of its disappearance, that her face remained immobile. He might have been telling her about yesterday's weather.

"An'," he added, "if you can prove to me that you were sittin' with the local bank president in his office on main street from a little after twelve until one-thirty— that's the time she was last seen to the time we found her, I'll retract every harsh word I said. If you can prove you were closeted with the minister in his study around two, when Dr. Cummings discovered the body was gone, I'll also eat every last inch of all them lamp cords, to boot!"

Miss Shearing took off her glasses, laid them on the table top, and told him, without change of expression, that his digestion was perfectly safe.

"Why? Where were you durin' the time she was killed, an' the time that her body was taken away?"

"I don't know, Mr. Mayo, and I'm beginning to feel afraid."

"What d'you mean, you don't *know?*" Asey demanded.

"I literally don't know! I was driving. I might have

been in any one of a dozen towns. I simply don't *know!* Look, have you ever been suddenly terrified? Because I am, now. Don't you see?" She got up and started to pace around the room. "That vase was planted there behind the tub! It was already there when I came in and found the water spurting—oh, don't you understand the real purpose of someone's causing that leak? The vase wasn't hidden there. It was put there to be found!"

"Wa-el," Asey began, "I s'pose—"

"Certainly," she went on, "there's no more effective way of calling attention to any given spot than to cause a flood in it. Whoever ultimately came to fix the pipe, whether it was one of the Smalleys, or a plumber, or some innocent bystander like yourself, would find that vase. And if by some chance they happened to miss it, it would be found by whoever ultimately took the wet towels away—and I remember now that I noticed that one of them had fallen down behind there even before I started to mop! Whether anyone put additional towels into that slosh or not, don't you see, one had already *been* put there. Even if everything else failed, that one towel would make things work—someone would surely reach over and pick it up and find the vase! And when this business of Mrs. Boone came to light, why *I'd* be suspected, immediately!"

Asey thought to himself that you could almost hear her brain ticking it out—Item One, Item Two, Item Two-A, Item Three, and so on to General Conclusion. Miss Shearing wasn't a one to bother with gestures, or posing, or what Cummings had called the dramatic hesitation. Her mind just bit into problems like a bull-dozer, and levelled them off with equal dispatch.

She sat down suddenly in the gilt rocker, as if her legs had given way.

But her mind hadn't. She went right on talking.

"No, Mr. Mayo, I didn't put the vase there to hide it from you. Someone else put it there to be found, and given to you. Look, we've got to review this situation, right from the start yesterday—*why* are you chuckling? What's so amusing?"

"I'm just sort of surprised," Asey said, "to find someone who knows where it started. Why yesterday?"

"Carolyn decided yesterday to come down here with Layne. She wanted to find out for herself why the projects were working out so badly, and why the crowd seemed to get into so much hot water. *I* knew why. I've theoretically been in charge of half a dozen of them —except that I've never had a single chance to be in charge!"

"How come?"

"Because the minute I arrive anywhere with them, I'm sent for by Carolyn and given some other job to do some other place. Without any restraining hand, those kids have raised simple hell! There's one girl—well, d'you know the phrase 'Hubba-hubba'?"

"You mean Gerty," Asey said. "We've met."

"I mean Gerty, and I should have guessed she'd meet you at once. Gerty doesn't mean to, but she treats every place we go to as if it were something just liberated from the fascist yoke," Miss Shearing said with a little grin, "and as if she had just fifteen minutes to see everything and meet everyone before she got her orders to march on. So she meets everyone, and she sees everything— and Gerty's infectious. The rest follow her, dumb with pleasure, and they have the time of their lives!"

"But not much work gets done?"

"Not very much. Cotton and Briggs and the older men are getting through next month, and they were scattered all over the world for the last three or four years—can you imagine what a violently glowing interest they take in projects like this one? Can't you just see them hurling themselves into a spirited investigation of garbage collections, and traffic problems, and the ethics and prejudices of towns under nine hundred population? It's a holy wonder to me that they've behaved half as well as they have!"

"Why didn't Mrs. Boone figure that out?" Asey asked. "Wouldn't that particular bunch have been better off without quite so much projectin' around? Couldn't they have done it all in a library?"

"Carolyn," Miss Shearing said, "would have referred to that as a reactionary statement, and told you that it's obsolete to learn by learning. You learn, Mr. Mayo, by *do*ing!"

"Oh?"

"She's written a splendid little pamphlet on the situation, and I'll gladly send you a free copy—provided that I'm in any position to have free access to the mails in the near future. What's done with leading female suspects these days, by the way? All I can think of is that series of terrible woodcuts of women sitting in cells and picking oakum."

"Almost anyone," Asey said gravely, "would refer to that as a reactionary notion. Oakum's obsolete. You'll probably learn a good useful trade, like permanent wavin', or spot weldin'."

"Elizabeth Shearing, Girl Welder—oh, I don't feel like japing, Mr. Mayo! But if I don't, I'll burst out into tears! Look, when I came today, Layne brought Carolyn to meet me. She had the inevitable errands for me to do, and I rebelled. It was such utter nonsense, my driving back to Boston to find out about something that could be settled with a simple phone call! So I told her that I'd go at once—but I didn't. I went into the telephone office, called Boston, got the information she wanted, and then I went gaily off, riding around the Cape!"

"Did anyone know that you didn't mean to go back to Boston?"

She shook her head. "I doubt it. I didn't tell anyone, and I turned as if I were going in that direction when I set out. Then this afternoon about—oh, I don't know exactly when—say around three o'clock, I telephoned the Douglass house and—"

"At long last!" Asey said. "At long last! Who'd you talk with?"

"Mrs. Framingham. Aunt Mary. I gave her the message for Carolyn."

"Exactly what," Asey said, "did you tell her? An' I mean—*exactly*!"

Miss Shearing thought for a moment.

"I said, tell Mrs. Boone everything's all right, and not to worry, and Shee's hair—"

"And *what?*"

"Hu Shee. Carolyn's poodle, you know. He was being clipped," she explained. "That was the crux of Carolyn's problem. That was why she wanted me to drive back to Boston, to find out about Shee. Anyway, I said that Shee's hair was okay. That's about as exact as I can be! I didn't repeat, and I didn't go into any detail, because I didn't really want to talk with Carolyn."

Asey tilted back in his rocker, stared up at the fruits and flowers on the ceiling, and shook his head.

"Mrs. Boone's all right," he murmured, "not to worry, an' she's here okay!"

"No, Mr. Mayo, you've got it wrong!" she protested. "*Tell* Mrs. Boone—"

"I've got," Asey said, "what Aunt Mary apparently got! Uh-huh, an' I see how it could happen, too!"

After all, he thought, Miss Shearing couldn't invent a poodle named Hu Shee on the spur of the moment!

"I do know where I phoned from," she remarked. "It was a little variety store in Chatham. They probably could tell you the time—except I'm sure it was long after two, and you don't care where I was then!"

"What did you do after givin' the message to Aunt Mary?" Asey asked.

"I went to a beach, and sat in the sun, and had as pleasant a time as you could wish for. I came back full of vigor and told off the project en masse—I'd never had the chance before," she said with a smile, "and I'd learned from a few carefully placed questions in the village that they'd been acting like demons! So there you are, Mr. Mayo! What would *you* do in my place? There on the table beside you is that vase, and I don't know where I was."

"Isn't there anything you can think of that would place you at any particular place at any particular time? Didn't you eat any lunch?"

"Yes, but it was some sandwiches that my housekeeper had put up for me. Oh," she said with a sigh, "if only I'd stopped to ask a two-headed woman the time! Or run over a cow as church bells were sounding! Or get stalled on a railroad track with the freight coming! But I didn't. There's always my speedometer, of course. The oil was changed yesterday, and they wrote down the mileage—no, I see from the look on your face that won't work!"

"Too many loopholes. You could've rewritten the figures," Asey said, "or rolled up mileage before you came here to account for what you claim you rolled up this afternoon."

"I suppose so! I'm afraid, Mr. Mayo." She got up and started to pace around the room again. "Not so much because I'm in such a horrible position, either. I didn't

kill Carolyn, I had nothing to do with it, and I'm sure
that you—or someone—will be able to prove it. I have
what amounts to a childish faith in the truth! What ter-
rifies me is that someone *planned* to put me in this hole!
It's the realization that someone must hate me so pro-
foundly—or do you suppose that I just appeared to be the
best bet? After all, for all that anyone knew, I might be
able to account for my time down to a split second!"

"Wa-el," Asey drawled, "d'you s'pose someone possibly might've figured out that maybe you had a motive
for killin' her?"

"I can't think why!" she retorted promptly.

"You were the head of Larrabee before Mrs. Boone
came there, weren't you?"

"Yes. Yes, I was," she said. "My father started it, you
know."

"An' Mrs. Boone displaced you?"

Miss Shearing perched on the arm of the easy chair,
and smiled.

"That depends on your point of view, Mr. Mayo. I
still run the place. I'm paid more than she is—although
frankly Carolyn doesn't—I mean, didn't—know that!
And I never felt that she'd stay at Larrabee forever.
Not," she added hastily, "that I anticipated anything like
this! But Carolyn wasn't a person who stayed put. She
always had a next step."

"You mean you think that Larrabee was just another
rung of the ladder for her?"

"Definitely. Writer, columnist, lecturer, judge, college
president—she wasn't going down, Mr. Mayo. She was
on the up, as Gerty would say."

"An' what," Asey said, "do you guess the next step
would've been?"

"The seat of the Honorable Willard P. Boone," Miss
Shearing said, "who isn't young, and probably not im-

mortal. College president, senator—you see my point."

Asey looked at her thoughtfully.

"Kind of awful philosophic about it all, aren't you?" he inquired.

She shrugged. "Admitting that she brought things to the college that I never could have is no discredit to me. Everything she did for it, everything she did to make it grow, only made my job grow, too. She didn't displace me, or hinder my career, or thwart me. On the contrary, Carolyn furthered my career, and I'm very well aware of the fact!"

"Just loved runnin' her errands, an' carryin' her Kleenex around, I s'pose," Asey commented, and noted that his thrust hit home. Miss Shearing's face was very pink, and her hands, as she lighted another cigarette, weren't as steady as they had been.

"Yes, I *have* been bored, and tried, and annoyed with some of her errands!" For the first time, she sounded on the defensive. "And yes, I've often bitterly resented being whistled at—oh, not literally, of course! Just that Fido-come-here-at-once-sir attitude of hers. But there are irritations in most jobs. Carolyn had the trustees on *her* neck, for example. She had to carry *their* Kleenex!"

"Tell me," Asey said suddenly, "what was she like? What did you think of her?"

Once again Miss Shearing's mind seemed to ply its bull-dozer tactics.

"She was invigorating, enthusiastic, one-minded, shrewd rather than terribly intelligent. She was an opportunist, and she took herself very seriously. D'you know that at one time, she offered quite seriously to mediate with Hitler? And at another time, she seriously suggested leading an expedition to comb Patagonia for him?"

"So?"

"And I remember sending out five hundred confidential wires and cables explaining to various government leaders her four-point program for permanent world peace. You've got to take yourself very seriously, you know, and feel that you really throw a lot of weight, to go in for that sort of thing! And yet she cried her eyes out the year she was left off the list of the ten best-dressed women!"

"An' did you like her?" Asey inquired.

"She could hurl herself at causes like that man who's launched from the cannon at the circus, she could grab headlines from anyone, and she must have had simply incredible glands! No, Mr. Mayo, I didn't particularly like her. But I got along with her very well. You could never complain," she said with a smile, "that life with Carolyn Barton Boone was ever dull!"

And that, Asey knew, was all he'd ever get from her on the topic of Mrs. Boone if he questioned her for a decade, and alternated thumbscrews and rubber hose with the Iron Maiden.

"Mind clearin' up some odds an' ends for me?" he asked. "Like did she have any other husbands besides Senator Boone?"

"One. A Mr. Branch, I believe."

"What became of him?"

"For all I know," Miss Shearing said, "she ate him."

"Ouch!" Asey said. "To me, that smacks of summin' her up in a very nasty little nutshell! What about her secretaries?"

Miss Shearing made a wry face.

"Frankly, all of them made me faintly nervous, Mr. Mayo. I always had the uncomfortable feeling that they were going to leap up and trim the back of my neck.

They're what I think of as hairdresser types. Amiable enough, but their principal task, of course, was to squire her around."

"Think she was ever seriously taken with any of 'em —Eric, maybe?"

"Never! Not Eric, nor *any* of the others—and I'm not insinuating that she preferred girls to boys, either," she added. "Actually, I don't think she liked women very much, unless she had something to gain from them and could use them. She used men more. Particularly the secretaries. Whatever the poor things advance to when she's tired of them, they've certainly earned it!"

"Was there any chance of Stinky or Briggs fallin' heir to Eric's job?" Asey said.

"You've done some probing, haven't you!" she sounded surprised. "Yes, I know that she asked them both, and they both very politely refused her. I think she meant to work on Jack Briggs, though. He has some important political connections."

"An' now tell me," Asey said, "why Gerty hates her so."

Miss Shearing shook her head. "How you must have probed to know that! It's a horrid little story. Carolyn accidentally discovered from the records that Gerty had practically never gone to school—she got into Larrabee on an intelligence test. Then she found out about Gerty's war record, and Bronze Stars, and battle stars, and saw the wonderful publicity angle. It was pretty grim."

"Boone turned the spotlight on her, huh?"

"The works, including newsreels. I couldn't stop her. I tried." She got up from the chair-arm. "Oh, you can imagine what it was like. This lovely illiterate. Orphan asylum. Night school. Chorus girl. Stage career. Wonderful army record. Real heroine. How many medals did you get, Gerty? Just a little louder, right into the mike!

Let's have your profile, Mrs. Boone—now the old smile, Mrs. Boone! Take her hand, Gerty. Kiss her, Gerty. Thank her for letting you get an education, Gerty. Smile!"

Asey whistled softly as he tilted back in his rocker.

"An' didn't Gerty black her eyes an' tear her ears off?" he asked in astonishment.

"Gerty wasn't in any position to, and she knew it. She had to take it. I heard her comment only once. She pointed down at the rug in Carolyn's outer office and said very softly, 'Don't those teeth look cute in that little heap!' I didn't catch on, and asked her what teeth she meant. She said, 'Oh, pardon me! I *did*n't kick 'em out, did I! Just a dreamer, that's me!' She handled it well, but it was tough on her. From then on, she was a marked girl. She couldn't move or speak without someone gawping at her."

"Waitin' for her to make a slip. I see," Asey said. "Lovely illiterate—huh! That explains why she's so sensitive about her grammar!"

"I saw her mimic Carolyn one day," Miss Shearing remarked reminiscently. "It made my blood run cold—but look here, Gerty has nothing to do with this business! I wouldn't believe otherwise if you'd found her standing over Carolyn's body with her hand clutching a smoking gun!"

"Smoking bud vase," Asey corrected her. "Matter of fact, she an' Layne were together on the beach most of the afternoon." But he made a mental note to check up again. "What about Eric—you seen him around today?"

"Eric? Here? No, but I'm not surprised to know he's been here. His idea of hard work is a display of intense activity—I've known him to take a plane to the west coast to see if Carolyn wanted certain letters signed with her initials, her first name, or her full name."

"Any reason you might suspect him? You see—" he went on to tell her of his meeting with Eric. "An' then he was seen around Pochet Point, an' variously described as sneakin', an' glowerin'."

"I'm quite sure," Miss Shearing said with a laugh, "you'll find out he wished to know whether invitations were to be printed on cream or ivory paper, and just what weight, and if the engraving was style eight, or nine. He could fret and glower just as much over a thing like that as I could about cholera breaking out among the sophomores. Why, a crooked centerpiece at a luncheon party can distress him for several days! Eric couldn't have had anything to do with this either, Mr. Mayo! He'd never kill the goose that's thrust his golden eggs on him!"

"Who would be your candidate?" Asey inquired.

"I've been racking my brains to remember if we have any pet cranks in this vicinity," she said. "There are a lot of them, you know, who write to people like Carolyn —sometimes they don't like what she's said, sometimes it's what she hasn't said, sometimes it's her clothes. But the really threatening letters have stopped entirely since the war, and I can't remember any cranks on the Cape, ever."

"Huh!" Asey said. "An' next to some crack-pot, who'd you pick?"

"None of the project," she told him with finality. "The undergraduates all worship the ground she walks on. And not the Douglasses. I know Harold and Louise disliked her, and I've heard Harold rant on about her, but that's only his jealousy. I feel guilty saying this, somehow," she hesitated, "but you asked me! I find myself thinking about Mrs. Framingham. Aunt Mary."

"Oh? An' why?"

"She loathes Carolyn. I don't think she's ever forgiven

her for getting the judgeship that her son was slated **for**," Miss Shearing said. "It was all dirty politics, and as **it** turned out, he went on to much bigger and better things. But in Aunt Mary's eyes, it was unquestionably Carolyn's own personal ruthless chicanery that did her son Ralph out of the position he deserved."

Asey stood up.

"I wonder," he said as he picked up the bud vase, "if you'll come downstairs an' call Eric from the pay station in the hall, an' see if you can find out what he wants Mrs. Boone for, an' why he came down here today."

Eric's problem, Miss Shearing informed him fifteen minutes later as she emerged from the telephone booth, was whether the Trustees' Annual Luncheon was to be held in the Blue Room or the Green Room.

"For that vital data, he drove down here," she continued, "and searched Pochet Point and combed the beach—because he'd called Carolyn quite early this morning about something else, and she said it was such a gorgeous day, she intended to spend it resting on the beach. He went to the Douglass's house once, but there was no one home. I told him the Blue Room, and he's now relaxed."

"Fine!" Asey said. "*If* you believe him!"

"I do, Mr. Mayo. He hasn't sufficient imagination to think up a story like that."

"Would Eric," Asey said, "be inclined to have one of Mrs. Boone's green scarves with him?"

"Oh, I'm sure he'd have one to tuck in his pocket before he met Carolyn," Miss Shearing returned. "Eric has tact. He wouldn't be found dead with it out of her presence, or without it in it, if you see what I mean—where are you going?" she added as Asey entered the lobby.

He pointed to the glass brick and mirrors.

"Must be some way to get through this to the back quarters without smashin' a path!" he said. "Which strip is a door, d'you s'pose? I want a door. I want to find a Smalley. *Any* Smalley!"

While locating the door proved to be difficult enough, they found the task simpler than locating any of the Smalley family. It took them the better part of ten minutes to find the oldest son inside the refrigerator out in a remote ell.

He stopped tinkering with an electric motor long enough to tell them that everybody else had gone to the moving pictures.

"Ma said she needed to relax after a day like today—anything I can do? Oh, I forgot all about your pipe, Miss Shearing! Gee, I'll go right up!"

"I've fixed it for the time bein'," Asey said. "But you'll need a plumber on that. Tell me, was there any callers for Miss Shearing, or any messages?"

"Gee, didn't you get 'em, Miss Shearing? Pa must of forgot. He meant to. I'll get 'em," he paused to wipe his fingers on some cotton waste, "right away! Pa'll feel awful sorry!"

He led the way back to the office in the lobby, pawed around under the glass brick counter, and finally came up with a fistful of telegrams, notes, and slips of paper.

"Trouble with these new glass walls," he said as he passed the collection to Miss Shearing, "is they had to take down our old pigeonholes. Things in those pigeonholes caught your eye, but this way, things slip your mind."

"I think—yes, they're all from Eric," Miss Shearing said as she ran through them. "Wires saying he was coming, and when he was coming, and for me to be here because he *was* coming. Notes saying he came and I wasn't in, and that he went to find Carolyn and couldn't, and that he had to go because he had to be back to make arrangements with a caterer—he murmured something on the phone about trying to find me. Want to see them?" She held the sheaf out to Asey.

"Say," young Smalley paused with his hand on the door. "Say, there was a caller I forgot to leave a note about. Just after dinner. I think you were out talking with some of the crowd in the orchard, only pa and ma thought you'd gone off in your car. I meant to write it down, but that ice chest has been—"

"Who?" Asey said.

"From the Douglasses. That aunt of theirs. Mrs. Frampton."

"Mrs. Framingham?" Miss Shearing demanded.

"I guess so. Big woman. She wanted to see you, but she was on her way to the movies and wouldn't wait. Anything else I can do? Ice water? I don't think we got any *ice*, but I could get some *cold*—"

"Thanks," Miss Shearing said, "I've had plenty of cold water!"

She looked quizzically at Asey as young Smalley, after two false grabs at a mirrored panel, at last found the door.

"Well?" she said. "Well? Aunt Mary called—and I go up to find the flood, and you find the bud vase. Well, Mr. Mayo?"

Asey looked at his watch.

"We might get to the second show an' catch her as she's leavin'—come on!"

"Me? Why? What for?"

Asey took her arm and hurried her outside to the roadster.

"What is this, protective custody?" she inquired as they started off.

"In a backhand sort of way," Asey said, "yes—doggone,

179

look at the stream of cars already headin' home—I'm afraid we've missed her!"

By the time they reached the theater, the home-going traffic had thinned to a trickle. Asey stopped and watched till it ceased almost entirely, and then he swung the roadster around to the parking space in the rear, and checked the dozen-odd beachwagons among the cars belonging to the second-show crowd.

The Douglass's beachwagon was not among them.

"Now what?" Miss Shearing said.

"Now," Asey told her with a grin, "we're goin' to step out. We're goin' to the juke joint."

He caught the sound of a smothered chuckle, but she looked surprised when they drew up a few minutes later in front of Mike's Place.

"Come on," Asey said as he locked the bud vase in the glove compartment. "We're goin' in."

He stood for a moment in the entrance, peering through the thick haze of tobacco smoke, and trying not to be distracted by the smell of frying onions and the deafening din of the juke box.

"I'm proud to see my little charges are reasonably quiet," Miss Shearing said, pointing to the corner where Gerty and Stinky sat with the fat boy and the girl with the bangs.

"I hoped they'd be here!" Asey beckoned to Gerty. "Golly, what a racket!"

"Isn't it ghastly? I wonder how they stand it."

Asey informed her drily that she was about to find out.

"Uh-huh," he went on as she stared at him questioningly, "in the interests of your own personal safety, Miss S., you're goin' to surround yourself with this group, an' stay surrounded by—hi, Gerty! Miss S., you trot over to the corner, please—you probably won't suffer anything that a couple of aspirin won't cure! So long! Gerty, come outside a second, will you?—how in thunder can you take that din!"

"You don't notice it after a while," Gerty said. "Or the air, either—say, how are things?"

"I haven't time to go into 'em with you," Asey said. "Look, you kids, an' particularly you, are to ride herd on Shearing! You're not to let her out of your sight. You—"

"Nun-uh, Mr. Mayo! Not *her!*" Gerty interrupted. "You're all wet! Shearing's okay! She never killed—"

"I don't think she did, either," Asey said quickly. "But it's possible she might be in a bit of danger. Don't you let her out of your sight till I say so! If she washes her hands, you wash yours—you see what I mean? You stick with her every second. If she complains, or tries to duck, knock her down an' sit on her. Okay? Now, one thing more. You an' Layne were on the beach from after twelve-fifteen or so. You left early—"

"That's right, a little before you found me there by the mud hole."

"Before you went to the beach, how long were you two together?"

"Why," Gerty said, "from the time we left your house! We were in her car!"

"You were together, as in each other's sight, all that time? She didn't leave you, an' you didn't leave her?" Asey persisted.

"Well," Gerty said slowly, "I *did* wander around and try to find some wild strawberries, but I gave it up because there was so much poison ivy—but Layne knew where I was. I could see her, so I guess she could see me. And she swam out further than I did, out to the raft and the boats—but hell, I saw her all the time! I don't know how we could've been any *more* together!"

"Know where Stinky or Jack was from around twelve to one?" Asey asked.

"Stinky was eating lunch somewhere in the town," Gerty said. "I don't know where Jack was. Stinky was just wondering about him. Said he hadn't seen him since early today."

"Okay—you mind Shearing, now! Watch over her!"

From Mike's place, Asey drove on to the church, where Jennie, who had apparently been watching for him, at once emerged bearing a paper plate with a small slab of ice cream on it.

"Refreshments," she said, handing him the plate and a wooden spoon. "Asey, nobody knows a thing about Sylvester! They've begun to make up stories about where they think he may have run away to, now. And there's nothing *to* the secret room business—nothing at all!"

"Doggone!" Asey stabbed at his ice cream. "Jennie, are you sure? I almost been countin' on that!"

"Mrs. Phinney says goodness knows the Hoveys were a queer lot, and one Hovey brought home a Chinese wife once, only she died of the fever, and one of the women wore pants—*real* pants—while everyone else was wearing proper hoopskirts," Jennie said. "But she says it's nonsense that they ever had any secret rooms. She's positive she'd've known if there was, because two of her brothers did carpentry work when they weren't at sea, and if there'd been any secret rooms being built, she thinks they'd've been pretty sure to tell her about 'em. Considering how much *else* I've had to listen to about other houses that got built about the same time, Asey, I *must* say I think she'd have known!"

"Wa-el," Asey said, "if someone didn't heft that body into a nice convenient secret room, then I s'pose someone took it somewheres else. Thanks, Jennie. Mind beggin' yourself a ride home? I'm goin' over to Pochet Point an' have a talk with Aunt Mary Framingham."

Jennie called him back as he started for the car.

"I don't know as it *mat*ters any, Asey, but I *do* keep wondering about Sylvester! Seems's if I couldn't get him off my mind. After all, he *lives* right over there at the point—"

"*What?*" Asey demanded. "At the point? I thought he lived over Skaket way!"

"Oh, he did till a few years ago, when they took over so much land for that radar station thing. Took his, too," Jennie said. "He owns a couple of acres right next the Douglasses, so he come over and built him a little shack there. Folks *said* he only did it to inveigle Douglass into buyin' his land up at a high price, but for all I know, that was only talk. No, if Sylvester still lived over in Skaket, Asey, I wouldn't think so much about him. But his being right *there*, as you might say—"

"Gives you," Asey said, "food for thought. Huh, it gives me food for thought, too! Golly, if I could only just figure out one thing! Well, maybe I can if I stick at it long enough! I'll be seein' you—"

She called him back again.

"When'll you be home?" she asked anxiously. "And don't you think you hadn't better go off alone? Shouldn't you take someone *with* you, like the doctor—or *me?*"

"I'll be back soon," Asey assured her. "I'm just goin' to see Aunt Mary. You might scare up somethin' for me to eat later, if it's not too much trouble."

Over at the point, he parked on the lane leading to the Douglass's house, and then got out and walked through the pine woods to the house.

His new roadster was on the turntable where he'd left it—shining almost as garishly in the moonlight, he

183

thought, as it did in the sunlight. The Douglass's beach-wagon was parked beyond it, and beyond that was a small convertible coupe—Layne's car, no doubt.

Walking closer to the house, he stood in the shadow of the lilacs and peered into the lighted living room.

Harold and Louise were busy playing gin rummy, their faces as grim and set as if they were about to take a beachhead from a landing barge. Layne sat by the table, turning the pages of a magazine. Aunt Mary, Asey decided with some annoyance, must have come home and gone straight to bed. He'd noticed a light in an upstairs bedroom.

Noiselessly, still keeping in the shadow of the lilacs, he made his way around to the rear of the house, and stood and looked reflectively at the Lulu Belle and the little engine, drawn up by the tiny, box-like station.

The whole place seemed even quieter than it had that afternoon during that strange period when everyone was somewhere else. The house, neat and white in the moonlight, had that same tomblike silence about it. The rolling marshes were just as forlorn—and even a little sinister with that slight mist rising from them and curling off over to the pines. You had to strain your ears to catch the pounding sound of the surf on the outer beach.

"An' it's all wrong, somehow!" he murmured to himself. "It bothers me—"

Was that the sound of footsteps in the woods near the station, or was he imagining things?

He'd never know, he thought, whether he'd actually heard anything or not, for the Town Hall clock suddenly started to peal out ten o'clock, and on its third stroke, an assortment of church clocks started to chime in with it.

Asey leaned back against an apple tree.

What had tipped someone off to planting that bud vase on Elizabeth Shearing? What was the reason for that sudden action? What was it that had set someone going? Or was it all the work of the mentally agile Miss Shearing and her bull-dozer mind?

Folding his arms, he settled back against the tree and considered Miss Shearing until another clock, the little station clock, started belatedly to chime ten.

Asey drew in his breath sharply and stood up as straight as if a bucket of ice water had suddenly been poured down his spine.

"Just about three an' a half minutes late!" he said out loud. "Golly, maybe what I been thinkin' isn't so crazy after all! I think—yessir, I know I'm right about that!"

13

CUMMINGS WOULD TELL him he was stark staring mad, Asey decided. And Cummings would have every right to.

"If only I could hitch that up—"

He took a step forward toward the Lulu Belle, and then stopped short.

There *were* footsteps, and they *were* behind the station.

Going away from the station, he amended. Someone *had* been behind there, as he'd thought a few minutes before, and now someone was leisurely leaving.

As if he were walking on eggs, Asey set out after the person.

In something less than sixty seconds, he discovered that the person was a man.

A tall, gangly man.

In short, it was Sylvester!

And he wasn't taking any particular care about how much noise his footsteps made. Not that he was advertising his presence by thrashing around violently, or kicking at trees, or singing loudly to himself. But under no circumstances could anyone truthfully describe his progress along the path as sneaking. To all intents and purposes, Sylvester was merely taking a little stroll before bedtime. And anyone, even Cummings, could trail him without having to think twice.

Keeping some distance behind, Asey followed him along the curving, rutted lane, waiting until Sylvester reached the door of the tar paper covered structure that was apparently his home, before he quickened his step.

Just as Sylvester's hand touched the knob, Asey noiselessly appeared beside him.

"Hi, Sylvester," he said casually.

"What the—my God, you scared me half to death! Who—" Sylvester peered at him. "Why, Asey Mayo! My God, so they got *you* out huntin' me, have they? Went an' put *you* to work findin' me!"

"I'm not huntin' for you at all," Asey said. "I just come over to see Harold Douglass on a little matter of business, but they was goin' to bed, an' when I heard footsteps, I wondered if it mightn't be you comin' home, an' so," he concluded, hoping that he sounded more convincing to Sylvester than he did to himself, "so it *was!*"

"Asey, what they goin' to *do* to me?"

"Who?"

"Why, *folks!*" Sylvester said plaintively. "What're they goin' to do to me for bein' late with the Bull Moose today? What're they goin' to *do?*"

"Nothin'," Asey said. "They just think it's kind of funny, your bein' late after bein' on time so long. If you'd take my advice, you'd make up a good yarn, like you got delayed watchin' the sea serpent over in Bottomless Pond, or something like that, an' they'll just laugh, an' it'll all brush over—you askin' me in?"

"Why, sure!"

Sylvester opened the door, lighted a match, went over to the table and lighted the old-fashioned kerosene lamp.

The inside of the shack, Asey thought, couldn't have been neater or better kept if Jennie herself had the care of it. The sink was free of dishes, the pump handle was polished like a mirror, the floor was swept, the white curtains were stiff with starch, and the bed was made.

"Kind of messy in here," Sylvester said. "Take a chair, Asey—that Boston rocker's the most comfortable. I hadn't much chance to tidy up today. I always say when you live alone like I do, you can't afford to get careless. About that Bull Moose business, now, Asey! Didn't they send you out to find me, honest? *Did*n't they?"

"No, honest," Asey said. "I just happened to drop by the Douglass's, like I said. Nice place you got here, Sylvester!"

"Well," Sylvester said with quiet pride, "*I* like it. Nothin' fancy, but—hm. 'Bout time! Where you been?"

He went to the door and let in an enormous white cat, who rubbed against his legs and purred loudly.

"Usually meets me on the path near the station," Sylvester went on. "I waited there for her just now—she was there all right, but she was bein' independent!"

"Nice cat," Asey said. "What's her name?"

"Lana Turner. Great company." Sylvester crossed over to a miniature ice chest and produced a tin of evaporated milk. "Great mouser. Here y'are, Lana. Fill up! Asey, ain't they awful sore about missin' the Quiz Question?"

"Wa-el," Asey said, "they were at first, but then they hunted around an' found people that *had* heard it, so it all worked out. They—"

"What was it?" Sylvester asked interestedly. "The Question, I mean. 'Course, there ain't much chance of

187

my bein' called an' asked it, me not havin' any phone, but I always like to *know*."

"I don't know exactly what the Question is," Asey told him, "but the answer is coypus—easy enough for you to remember. Just think of Lana. Coypus. Look, Syl, what really *did* happen to make you late today?"

Sylvester shook his head as he sat down at the table.

"Asey, I tell you, I don't understand it yet! I set my watch, just like I do every single day—"

"You mean," Asey said, "by the clock on the Douglass's station?"

He held his breath while Sylvester got up, picked up the cat's empty milk saucer, and put it in the sink.

"Thirstiest cat I ever seen! Yes, that's it. That clock's an old railroad station clock they got there, you know, and railroad station clocks are *always* right!" Sylvester said seriously. "It's electric, too, and so there isn't any chance of its ever bein' wrong—an' by golly, it never *was* wrong, either, all the time I've used it to set my old turnip by! Why, I left the point here in plenty of time, an' I got to town early, an' at one o'clock, why I *binged* her! Didn't think nothin' about it. Didn't have any notion in the world that I wasn't smack on time!"

"Didn't you hear the Town Hall clock, or any of the church clocks strikin' one?" Asey asked curiously.

"Wind," Sylvester said laconically. "You can't hear any of them things a foot away if the wind ain't just right, or less there ain't no wind blowin' attall, like tonight. Besides, I wasn't listenin' for 'em. Don't know what made me look over across towards the Town Hall clock as I come out of the Fire House. One-six, 'twas. One-*six?* I says to myself. Ain't never been more'n one-two or one-three before! Then Lizzie Hampton seen me an' starts yellin' she missed the Question, all on account of I was late with the Bull Moose, an' what's the matter with me, anyways! An' then—"

In detail, he recounted how he'd checked up on every available clock, and of his ultimate conclusion that his own watch was slow.

"Three minutes, an' most a half! Well, sir, I can tell you I skipped out of town *so* quick!"

"How'd you skip?" Asey inquired.

"Hitched me a ride on a truck clear to New Bedford!" Sylvester told him. "Don't know *when* I been so far away from the Cape before. Twenty years, I guess. I sort of had it in mind to keep right on goin', but then I remembered I hadn't locked up my front door, an' who'd take care of Lana?"

The white cat, purring furiously, jumped up on his lap at the mention of her name.

"So," Asey said, "you hitched back?"

"Yessir, I hitched back. After all, there ain't no place like home!"

"I always feel that way," Asey said sympathetically, "every time I get back. Say, I hear you been havin' famous visitors out this way today!"

"Who's that?"

"Carolyn Barton Boone," Asey said.

"Oh, that woman! *Her!*" Sylvester said with so much force that Lana stopped washing her face and looked up at him. "That woman! *Dyed* hair, an' her face all painted up—honest, I don't know what the country's comin' to when women like that get into the papers, an' folks listen to 'em, an' think they *are* somethin'!"

"Where'd you see her?" Asey asked. "Up town?"

"No, here, at the point. I was standin' up in a sugar line for Mrs. Winters, see," he explained, "when I heard that Boone woman was in town—you know, Asey, there's one thing you can say for the way they gone an' botched things up so. An old feller like me can make a pretty good livin' standin' in lines for people! An' a lot easier than quohauggin', I must say! Well, so I heard she was in town, but nobody told me where she was stayin' or anythin'. An' when I got through gettin' Mrs. Winters's sugar, I came back here—by golly, wasn't I surprised to see her over at the Douglasses! I recognized her right away, in that white suit of hers!"

"Douglass was givin' her a ride on the railroad, I s'pose."

Asey held his breath again and decided that this was, in its way, the most completely nerve-wracking interview he'd had.

"Yup, he was. Say, that's some railroad, ain't it? Once in a while when they got a crowd there, I put on a white jacket an' a cap he's got, an' take a basket over my arm an' pretend to be a butcher for him. You know, I go up an' down the aisle sayin' '*Her*-shey bahs! *Al*-mond bahs!'" Sylvester's imitation of himself being a butcher sent Lana scuttling down to the floor. "Come back you! Hop up here! Of course, mostly it's just little peanut bars from the A & P we had lately, but they *used* to say Hershey bars an' almond bars, so I do."

Asey had to dig his fingernails into the palms of his hands to keep himself from screaming out question after question. But he knew it would never do. Not with someone like Sylvester!

"Guess even a person like Mrs. Boone was kind of impressed with folks havin' a railroad in their back yard for her to ride on," he remarked.

"She ought to be! I bet," Sylvester said with scorn, "I bet *her* grandfather never *owned* any railroads! I bet he never even had a *ride* on one!"

"Did that really belong to Mrs. Douglass's grandfather, like I heard?"

"Why, sure! It'd kind of gone to seed," Sylvester said. "You know how things got with some railroads after cars got to be so common. An' Mrs. Douglass didn't want it sold to the Japs for scrap, so she bought it up, an' they had it brought down here. She thought her grandfather'd like it better that way—you know how they are about old things, so careful with Aunt Della Hovey's stuff an' all."

"So," Asey said, "Mrs. Boone got a ride. She seem to be enjoyin' it?"

Sylvester said he wouldn't know.

"Douglass helped her on, an' they went inside—I s'pose he punched her ticket—an' then he come out an' went into that little lean-to he's got where he changes his coats an' caps, an' then Mrs. Boone hopped out an' ran indoors. After a while, Douglass came an' looked in, an' then he went off to the house—after her, I s'pose. An' then Mrs. Boone came back—an' by golly, *did*n't I want to go tell that woman what I *thought* of her! I don't think *much* of her, if you want to know, Asey! Yessir, wouldn't I liked to of gone an' told her a thing or two!"

"Why didn't you?" Asey asked.

"Why, land's sakes, how could I? There wasn't the time! I always plan on bein' up to the Bull Moose at *least* half an hour early, anyway," Sylvester said. "I got my reputation to keep up! An' it was after twelve, then. I had to come here an' make me a sandwich, an' be back to town by twelve-thirty!"

"But you *could*n't eat an' get back to town on foot by twelve-thirty!" Asey said.

"You couldn't by the road, but you can the way *I* go," Sylvester told him with a smile. "People always sort of get mixed up out here, thinkin' it's such a long ways to everywhere, an' all these lanes twistin' around to confuse 'em, an' the main road windin' so. Nossir, you just cut across lots by the shore, an' it's less'n a ten-minute walk for me. 'Course sometimes I get my feet wet, an' some of the steppin' stones are pretty barnacly an' hard on shoe leather. But I can do it easy. You just have to know the right places to go, that's all!"

"So you seen her come back to the Lulu Belle—an' then you went off!" Asey said with genuine regret in his voice. "Huh!"

"Why, I had to!" Sylvester said earnestly. "I got a *name* for bein' prompt! I got my sandwich, an' then on the way back, I set my watch an' hustled along—you know, I wonder if Douglass really did give her the ride after all, Asey! I'd of been sure to of seen the train, or heard it toot, but I never did!"

Had Douglass returned from the house, Asey asked himself, looked at the car and thought it empty—since by then Mrs. Boone was lying on the floor, dead?

Or had Douglass himself returned and killed her?

"I always felt pretty sorry for ole Senator Boone," Sylvester went on conversationally. "Him in Washington, an' his wife kitin' around the country, an' him as like as not never gettin' a good, proper, hot, home-cooked meal! I always kind of figgered that was why he voted so dumb, sometimes. No wife to look after him proper. But after I seen that dyed yellow hair an' painted face of hers, I decided maybe he was just as well off! She sure didn't look to me like anyone it wouldn't be better if you didn't have 'em around attall!"

"Always seemed to *me*," Asey tried to draw a line between sounding casual and owning to a conviction, "she was the sort of woman this world would be a whole lot better off without!"

Sylvester promptly bit.

"That's just what I was tellin' Amy Waters that was standin' next to me in the sugar line! *I* said if all the busy-body women like her was killed off in one swoop, why it'd be the best thing ever happened to this country! I said I'd like to do it myself—an' by gum, if I'd had just a little *mite* more time this noon, I'd of given her a good piece of my mind! I'm not sure maybe I won't yet, if she stays around very long. Some day I'd like to get hold of one of those women that shoots their mouths off so, an' *tell* 'em a thing or two!"

Asey looked over at him thoughtfully as he sat by the table, stroking the white cat who was curled up on his knee.

"Wa-el," he said, "you can't ever tell—I mean, if you'd do any good or not. They probably wouldn't listen to folks like us—say, Sylvester, you'd be just the feller to know! Yup, I bet you *would* be just the feller who could tell me!"

"What?"

"Jennie an' me," Asey said, "was havin' an argument about ole houses tonight. I said there *was* a secret room at the Douglasses, an' she said I was crazy. To tell you the truth, *that*'s the errand I had over here. Jennie an' I got so hot under the collar, I said I'd just get right into my car an' go find out from Harold Douglass!"

"You wouldn't of got much satisfaction from *him!*" Sylvester said. "*I* can tell you that!"

"Just the samey," Asey said, "I'm dead sure I'm right! I'm sure I heard my grandfather say somethin' about it, an' it seems to me the last time I was home, or maybe the time before, I got to talkin' with Mrs. Framingham, an' we somehow mentioned secret rooms, an'—"

"Oh, *her!*" Sylvester smiled as he rubbed the cat's ear. "*That*'s different! But she wouldn't of let on a thing if

193

you'd asked her or talked about it in front of the rest, you know. Not a *hint* of it. No, sireebob! Not after the way they kidded her so about tryin' to find it!"

Asey ordered himself not to jump out of the Boston rocker and shake the whole story out of Sylvester in one lump. To make sure he wouldn't move, he wound his feet around the rocker rungs. At this point, he couldn't afford to spoil things!

"She was awful wary about it, as I remember," he said. "Didn't say there *was* a secret room, you understand, but she didn't say there *wasn't*. Didn't tell me *where*, or anything like that! 'Course, Jennie says if she didn't say more'n that, why, there just plain couldn't be any."

"That's just where Jennie's dead *wrong!*" Sylvester said. "But I don't know how you can prove it to her just now, on account of—well, you see, Asey, since I been livin' over this way, I work around the Douglass's place some. Gardenin', an' helpin' keep the place tidy. Ordinarily, I don't like that kind of work, but things're so neat there, it's a pleasure. Everythin' to work with, too, like a motor lawnmower. Well, Aunt Mary an' me, we worked together around the flower gardens a lot, an' she kept talkin' about this secret room to me—sounded awful kind of crazy to me at first. Then I said to myself, why not? The Hoveys did plenty of other crazy things. They were *queer!*"

Asey mentally recalled Cummings's statement about queerness being comparative.

"You mean like that Chinese wife," he said, "an' the woman that wore pants."

"Just so. An' then, by golly, one day me an' Aunt Mary, we found it!" Sylvester said reminiscently. "Remember it like it was yesterday. Nice fall day, not too cold—"

Asey sat with a fixed smile on his face while Sylvester

went into detail on the chrysanthemums, the picking of the McIntosh reds, and the ten barrow-loads of punkins he'd carted out of the west garden.

"I always like the fall of the year," he concluded cheerfully. "You can have the spring, I always say—you get to it from the *outside*, you know, Asey!"

"Is that right, now!" Asey felt the fixed smile crack and widen into a genuine beam of pleasure. "Well, well, well!"

"Yes, sir, that's where me an' Aunt Mary went wrong for a long while! *We* was all the time huntin' from the *in*side—while the Douglasses was away, of course."

"On the outside!" Asey said. "Huh—now let me think." He closed his eyes, figured what portion of the house would be nearest the Lulu Belle, and made a guess. "Say, I bet you—uh-huh, I bet you it's somewhere on the west side of the kitchen door!"

He opened his eyes to find Sylvester staring at him in open-mouthed bewilderment.

"I must say, Asey, you beat *me!*" he said. " 'Course whenever they talk about what a great feller you are these days, I always tell 'em I understand how you got way up in Porter Motors—never was any young feller around here that could tinker any better'n you could! But on this detectin' business, I always said, I don't *know!* I always admitted your grandfather was a sharp man— they didn't call him David Razor for nothin'! But I never seen how you—now looky, just how *did* you detect where that door was, after all the months an' months me an' Aunt Mary spent huntin' for it?"

"Why, *I* don't deserve any credit, Syl!" Asey said truthfully. "It's kind of like Columbus standin' that egg up on its end. Easy enough when someone tells you—I mean, *shows* you! An' it seemed to me if it was an outside job, it couldn't hardly be on the front side of the house. Don't you forget, *you* can walk right to it, an' open it. I can't. I only just know where it is in a general way!"

"Oh, sure you could open it!" Sylvester said. "Anyone could, now we got it oiled up an' eased up. You see how it happened—Aunt Mary said she was givin' up the hunt. Said she'd always wanted to find a secret room there, but she was through. I asked her why she was so keen about it anyway, an' she grinned—great sense of humor, she has!—an' she said, she wanted to find it, an' fix it up, an' invite the Douglass family in! But she said she guessed she never would, now, unless a wall fell in—an' by golly, Asey, *what* do you think?"

"A wall fell in," Asey said promptly.

"No, but where I was leanin' against it, there by the back door, I felt it *give!* What it amounts to, see, is a door cut there," Sylvester said. "It was hinged on the inside, see, an' the old hinges was givin' way under my weight."

"Oh, now wait!" Asey said. "You'd *see* a door cut there! You couldn't miss it!"

"Nope, you could! *We* did. Everybody did. Everybody does, as far's that goes. There ain't no latch, or handle, just a little hook you put your finger in, so—"

"But you could *see* that!"

"Well, I *s'pose* you could!" Sylvester retorted. "*If* you knew there *was* a hook, an' *if* you was huntin' for it, an' *if* you knew just *where* to hunt, an' *if* you knew how to shove the wistaria to one side! An' *if* you knew in the first place it was behind the drain pipe all the time! Why, sure, I s'pose you *could* see it—only if you want to know what I think, I don't think you could!"

"But whyn't you see the *other* side of the door? I mean, if it's cut there—"

"Why, the side where the hinges are, there's this beam

runnin' down that laps over the cut, see?" Sylvester explained. "You wouldn't never notice *that* side of that door if you stared at it for a hundred years! The door shoves inwards, see—"

"Hey, it goes to the end of—of somethin' off the dinin' room!" Asey couldn't recall just what from his tour of the house that afternoon. "A pantry, isn't it, or a closet?"

"A pantry—that's right! Aunt Della's best-dish pantry. Kept the best china there. Still *do*. This secret room backs smack against that pantry's long side—room itself runs the length of the pantry, an' it's about three feet an' a half wide. Maybe a little less. Ain't big, but it's a room, an' it sure is a secret!"

"More'n three feet—why in time didn't someone ever spot that from the inside?" Asey demanded.

"I tell you why," Sylvester said. "You go into that pantry from the dinin' room, an' what do you notice? First you got to take a step down. Then what? You got to grope around for the light. No windows in that pantry! Then what do you notice? Dishes, an' shelves, an' shelves, an' dishes! Secret room's sittin' there to your left. But do you think of it? No, sir!"

"But you got more'n three feet extra stickin' out beyond the shelves to the left!" Asey said. "You'd think it'd be noticed right off, in the dinin' room!"

"An' you know why you don't? I'll tell you! Because you got a built-in corner cupboard there, that's why!" Sylvester said. "You don't notice no three an' a half extry feet! *Ain't* no extry feet—why, Aunt Mary never noticed, an' she went all over that house with a tape measure! If the corner cupboard wasn't there, an' if she'd measured straight, she'd probably of found that extra footage beyond the width of the pantry. But she said it was one place she hadn't dreamed of botherin' with.

An' if she didn't spot it, nobody would of! Nope, I don't think even *you*'d detect that from the inside—*or* the outside!"

"Let's see!" Asey said. "One long side's the pantry, an' the other long side's the outside of the house. One short side's the dinin' room an' corner cupboard—what's the fourth side? What's that back up against?"

"Shelves," Sylvester told him. "Wall shelves in the kitchen—more shelves back of the pantry, too. I tell you, Aunt Mary nearly had a conniption fit when the Douglasses talked about cuttin' a window in the best-dish pantry this year, on account of it was so dark in there! She had to speak up quick! Told 'em it unquestionably was a lot of nonsense, an' probably the wall'd fall in if they fussed with it that much, an' she was *sure* Aunt Della wouldn't ever approve. She talked 'em out of it finally!"

"Why's she keepin' this such a secret for so long?" Asey wanted to know.

"Because she's furnishin' it! Kind of slow goin', because she can't do nothin' unless the Douglasses are away, see? We'd never of got the floor painted an' spattered if they hadn't gone off for a weekend in New Hampshire —an' then we had to cover up the smell of paint by touchin' up the trellis by the back door, an' all! When she gets it all fixed up an' furnished complete, she's goin' to invite 'em in, an' have like a party."

"Well, well!" Asey said. "An' nobody knows about it!"

"Just her an' me! We kind of aim," Sylvester said, "to have the grand openin' on the Fourth of July. With cannon-crackers an' a lot of noise."

"Speakin' of noise," Asey said, "don't that door kind of scrape an' groan some?"

"Not if you know how to work it, an' do it right, an'

take your time. After you got your finger in the hook, see, you give it a little boost—get up, Lana, while I show him!" Sylvester deposited the cat on the floor and got to his feet. "See, it's like this!" he demonstrated. "You push a mite with your knee, an' pull up a little with your hand—so!"

Asey watched the demonstration very, very carefully.

"If you don't do it just that way," Sylvester continued as he sat down again and snapped his fingers at the cat, "why, you're liable to get mixed up in the wistaria, an' then *that* jerks the lattice, an' the lattice catches the gutter, an' the drain pipe—my, what an awful sound it makes! Kind of a scrape an' a grate, an' a whine—Aunt Mary says it's the strangest noise you ever heard, if you're in the house. She was indoors once when the Douglasses come back sooner'n we expected, an' I had to shut the door in a hurry."

As Lana stalked past him on her way back to Sylvester's knee, Asey reached down and patted her. He felt like patting someone on the head.

"Seems funny you don't put a lock on that door," he said.

"Don't need to, the way it fits. After all, nobody'd found it for I don't know how many years before *we* did, an' it wasn't locked all that time!" Sylvester said. "Besides, Aunt Mary says there's no sense in puttin' on a lock an' advertisin' it till she's ready to show it—look, Asey, what I *started* to say to you was, of course you're dead right about the secret room, but I don't know how you can prove it to Jennie without lettin' out what Aunt Mary wants to keep a secret! So, you won't tell her, will you? I never mentioned it to no one before—but then, you really knew all about it, anyway!"

"Tell you what," Asey said as he rose from the Boston rocker, "I'll just tell Jennie that the Douglasses had gone to bed, an' for her to ask Mrs. Framingham herself. Then, if she wants to confide in Jennie, she can. If she don't—wa-el, when she has her grand openin', Jennie'll know that I was right all along! Golly, it's gettin' late, an' I shouldn't be keepin' you up, after the day you had! I had a real pleasant visit with you, Sylvester!"

Sylvester said Asey could drop in any time he wanted to.

"An' say, what was the answer to that Question again, now? Smart puss?"

"Coypus," Asey said. "So long!"

The assorted town clocks were striking eleven when Asey swung his roadster into Cummings's driveway.

Before he could turn the motor off, the doctor appeared in the doorway of his office.

"Been expecting you!" he said. "I knew in my deepmost heart that you couldn't continue inspecting quohaugs by yourself. You haven't my flair for rapid improvisat—" he broke off as Asey entered the office. "What's happened, man! What's the *matter*? I never saw you look shattered before!"

"I am," Asey said. "Some of it's due to puttin' myself through a wringer with Sylvester Nickerson. An' the other ninety-nine per-cent—listen, doc!"

Cummings stared at him as he concluded his summary of his interview with Sylvester.

"My God!" he said. "So there *is* a secret room! And you went there at once, of course!"

Asey nodded.

"And you found Mrs. Boone's body in there, of course!"

"No," Asey said. "Not Mrs. Boone's. Aunt Mary's."

14

"MRS. BOONE'S," Asey continued, "is back in the Lulu
Belle—not just exactly where we found her, an' not in
exactly the same position. But almost."

Cummings turned on his heel and strode out of the
room for a moment. When he returned, he was shaking
his head.

"Just looking to see if I had anything in the dispensary
I thought could cope with the situation," he said. "I
haven't."

"Do I look *that* shattered?" Asey demanded.

"Who said anything about you? I want it for myself!" Cummings returned. "Aunt Mary's body—her
body—is in the secret room! Mrs. *Boone*'s is back where
we originally found it—oh, it's too awful! It's too damn
fantastic! It's—frankly, I'm speechless! Mother Gaston
never thought up anything like this! What's it all *mean?*"

He looked even more surprised when Asey started to
tell him what he thought it meant.

"Mrs. Boone, I'd say, was supposed to be found tomorrow. Or tonight, if anything happened that someone
went into the Lulu Belle. Or any time."

"Oh?" Cummings said with rising inflection. "Indeed!
And when d'you think Aunt Mary was supposed to be
disinterred? August tenth, at four, possibly?"

"Nope, I don't think that Aunt Mary was s'posed to
be found at all," Asey said.

"I'm sure there's nothing in the dispensary that can
cure *that* type of thinking!" Cummings said. "Wasn't
supposed to be found at *all!* What d'you *mean?*"

"Mrs. Boone gets found. Who killed Mrs. Boone?

Aunt Mary's missin'. No one'll ever forgive themselves for thinkin' Aunt Mary might've done it—but Aunt Mary's missin'. Think it over. Consider it. S'pose in a few days, Aunt Mary's body gets washed up by the tide. Did Aunt Mary kill Mrs. Boone an' then kill herself?"

Cummings slammed himself down in his swivel chair.

"Oh, you're right, of course!" he said. "It's too diabolically simple not to be right! What happened to her?"

"Same thing," Asey said. "Blow on the head. Nastier than Mrs. Boone's. She was a big husky woman, an' no one was takin' any chances at all."

"Not another bud vase!"

"Milk bottle," Asey said.

"In there, in the room?"

Asey nodded. "Way I see it, doc, sometime after she came back from the movies, she went inside that room—maybe the door was open, maybe she opened it, I wouldn't know."

"And Boone's body was there, and the murderer was there—or," Cummings said, "as she discovered Boone's body, the murderer arrived on the scene. Exit Aunt Mary, and I'm frank to say I'm sorry. Asey, I begin to see what you meant by saying whether we had the body or not didn't matter so much. My God, now we've got two—and it's worse than not having any! If it wasn't Aunt Mary I followed down to the boat house, who the hell was it?"

"Someone else," Asey said. "An' was that flat tire a fake, or did someone stymie Aunt Mary by givin' her a flat tire? Seems to me like someone must have. An' who planted the bud vase in behind Shearing's tub?"

"If you say that last sentence to yourself several times," Cummings said, "you can experience the earlier sensations of madness. May I remind you I haven't seen you since way back there at the traffic lights? Catch me up."

"Jennie," Asey said, "Billy's wife, Stinky, Shearing, data on Eric, data on Aunt Mary, juke joint, Sylvester—I'll do it if you promise not to open your mouth till I'm through."

When he finished, Cummings said he *could*n't open his mouth.

"And if I could, all that could come out of it is—you're licked, Asey! I'll call Halbert—he can bring in his fancy truck with the pretty equipment. This is the sort of thing where you need gamma rays and snippets of uranium."

"We'll call him," Asey said, "but it ain't that hard, doc. Most important thing is that station clock bein' three an' a half minutes slow, you know. You don't need atomic energy to solve that one."

"*What?*"

"Sure. I been broodin' about them three an' a half minutes," Asey said, "since—oh, since long before I slewed you around the road there, comin' back from Douglass's. Only it seemed too crazy to talk about."

"It still does," Cummings said with infinite gentleness.

"Look," Asey said, "what's the first thing someone thinks of for an alibi? Time. Little bits of time! Split-second—"

"Yes, yes, I know! But you said no one in this whole crew knew when they did anything, or when anything happened! You definitely gave it as your opinion that they couldn't *tell* time!" Cummings said. "So what's three and a half minutes got to do with it? Nobody's three and a half minutes short, or over, or anything—well, *are* they?"

"Nope," Asey said with a grin. "Nobody. It's not a

bit important except Sylvester set his watch wrong, an' told the town his watch was wrong, an' everybody missed the Quick Quiz Question!"

"Coypus!" Cummings snorted. "That's a good word to sum up what I think! *Coypus.* Sheer, unadulterated coypus!"

"Mean you don't get it?" Asey said. "Wa-el, think, Dr. Muldoon, think! How does an electric clock get to be three an' a half minutes slow? How d'you stop one of 'em?"

"You stop the electricity, I suppose!" Cummings retorted. "Good God, I don't know how you stop 'em! My primary preoccupation has always been to keep the damn things going. I never tried stopping one. I—look, you've got Shearing and the murder weapon, and a dandy motive, and—"

"Only Boone bettered her career, don't forget."

"Well, you've got this ass Eric wandering around—"

"But Boone was more important to him alive," Asey said, "than dead. He isn't *any*body's secretary now!"

"What about that Stinky fellow? Suppose," Cummings said, "that Boone's offer of a job made him sore. Suppose he resented the insinuation that he was the Eric type. Suppose Boone even blackmailed him a bit—you take that job, or you get booted out of Larrabee. Or, in view of the Gerty angle, you take the job, or I harry Gerty!"

"The Gerty angle's most likely," Asey said. "An' don't forget Sylvester. After all, he *knew* about that room! He didn't like Boone. He—"

"Bah!" Cummings interrupted. "Stop kidding me! And that Briggs—didn't he tell you he was on the beach all afternoon? Well, I've been thinking—he couldn't have been there all the time, and still have got my lighter! If the lighter'd been there on the stump all afternoon, you'd have noticed it when you came. He was lying about that!"

"Uh-huh," Asey said. "I know it. I think he came back at least once. I think—"

"Look here," Cummings said, "we can't sit and play quohaug inspector with two corpses sitting out there at the point! I'm going to call Halbert!"

"Hurry up about it," Asey said, "because we're goin' to need him! This is goin' to take quite a lot of stage managin', doc, an' I think that the quicker we get to it, the better. People get a taste of bashin' their fellow men, an' it goes to their heads. You can't tell where they'll stop. I keep thinkin'," he added gravely, "if I'd managed to get hold of Aunt Mary sooner, I might've saved her —but on the other hand, no matter what I found out or didn't find out from her, I couldn't have kept her from goin' into that room if she'd wanted to go, an' I'd never have known about the secret room, or found out what'd happened to her if I hadn't gone through that wringer with Sylvester first—call Halbert, doc."

"Look here!" Cummings paused with his hand on the phone, "d'you mean you *know* who's responsible for this?"

"Sure," Asey said. "I know. Only I want to prove it quick before anything else happens. Halbert can't do it quick enough. *We* can."

"And while we're proving it, as you so humorously phrase it," Cummings said, "what's to prevent someone from taking *both* those corpses away?"

"Wa-el," Asey said, "Sylvester, for one thing. He's parked on a stump beyond the station with a loaded shotgun. He looked on Aunt Mary as one of his best friends, an' I don't *think* he's goin' to permit anyone to do any serious body-movin', like over to that mud hole!

An' I think he'll know if anyone tries to fix that clock. His orders are just to watch, an' only to shoot as a last resort—but I don't think anyone's goin' to try any tricks. Nobody needs to, with the set-up they got. But Sylvester's there, an' then Jennie's coupe is actin' as a road block across the lane off the main road. In a nutshell, I'm not worryin' about losin' any more bodies!"

"I suppose," Cummings picked up the phone, "that we stage manage so that at a given signal—hullo, this Sophie? Cummings speaking. Can you get me Halbert, the cop who replaced Hanson—what? He is? Well, put him on!" He turned to Asey. "Halbert's in town. Just came into the phone office. Hello! *What?*" A grin spread over his face as he listened. "Okay, I'll tell him. By the merest coincidence, he's here in my office. Halbert, we have a little surprise for you—several of 'em, in fact. Yes, suppose you come over, right away!"

"What's he doin' in town?" Asey asked as the doctor hung up.

"Seems he was just passing through," Cummings, said, "when he was virtually annihilated by a jet-propelled roadster driven by a man with a yachting cap. He recognized you. He's struggled with his conscience, and he was about to call me to ask if I'd tactfully request you to slow down just a little. Said very deferentially he wouldn't dream of bothering you himself, but he thought maybe a tactful word from me might—humpf! You've got that young man thoroughly overawed at the start, which is probably just as well! *I'd* rather have suspected he'd go screaming after you with drawn gun—what about this stage-managing, now? I suppose that at a given signal, the railroad starts up, the water tower falls down, the secret room bursts open, and you, dear Superman, swoop down from the starry heavens and pounce on our victim —whoever the hell our victim *is!*"

"No, kindly old Doctor Muldoon," Asey said. "No! But—wa-el, al*most!* Our victim's now so doggone sure everything's all set, I think a little harryin' might work out as the quickest way to wind this up. I even think that just *suggest*in' that we already know everything will do it. An' thanks for remindin' me of the water tower, doc. That's where they are, I'm sure. Now, with some cooperation from Halbert an' some of his boys—"

As the station clock struck two, the Douglass's old water tower toppled to the ground with a crash that amazed Asey and Cummings, even though they'd been standing in the pine woods waiting for it.

"*That* got 'em all right!" Cummings pointed toward the house. "Knocked 'em out of bed—and why not! It nearly knocked *me* off my feet! See the lights go on! Hall, downstairs, kitchen—there goes Douglass, rushing out! There go Louise and Layne—let's move over nearer. I want to hear what they're saying!"

While the flashlights of the Douglass family played excitedly about the debris of the tower, Asey and the doctor edged as near as they dared.

Louise, her voice shrill with excitement, was ascribing the tower's downfall to the project.

"Over it like flies all afternoon—certainly a miracle it didn't topple with them on it! For the—Harold! Look! *Look* what's tied on this piece of railing! With a red ribbon bow tied on them! What on *earth* are those rubber bathing shoes doing there! With their soles all cut—how utterly strange! They're quite new-looking otherwise! Now *why* would any of those project children tie red ribbons—"

"The red ribbon bow," Cummings said in Asey's ear, "was a stroke of genius, and I congratulate you for thinking of it! If I'd put *my* murdering shoes away forever on a deserted, abandoned water tower, and they suddenly had them turn up at my feet with a red ribbon bow on 'em! Wow!"

"What's keepin' that cop of Halbert's?" Asey muttered. "As soon as Sylvester an' Stinky jerked that tower down, he was to count to—oho, there he goes!"

"How Aunt Mary could sleep through this! I'm *sure* now that she's getting deaf—oh, look! *Look!*" Louise's voice rose to a scream. "Harold, look! The Lulu Belle— is it on *fire?* It's all lighted *up!* Layne! Harold! Quick —look at it!"

The Douglasses stared toward the Pullman, and then Harold started to run toward it.

But suddenly he stopped short.

Louise, racing along behind him, stopped and clutched at his arm.

"Harold! The side of the house—look, it's *opening!*"

Asey and Cummings could hear her easily even from where they stood.

"Harold, what can—Layne, come look *here!* It's a *door!* Where did she go, Harold, to get a fire extinguisher from the barn? She's gone—"

Cummings turned on his heel.

"And there," he said to Asey, at the sound of a car starting, "there Layne goes! She grabbed those shoes— notice that? Rushed to her car—no keys. Beachwagon —no keys. Your roadster—keys! Complete state of panic. She should've remembered seeing you take the keys out this evening, and *know* it's a trap! Does the little fool think we're going to let her streak away?"

"If she does," Asey said, "she'll soon find it's parade speed into the arms of Halbert himself, around the curve in the lane! Huh, I s'pose it's nicer that the Douglasses don't have to witness that scene—not after Aunt Mary!

The cop who opened that door is just shooin' 'em out of the room, see? I guess, doc, you'd better take 'em over now. I'm goin' home. You an' Halbert can—"

"Asey, you can't leave me here to tell 'em! I can't do it!" Cummings protested.

"You told it to *me*," Asey said. "Or most of it, anyway. You set me to thinkin' of her. Begin with that stuff about reversal, doc—how sometimes when you seem to be workin' so hard adorin' someone, you sometimes really hate 'em. Go on about roots—Layne hadn't any. She didn't understand 'em. She didn't begin to understand about Aunt Della's things. They know that. She never belonged—anywhere, or to anybody. Go on to how Boone was usin' her to get Jack Briggs as a secretary, an' how it tore Layne apart—because if Boone got him, she lost Jack, an' if Boone didn't, she lost Boone. Tell 'em how Boone used her—"

"That's another thing they certainly know!"

"Uh-huh, but I doubt if they know it all. Tell 'em what Shearing an' Gerty told us a while ago—how Layne wrote all her speeches an' articles, an' how Boone just took 'em over for her own. Explain—"

"What *do* you think was the last straw?" Cummings interrupted. "I mean, the thing that goaded her to it?"

"I concur with Gerty," Asey said. "She must have overheard Boone makin' that date with Jack Briggs for the beach, when the project came this mornin'. Explain about Aunt Mary—but they won't need any more explanations than that, doc!"

"Except one, maybe," Cummings said slowly. "That Aunt Mary *was* getting deaf. She knew it. Made a date to see me about it next week—I'd completely forgotten till I noticed her name on my date book in the office tonight, when I was hanging around for you. That's why she botched Shearing's message. Probably it's how Layne caught her tonight—Aunt Mary didn't hear her. Okay, I'll do what I can! Where's Jennie?"

"I told her to stick by that cop with the floodlights, over by the Lulu Belle," Asey said, "but there she is, pokin' her nose into the secret room! Jennie! Hey, we're leavin' now!"

"I suppose," Cummings said, "I really have the easier job. I've only got to explain motivation to the Douglasses, and commiserate. You've got to clear up every last question in Jennie's mind!"

But Jennie never spoke on the trip home until Asey was swinging the old roadster up the oystershell driveway of his own house.

"I can't hold in any longer!" she said as the car came to a stop. "*I* saw her there in the lane with Halbert, as we went past! She wasn't repenting any, was she? Spitting like a cat—ugh! Asey, if she was with Gerty all the time, how *could* she have done it?"

"Layne swam out to the raft, an' beyond that out to the moored boats," Asey said. "Gerty thought she saw her all the time, but she only saw Layne's bathin' cap. Layne knew Gerty wasn't much of a swimmer, an' wouldn't be venturin' out that far. So she draped her cap on one of the boats, swam around that far point, an' hopped across the rocks back to the Douglass's. Remember I told you how surprised the doc was to find the boat house so near the Douglass's? An' then Sylvester ran on about his short-cuttin'—"

"But it's a *long* way to the outer beach!"

"Uh-huh, Briggs an' Gerty both got lost. But Layne knew—look, Jennie, if you go up an' down three fingers of your hand, say, that's a long way. Cut across the knuckles, an' it isn't. See? Layne went to the beach, swam out, an' was back at the house there inside of five or six minutes. She knew Douglass was takin' Mrs. Boone for a ride on the train, so she slipped into the station—"

"What was all that business of seeing that nobody touched the station clock? And it's being three and a half minutes slow?"

"How d'you stop an electric clock?" Asey asked with a laugh. "Why is our hall clock sometimes slow?"

Jennie said she wished he wouldn't harp on that old hall clock. "I have to unplug it to use the vacuum in that socket, and I *try* to remember to set it ahead when I plug it back, but I *do* sometimes forget, and it's slow— oh!" she said. "You mean someone pulled the plug out for three and a half minutes—but they certainly weren't cleaning!"

"Nope, but you got the principle of the thing," Asey said. "Layne hid in the station, an' accidentally pulled the plug out—tripped over it, we think—as she slipped out an' into the Lulu Belle after Mrs. Boone. After killin' her, she slipped back into the station again—I think she was duckin' Douglass, who was by then huntin' Mrs. Boone. She saw what she'd done, an' put the plug back in. She hadn't the time or the chance to stand up on one of the settees an' put the clock ahead—an' she probably wouldn't have known exactly how long she'd been gone, anyway."

"But what did that three and a half minutes *matter?*"

"Only that Sylvester, goin' back to town, set his watch by that clock, an' set it three an' a half minutes slow," Asey said, "an' told the world about it! An' it kept botherin' me. I kept workin' back, an' finally got it— three an' a half minutes seemed to me about as long as the whole business would take anyone!"

"I'm sure it bothered *me*," Jennie said, "when it lost

me the Question, but I'd never dream of connecting it with any of this—what did Layne do then, go back to the beach?"

"Uh-huh. Took her cap, swam back to shore, chatted with Gerty, ate lunch, lay in the sun. Later she took her sketch pad an' pencil in a waterproof case an' swam out to the boats again—to sketch from out there, she said. Only she didn't."

"Seems funny Gerty didn't ask to see what she'd been drawing!" Jennie said. "*I* would have!"

"Gerty did, an' Layne showed her—how was Gerty to know it was an old sketch she'd done long ago?"

"How did *you* know?" Jennie demanded.

"What Gerty described," Asey said, "an' what she drew for me from memory, was the shore line before the hurricane hit—steeples, an' big trees, an' a wharf. Wa-el, durin' that so-called sketchin' period, Layne came back to the house again. I think she only wanted to see what was goin' on, an' then she meant to pop back to the beach again. But when she got to the house, there didn't seem to be a soul around—no car on the turntable, no sign of anyone. I think she concluded they'd missed finding Boone entirely, an' had probably gone off uptown on errands, as they always did after lunch. I think she acted on impulse when she put that body into the secret room. Took her only a few minutes, includin' scrubbin' that carpet, as I figured—"

"Where'd she get *water?*" Jennie interrupted. "And why'd she put her *there*, where Aunt Mary'd been sure to find her?"

"There's a tap by the station," Asey said, "an' Aunt Mary wouldn't necessarily have found her, an' not necessarily at once. Certainly the body wouldn't be found there as quick as in the Lulu Belle! But she made that noise with the door, an' Cummings heard, an' went out."

"How'd Layne *know* about the room, anyway?"

"She'd either spotted it herself, or else seen Aunt Mary comin' or goin', an' just decided not to say anything to spoil Aunt Mary's fun. Anyway, she lured the doc down to the boat house—"

"What about that business of the flat tire?" Jennie broke in.

"I meant to ask Layne about that," Asey said, "but as you saw, she wasn't in a mood to answer questions. I don't know when or how she happened on the beach-wagon. Probably after shuttin' the doc up. Probably she got a glimpse of Aunt Mary, who was huntin' around for Boone. I suspect Layne mistrusted her as bein' the sharpest one about, an' thought it'd be a good thing if she was kept busy with a flat tire instead of comin' to the beach, or pokin' her nose around too much. That was the point of it. Could be, of course, that she meant all along to implicate Aunt Mary if she could."

"Nice way to treat your own family, I must say!"

"But it wasn't her own family, an' she didn't waste much affection on 'em. That's all Layne did," Asey said, "till she put that vase behind Shearing's tub. I been broodin' about what impelled her to start counter-actin', an' though I'll probably never know, I think Cummings asked her too many questions when she drove him back from the boat house. I think he tipped her off we were at work on things. She had to take Briggs up later, an' that's when she did the plantin'—he said she left him in the village, an' she must've gone right on to the inn."

"Why'd she plant it on Miss Shearing?"

"Why not? Next to Aunt Mary," Asey said, "she was a good, likely suspect!"

"I heard Harold Douglass tell that cop Aunt Mary'd

come from the movies and gone straight to bed—you think she sneaked down to that room instead?"

Asey nodded. "I think Aunt Mary suspected something. I'm sure something was bothering her, anyway, for her to go call on Shearing. Maybe she wanted to check on that telephone call, or on Boone's whereabouts —I wondered why the Douglasses wasn't more bothered about where she was, an' then I decided probably Layne was responsible for that. Probably kept sayin' what she said to the doc an' me, a lot of stuff about not wantin' ever to bother dear Carolyn when she was busy with her schedule. Now, let's get in an' get to bed! I'm—"

"Those shoes!" Jennie said.

"Oh. Well, I thought about the only clue would be her shoes—she couldn't have short-cutted over those barnacly rocks in her bare feet, an' she couldn't have worn much else on 'em but bathing shoes. I honestly never expected to find 'em, but when Cummings quipped about the water tower, why I went up—an' there they were! You can't burn rubber shoes up without lettin' folks know, an' in that gardenin' family, I s'pose she'd have hesitated to bury 'em—Jennie, that's all!"

"Listen!" she said. "Isn't that—yes, the phone's ringing indoors—you run in and answer, Asey. I'm sure it's for you—oh, and shall I bring in that bottle of medicine that's on the seat here, that Mrs. Gill gave you?"

"If you want," Asey said with a chuckle as he got out of the roadster. "Never can tell when it might come in handy—"

Jennie paused curiously by the phone when she came in a moment later.

"How's that?" Asey was saying. "*What?* What's *nutria*? Say, what in time are you callin' to ask me a fool thing—oh. Oh, I see. Well, by the merest chance, sir, I *do* happen to know the answer. Coypus!"

Jennie's gasp of surprise nearly deafened him.

"What? Can I recite the rest of what old rhyme—just a minute, please! Jennie," he said in an undertone, "unwrap that bottle of medicine, an' take a swallow! Now, sir, the rest of what rhyme? *What?*"

"It's the *Doubler!*" Jennie's voice was an octave above normal. "It's the Question that doubles *everything* you get!"

> 'Punch, conductor, punch with care,
> Punch in the presence of the passen-jaire.
> A blue trip-slip for an eight-cent fare,
> A buff trip-slip for a six-cent fare,
> A pink trip-slip for a five-cent fare,
> Punch in the presence of the passen-jaire!
> Punch, brothers, punch with care!
> Punch in the presence of the passen-jaire!' "

Jennie screamed.

"What's that, sir?" Asey said. "Oh. Send all the loot to Jennie Mayo, thank you. Our reaction? Owin' to the handy presence of some faintin' medicine, we averted casualties. But what with one thing an' another, I think you could sum us up as—punch-drunk! Good night!"